The Witches of Salix Pointe

Not everything that's good is good and not everything that's evil is evil...

Singleton's Press Publishing

ISBN: 978-1-955916-04-2

CHAPTER 1:
ELISA

Rain poured down in sheets as I rushed into my coffee shop. It was yet dark outside at six in the morning, and I felt as if the wind was assaulting me. It whipped the trees left and right, to and froe, making them appear to be doing an angry tango.

The weather had been on its worst behavior since the day Ms. Noreen Chadwick had died. She had been the town's quirky matriarch. Her family had been in Salix Pointe for generations upon generations. It was even speculated that her family had been some of the first freed people to settle here. She had been pivotal in the upkeep of the town. Even the mayor didn't do things without her approval.

Ms. Noreen's passing had caught us all by surprise as she had been active the day before. She was her usual self. She had opened her bookstore and did everything as she normally would. So, when she was found on her porch, in her rocker, unresponsive, the whole town had been stunned. I guess the good part of it was she had passed on peacefully. No pain according to the town's medical examiner, Doc Benu.

Last Tuesday, her niece had driven in and made the arrangements for her estate. I remembered her niece from when she would visit during the summer, but that was about it. She never hung with any of the local kids, choosing to stay locked way in the bookstore with Ms. Noreen most of the time or she was always off reading books in the library or she just stayed at home all the other times. She never bothered to interact with the rest of us kids back then nor when she came for the annual family reunion Ms. Noreen and her family threw here, so it was no wonder she was a complete stranger to most of us now.

As the town said goodbye to Ms. Noreen, I couldn't help but feel as if the heart of the community had been ripped out. And the weather seemed to fit the way we all had felt; dismal, dreary, and dark.

As soon as I closed the door and locked it behind me, thunder clapped across the sky, scaring what Jesus I may have had in me out.

"Good grief," I mumbled after I'd startled so hard I almost tripped over my own feet.

A violent flash of lightning danced across the ground, lighting up the dark street and almost made me rethink opening the shop today. I dropped my wet umbrella into the tall tin umbrella apparatus then ridded myself of my wet trench coat. I took a deep breath before disarming the alarm and flipping the lights on.

I couldn't help but smile at what I saw. My coffee shop was everything I'd dreamed of. Small and cozy with a dash of modern taste so it wouldn't feel too old-fashioned. Round tables decorated the middle open space. Four booths sat against the wall on either side of the cafe. Since Halloween was coming, I'd decorated the place accordingly. All the tables had black and orange tablecloths. The windows had ghosts, witches, and bats painted on them. The curtains were black, sheer and frilly. It looked as if a werewolf had taken its claws through them.

Outside were large pumpkins that I'd carved myself. To the right of the front door stood a life-sized witch with a cauldron full of different candies like bite-sized Snickers, Kit-Kats, Milkyways, tootsie rolls, and the like. On the walls throughout the place were faux spider webs with real live looking spiders and other bugs.

On the accent wall was a painting of the first woman to be accused of witchcraft in Salem; Tituba. I didn't know why, but that picture gave me chills today. I'd been drawn to it when I first saw it for sale in Salem. It was as if it called to me. I couldn't leave the antique shop without purchasing it. I stared at it for a while before turning my eyes elsewhere.

To the left was the pastry counter that had yet to be filled with the day's fresh pastries. I stood behind the coffee bar that housed the cash registers and fancy coffee machines. Elisa's Coffee Press was everything I'd envisioned it to be.

As the rain let up, I went about my normal routine of pre-heating the ovens for the pastries which I'd prepped the night before. I grinded coffees and set out teas. Made the dough for the fresh cookies I served daily. After all of my prepping and baking were done, it was time to open. The rain had let up. Dawn was peeking through the clouds, although they were still gray. I walked to my front door and looked to the left. Most of the small businesses on Main Street were starting to open. A few lights were on in some of the connecting shops.

After I unlocked my front door and set the small round wrought-iron tables and chairs outside—I hoped it didn't rain any more today— that some of my patrons liked to use, I looked at the bookstore. I was going to miss Ms. Noreen. She was always my second customer of the day. The first was the ever elusive and mysterious Dr. Dafari Battle. Every morning like clockwork, he was the first customer inside of my shop.

Dr. Battle always ordered the same things; a large white chocolate mocha, an almond filled croissant, and two chocolate chip cookies. He was a bachelor whom every single woman—and some not so single women—wanted. He also happened to be our town's veterinarian.

At times, I didn't know what to make of him. He carried this darkness about him. It was as if no matter how nice he was, just behind his eyes danced something that I was sure I didn't want any parts of…no matter how fine he was. And the man was drop dead gorgeous.

With skin as dark and rich as the finest chocolate, Dr. Battle looked delectable. He had long jet-black wavy hair that cascaded down his back which he always wore in a ponytail. He was thick and sinewy with muscles in all the right places. That man could wear a turtleneck and make me want to throw caution to the wind. His golden eyes always ensnared me. It was as if he could look right into my thoughts and know what I was thinking. I hated that.

He came with a devilishly handsome smile that I'd only seen once and that was when he smiled at a child who had lost her dog. His dimples reeled me in, but the absolute masculine way in which he carried himself made the pure animalistic lust that overtook my senses anytime he came near scare me to my wits end. I was not some damsel in distress. I did not faint like some little love-sick woman from a 'Gone with the Wind' novel. However, there was something about the man that made me want to do all the carnal things my Elders had warned no respectable woman should even think about.

By God, woman, get a hold of yourself, I chided myself mentally.

Anytime he spoke, every woman in close vicinity seemed to lose their good sense. I admit, his voice was deep and melodic and carried a honeyed undertone that not many men in our sleepy town possessed. Thinking about it annoyed me for some reason. A reason I had no desire to explore at the moment.

I was about to go back inside until I saw the light come on inside the bookstore. My curiosity was piqued. I stepped closer to the street when I saw a figure in the window. It was a feminine one. She was short and a bit curvy just as Ms. Noreen had been. I watched curiously as she pulled the curtains back…then my spine went statue straight. I gasped in shock. It looked as if a younger version of Ms. Noreen was standing in the window of her bookstore. The resemblance was so uncanny that it took me a minute to get my wits about me.

Now I knew a lot of strange things happened at and around Ms. Noreen's bookstore, The Book Nook. It had always been the epicenter of all things weird—a few years ago, some skeletons had been found in the walls of the underground cellar and there were claims of a few ghosts walking through the bookstore at night— but seeing what looked to be a young Ms. Noreen inside of the bookstore just days after her homegoing sent chills up and down my spine. Maybe the ghost stories had been true?

As the thought crossed my mind, the wind picked up. Fallen leaves whipped around me as the rain started to pour heavily again. I needed to get back inside, but for the life of me, I couldn't get passed what I'd just seen. I heard the bells chime to my front door, the ones that alerted me that a customer had walked in. I turned to look behind me, but no one was there. The hairs on the back of my neck stood up and I got the eerie feeling that someone was watching me.

I turned my attention back to the window of the bookstore to find it empty. Whoever, or whatever, had been standing there was now gone. I took a deep breath and then made my way back inside my cafe. For some reason, I decided to lock the door. I didn't think I'd be getting any customers anytime soon in this weather anyway. It always took Salix Pointe a while to come to life in these weather conditions. On days like this, we were the proverbial sleepy, small town.

I walked behind the counter, all set to start on the dough for some new pastries when I heard, "Good morning, Ms. Hunte."

I dropped the glass bowl in my hand, heard it shatter as I turned to find a man standing there. I'd never seen him before, but he looked oddly familiar. He had a face that I could have sworn I'd seen before.

"How—"

I stopped myself. I was set to ask him how he'd gotten into my cafe but didn't want to seem crazy. I mean, of course he had walked through the door. Only… I hadn't heard the normal chime of the bell that sounded when someone walked in—well I'd heard it while standing outside, but— and hadn't I locked the door?

My heart raced, and breath caught in my throat. The man's eyes were so startlingly black that it looked as if I was staring up into a never-ending abyss. His jet-black hair, which had been lined and tapered to perfection, sat in a low cut of thick curls. His burnt honey colored skin had an unnatural glow that made me want to reach out and touch him. He stood well over six feet which was apparent by the way he towered over my five-seven frame. Broad shoulders and a well-defined, muscled physique stood out to me. He was dressed in black slacks that called attention to the muscles in his thighs. The black collarless dress shirt he had on caressed the muscles in his chest and arms, and the black trench coat made him look as if he had just stepped off a runway in Milan.

And even with all of that, I still wondered just how the heck he'd gotten into my cafe.

As if he'd read my mind, he said, "I walked in and no one was in here, so I excused myself to the privy."

As soon as he said the word privy, I took note of his British accent. Something that hadn't registered with me until that moment. I nodded as I laid a hand over my heart. It was a relief to know I wasn't crazy.

"Oh, goodness. I'm so sorry. Please forgive me. I'd stepped out for only a moment and then I looked and saw—" I stopped talking when I realized I was babbling, and I was babbling because the beautiful stranger inside my store had unnerved me. "That's neither here nor there," I said. "What can I get for you this morning?"

"Give me a moment," he answered.

I nodded and went to grab my broom and dustpan, so I could clean up the glass bowl I'd broken. It took me all of a second to do that. Once I was done, I walked back to the counter and smiled up at my customer.

"Are you new in town?" I asked while he looked above my head, browsing the menu that I'd handwritten on small chalkboards on the wall behind me.

His black eyes found mine. "You can say that."

"Oh," I said with a smile. "What brings you to our neck of the woods? People normally pass right on by us."

"Family," he said. "I've got a brother here. We haven't seen one another in ages."

And then it hit me like a ton of bricks. That's where I'd seen his face before. "Is Dr. Battle your brother?" I asked, completely stunned.

"He is indeed," he said then held his hand out to me. "I'm Octavian."

I took his hand, a bit in awe. "I'm Elisa. Dr. Battle never told us he had a brother…"

As his big hand enveloped mine, a cool heat—if that made any sense—settled over me. I felt calm and relaxed. It was as if all was well in my world. I felt a peace I'd never known before.

Octavian gave a smile similar to his brother's…only Octavian's smile in no way alarmed me.

"I just bet he didn't," he said as he shook my hand then eased my hand out of his.

There was something hidden in the way he'd said that. I didn't know what it was, but I was sure it was something that was between him and his brother.

Octavian ordered a tall black coffee and a honey and almond filled croissant.

After he paid and after I'd served him, he walked to the front door and asked, "Do you know what time that bookstore next door opens?"

I shook my head. "I'm not sure if it will. The owner just passed a few days ago. I hear her niece is here to get things squared away."

He smiled then nodded his head on the way out the door. I was so caught up in the fact that Octavian was Dr. Battle's brother that it didn't occur to me to ask Octavian how he knew my name.

CHAPTER 2:
TASMIN

About five hours travel between La Guardia International Airport in New York to Brunswick Golden Isles Airport in Georgia, followed by an excruciating forty-minute drive. That was how long it took to get to Salix Pointe, the home of my aunt, Noreen Chadwick. The same town where I had spent many long, hot summers wishing I was back in Brooklyn, New York. Don't get me wrong; I loved my aunt dearly, and I loved spending time with her, I just hated where she lived.

Salix Pointe; a sleepy little island that sat between Little St. Simons Island and Jekyll Island, both of which are part of a larger group collectively known as the Golden Isles of Georgia. It was so small it didn't appear on any map, nor was it mentioned in any tourist guide. Strange thing was the only people who really knew about it were those whom either grew up there, or whom had ancestors that lived on either of the surrounding islands.

Another weird fact was that the population size never, ever changed. It was always a constant at seven hundred seventy-seven. How that could happen I couldn't begin to explain. One would think it was impossible considering that babies were born, and people died, but I learned a long time ago that Salix Pointe was unlike any other place I'd ever been to before. This, along with a myriad of other reasons, was why I needed to finish up my dealings, and get back to New York as soon as humanly possible.

If it hadn't been for the untimely death of my grand-aunt, I probably never would have set foot back on this godforsaken rock. Unfortunately, not only had she named me as the executor of her estate, she had also gifted me her bookstore, The Book Nook. I had no idea that she had done any of this until I received a message one week ago from the town's resident attorney, Porshia Achebe, from the law firm of Achebe-Daystar, asking me to call her at my earliest convenience.

"Hi, may I speak to Porshia Achebe?" I asked, calling her once I got home from work. "This is Tasmin Pettiford returning her call."

"This is Porshia Achebe. Thank you for calling me back so promptly. It is with a very heavy heart that I must inform you of the passing of your aunt, Noreen Chadwick. Her death is a great loss to our community, in more ways than you know," she stated. "I'm contacting you because you are listed as her next of kin, and the executor of her estate."

"Wait, what?" I stammered. "When did she pass? How did she pass? I just spoke to her a few days ago and she seemed fine."

Miss Achebe's statement about Auntie's death being a great loss to the community, particularly that last part, wasn't lost on me, but that wasn't the time to address it.

"Ms. Chadwick transitioned early this morning. According to the medical examiner, she died peacefully of natural causes," remarked Attorney Achebe.

"And she put me in charge of her affairs?" I asked perplexed, still trying to wrap my head around the fact that my aunt was gone.

While Auntie Noreen had never been married nor had any children, she did have three sisters and three brothers, seven nieces and nephews, including my mom, and six other grand-nieces and grand-nephews, all of whom were living. Even though I had spent much of my childhood, and a good amount of time as an adult, being around her, the last thing I ever expected was to be put in charge of her final affairs. Then again, I never expected her to leave this world so early.

While Miss Achebe droned on regarding the specifics of Auntie Noreen's will, I was busy figuring out how I was going to reschedule all of my appointments for at least the next week, as well as booking my unexpected travel plans.

Fast forward and here I was, completing the rest of the meticulously detailed instructions outlined in her will, with one caveat. Despite Auntie willing it to me, I planned to offload the bookstore. I had no intentions of keeping it, or staying in Salix Pointe, any longer than I had to, mainly because I had a business of my own that demanded my attention. I ran a very successful complementary medicine practice in Brooklyn's Park Slope area, and I wanted to get back to my patients as soon as possible. Besides, Salix Pointe was a far cry from New York, and was not my idea of a good time.

I started my day early, with the plan of inventorying the bookstore, but I quickly got distracted. Sitting at the front desk, I found myself half-heartedly flipping through an old book on Salix Pointe's history. I allowed my mind to wander, reflecting on my own family's history, what little I knew of it anyway. From what I had been told, our family had been in Salix Pointe for at least one hundred and fifty years. It was even rumored that some of my ancestors were town founders. One thing I knew for sure was that my clan always had high standing in the community.

Auntie grew up in Salix Pointe, as did all of her siblings. However, she was the only one to remain here. The other six headed for big cities; New York City, Detroit, Los Angeles, Miami, Seattle, and Houston, to be exact. Although they were spread far and wide, the siblings always came back to Salix

Pointe for our annual family reunion. For as long as I could remember, Auntie Noreen hosted the gathering, as she had plenty of room in her expansive home for everyone.

We all had roles to play; whether it be cooking, baking, manning the barbeque grills, preparing beverages, setting up tables and chairs outside, or handling the place settings, no one was allowed to slack off when it came time for the family reunion. The best part, in my opinion, was game time, where we'd split into teams and play games such as football, dominoes, spades, relay races, and tug-of-war. Those were some of my fondest childhood memories.

My visits would have been fine if they had ended with the family reunion, but my parents, in their infinite wisdom, thought it would be a 'great learning experience' if I stayed with Auntie Noreen for the summer, the *entire* summer. Despite my numerous protestations, my staying in Salix Pointe for the summer was nonnegotiable.

"I spent every summer in Salix Pointe, and enjoyed every minute of it," my mom would say. "If it wasn't for Aunt Noreen, I probably wouldn't be the nurse midwife I am today. Plus, you could use some good, clean, fresh air."

Auntie was the town's 'everything person'. From delivering babies to preparing home remedies for various ailments, she did it all. Some say that many of the townsfolk sought healing from her more than they did from the town's doctor.

"I'm not you, Mom," I remember saying back to her. "I don't want to deliver babies, and I don't like the country, clean air or not. I'll take the hazy days of Brooklyn any day of the week."

"Well, young lady, until you have a job of your own, and until your father and I say otherwise, you'll be spending your summers in Salix Pointe, end of discussion."

When Mom said end of discussion, it most definitely was the end of the discussion.

And so it went for most of my childhood; summers in hot-as-Africa, mosquito-ridden Salix Pointe. It was only when I turned fifteen did I show them. I was finally able to get a summer job, which meant no more Salix Point for me, unless I wanted to go. While neither of my parents was thrilled with me spending most of my summers in Brooklyn, they did respect my initiative.

Truth be told, affection for my aunt notwithstanding, I found Salix Pointe creepy. Unexplainable things happened in the town; things that would make one want to hide under their bed at night, and not come out until daylight the next morning.

For example, a few years ago, the local veterinarian Dr. Adofo Ange-Diable, affectionately

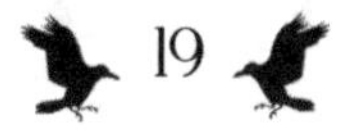

known to townspeople as Doc, just up and disappeared. He hadn't moved, hadn't gone on vacation, he just…disappeared. One day Doc was there, the next day he wasn't, leaving all of his belongings behind. He had been the town's veterinarian for decades, and he loved the town, its people, and its animals. He especially cared for Auntie Noreen; as such, everyone was baffled by his sudden disappearance. Even Auntie, who knew any and everything that went on in Salix Pointe, and knew Doc better than anyone, was at a loss as to what had happened to the good doctor.

A tall, well-built man, with a clean-shaven head, and nicely trimmed mustache and goatee, he could have been a dead ringer for an older Boris Kodjoe, which made him very popular with the townsfolk. Despite his many admirers, women and men alike, he took a particular shine to Auntie Noreen, and while they never made anything official, there seemed to be a clear understanding that they were an item, and off limits to other suitors.

While all of Auntie's siblings were married, the dynamics of her relationship with Doc worked for them, so no one in the family questioned it. During my summer visits, I saw how happy he made her, doting on her like she was a queen, and being protective of her in a way that I found a bit abnormal.

But hey, she liked it, so I loved it. That was why, in my heart of hearts, I found his disappearance extremely suspicious.

No sooner had Doc been missing, only a few days later did Dafari Battle drift into town. He just showed up out of the blue and, ironically, was also a veterinarian, as if the Universe had put out a cosmic job posting. Quickly taking over Doc's sizable practice, he strangely became one the town's favorite sons, although no one really knew anything about the extremely evasive man.

Something about Dr. Battle made me very uneasy. When he looked me in the eyes, it was as if he was looking through me, looking right into my inner being, which I found rather unnerving. This made me give him a wide berth. Auntie got along with him just fine; then again, she could get along with anyone. I always felt that she could befriend the Devil himself and could convince everyone that he was just misunderstood. In the back of my mind, I had wondered if Dr. Battle had something to do with Doc's disappearance. Since I had no proof, I let it go.

Auntie Noreen was so beloved by the Salix Pointe community that when it came time to make arrangements for her home-going, I found that I had very little to do. The townsfolk had done much of the preparations; from planning the wake and funeral service, writing and printing her obituary, picking the venue and flowers, preparing the food for the repast, and scheduling the viewing of the body; they had it covered.

I had to admit, without the help of the residents, it would have been a lot of work. As it stood, the way the community took charge of everything, all I had to do was show up. I was hesitant to call a funeral beautiful, but it was. Many of her friends and neighbors gave glowing testimonials, attesting to my aunt's kindness. Even Dr. Battle gave a rousing tribute, lauding her great generosity, and speaking to how welcoming she was when he first arrived in Salix Pointe. I didn't know what it was about him, but even after several years, I still found his presence disturbing.

At Auntie's behest, she was cremated right after the funeral. She always said the body was just a temporary vessel to house the soul, which was why she decided on cremation after death. She wanted her ashes to be spread around the largest willow tree on her property.

I didn't mind being tasked with the responsibility of dispersing her ashes. What I did mind was *when* she wanted it done. She wanted the ceremony performed the first night of the waning moon. Since the waning moon was a time of letting go, I understood the significance. I was letting go of Auntie on the physical plane, so it made perfect sense. But doing it at night, by that tree, left me feeling ill at ease, mainly because of the tree itself.

As a child, that same tree was clearly visible from my bedroom window. It never bothered me during the day, but at night, it seemed to come to life. At times, that willow tree reminded it me of the Weeping Angels, aliens who looked like angel statues, from the Doctor Who episode *Blink*. When someone looked at a Weeping Angel, it appeared to be frozen in one spot. However, literally in the blink of an eye, it would move closer and closer to the victim.

Just like that Weeping Angel, at night, that willow tree appeared to be moving closer to the house. It scared me to no end. I never told anyone about my fear, since I knew they would dismiss it as the musings of a child's overactive imagination. I was finally able to push my childhood terror to the back mind once I stopped spending summers in Salix Pointe; but now, it was all coming back. I had to find some way to get past it before the waning moon if I was going to fulfill Auntie Noreen's wishes.

I finally put the history book away, intent on getting some work done, when I realized how hungry I was. Since there was a coffee shop a few feet away, I figured I'd walk over and quickly grab something.

As my bad luck would have it, it started to rain, and, of course, I didn't have an umbrella. I was all set to make a run for it until I saw a familiar resident heading in the same direction. It was Dr. Battle, on his way to the same coffee shop. The rain was now coming down in sheets, yet it appeared to not touch Dr. Battle, who didn't have an umbrella. It was as if even rain avoided him. I was extremely tired and hungry, and thought I may have been hallucinating. I rubbed my eyes a few times to make sure, but the visual didn't change. It was then that I decided to continue the inventory. Food could wait.

CHAPTER 3:

OCTAVIAN

"Why are you here?" greeted me as soon as I walked into my brother's vet office.

"It is nice to see you as well, Brother," I said.

"Rest assured the pleasure isn't mine at all," he said through a snarl.

I watched as he placed a small rabbit back in its cage. It was odd seeing my brother in such a light, in any light to be honest. He was born of the dark so to see him thriving in this little sleepy town amongst mere humans gave me pause. It shouldn't have, being that Salix Pointe had a few secrets of its own.

I studied my brother. He still looked the same. Long thick wavy black hair he inherited from his father. His eyes were still just as golden as his father's. Skin as dark as night, courtesy of our mother. He was still built like a battle angel, shoulders broad and body sinewy with muscles. He was older than I by a mere seven years, but one would have thought it was by hundreds of years with the way he carried on. Last time we were in the other's presence, he'd called me archaic, but I had a few choice words I could use to describe him. Arsehole came to mind.

Dafari brushed past me. Dogs barked incessantly. Cats mewled. Birds squawked and flew around their cages. A variety of chirps, clicks, and squeaks from lizards blended in with the noise, most of those sounds would be inaudible to the naked human ear. The room was small. White walls made it look bigger than it was. Cages of all sizes and shapes lined the walls. It smelled of animals which didn't seem to bother my dear brother at all. That didn't surprise me.

"Quiet," Dafari said to the room.

The animals' incessant noise ceased immediately. He flipped the light off in the room then walked to a door with his name on the plague, his office I assumed.

"It has taken me a hundred years to track you down," I said, following him to the office.

"Clearly I didn't want to be found."

"That is not how the order of things—"

"Screw your order, Octavian!" His eyes flashed golden as he rolled his shoulders.

"You know how things are supposed to go with us, Brother," I said. "You came to this town because you knew the powers here would hide yours. Only amongst other powerful entities and beings can you camouflage so easily."

"There is no crime in wanting peace, Octavian."

"It is a crime to have your presence cause the death of one of the most powerful witches in the world..."

Dafari stood at his full height, eyes blazing from gold to fire red. My brother's powers could frighten the most powerful of angels and demons, but he didn't frighten me. He and I had come from the same womb, with equal powers. We were the literal definition of good and evil, light and dark...the yin and the yang.

The air chilled in the room as the lights flickered on and off.

"Simmer down, dear brother," I said. "You're bloody well not going to fight me for the whole town to see, are you?"

"What do you mean my presence caused her death?"

"Noreen Chadwick of the Bloodline Tituba did not die of natural causes. She was murdered by an entity that followed your trail to Salix Pointe."

"The only entity who is able to track me is you."

"This is what running and hiding for over a hundred years does to you. Things have changed, dear old brother."

I saw his eyes go cold and flinty. The raging fire behind his eyes simmering. "Will you stop talking in riddles and say what it is you need to say? Who murdered Noreen? And how would they know she's of the Bloodline Tituba?"

"Perhaps if you took calls from Mother more than every fifty years or so, you'd know—"

"Know what?"

"That your father has escaped."

"What?"

"He has escaped. His last known energy trail led me right to you which means…he's been here in Salix Pointe and that Noreen Chadwick was his first victim."

Dafari plopped down in the chair behind his desk. His eyes darted around the room as his mind processed what I'd just told him.

"That's not all," I said.

"Speak."

"There is also a witch of the Bloodline Leveaux here."

When he didn't look surprised, but his fists clenched, it was my turn to ask questions.

"You knew she was of the Bloodline Leveaux, didn't you? It's why you chose this town specifically. Bloody hell, Brother, you've led him right to their door," I snapped.

"How was I supposed to know he was trailing me? He's was to be chained to the side of a mountain for all eternity."

"Why have you blocked Mother from contacting you?"

"It's safer that way."

"Codswallop!"

"It is and you know it."

"You avoid her because you're still angry with her."

Our family history was a sullied one, one my brother tended to only revisit when it suited him.

I kept going. "If you hadn't all but shut us out of your life, Mother would have told you that your father had visited her upon his escape."

Dafari's heated gaze settled on me. I didn't have to tell him what that meant. I was sure he knew the mad demon his father was.

"Where was your father?" he asked. "Why wasn't he there to protect her?"

"Another thing that has changed since you shut Mother out…They're no longer together."

Dafari's brows shot in the air. Something akin to shock registered on his face or it could have been skepticism. "What do you mean?" he asked.

"During the years, since you cut Mother off, their relationship took a dive. Loads of argy-bargy between the two before Dad gave up…and Mother simply clocked out of the marriage all together. Don't ask me anything further as it isn't my story to tell and that's all I know," I said.

That last part was a lie. Because of that lie, my palms burned, and my ears had a ringing that caused the dogs in the back to start barking and howling again. I placed my hands behind my back and looked over my brother's head out the window.

"You're lying, Octavian," he said then rounded the desk. He stood right next to me, staring at my profile while waiting for me to confirm or deny my lying.

"Mother is the last of our worries at the moment. Neither the café owner nor the niece know what they are. They're completely clueless to their powers and the fact that their lives are in danger. That should be our focus." I turned to face my brother. His eyes fiery red again. "Tell me, dear brother, how is that you've been in this town for years now and you haven't managed to finagle your way into the café owner's breeches?"

Dafari growled then sucked his teeth. It was his turn to show me his profile as he turned to the window. He stood rigid, hands behind his back, standing at attention like a soldier. I walked over to his bookcase and picked up an old bottle of rum. It was from the 1700s which made me appreciate my brother's unique tastes and tendencies to hoard even more. I popped the topper and then inhaled. Pure molasses fermented for an extended amount of time and judging by the woodsy aroma it was distilled and then aged in an oak barrel.

"You're a cad," my brother said.

I chuckled as I poured myself a finger of the liquor. "That is a valid question, is it not?" I took a sip.

"I haven't touched a woman, human or otherwise, in seven years."

The heavenly spirit—not the one modern day religious folk believed in—got stuck in my throat. I coughed as it burned going down. I sputtered and tried to focus on getting my breathing together. "Pardon?" I croaked out once I found my voice again.

Dafari cut his eyes at me.

"You… you're a—"

"I know what I am," he said, cutting me off.

"Well then how is that possible? *Is* that possible without causing yourself severe damage?"

"I should clarify and say I haven't been with a woman on the earthly plane in seven years."

"So you've gone to hell to get—"

"No. Astral—"

"You've invaded her dreams? You bloody wanker. Isn't that against some kind of preternatural law? Don't you have to get consent?"

"She never remembers them."

"How do you know?"

He turned red eyes to me. "Trust me, I see her every morning. If she remembered half the things we do in those dreams, she wouldn't be able to face me. As far as consent, she invites me into her subconscious every night…while having no idea she's doing it."

I laughed. "Bloody hell…and that has sustained your natural side for seven years?"

"For three. She's only been doing it for three years…"

"And it's keeping you sated? Well she is a right crumpet so I can see how…" I cleared my throat and stopped talking once I realized my dear brother was bulking in size. "Get a hold of your senses, man," I taunted him. "You don't see me losing my cool over…Tasmin. Although she smells divine… Perhaps, Dafari, you can give me pointers on how to invade her dreams later?"

No sooner than the words had left my mouth, I went flying backwards and out the window of my brother's office. I landed with a hard thud in the middle of the street.

I was face up, looking toward the heavens. "I was talking about Tasmin, you arse," I yelled. "You and your temper," I mumbled then stood.

I stood there a moment, gathering my thoughts. I saw when my brother left his office and headed into the coffee shop. Saw when he finally left back out and wondered if Elisa had any idea as to what he truly was.

Finally, I brushed my shoulders off then looked toward the Book Nook and saw Elisa rushing inside from the rain. I'd been in the establishment earlier. Tasmin hadn't even sensed my presence or known I was there. I smiled. It was time to change that.

CHAPTER 4:

ELISA

I knew he'd walked in without having to look up. I didn't even hear the bell on the door chime. I felt him, as I always had. I looked up from packaging the box of pastries and sandwiches I intended to take to Ms. Noreen's niece next door. Dr. Battle didn't smile as he walked up to the counter. His hair was loose, flowing down his back. He was dressed in black slacks that fit him far too well and a red turtleneck that hugged the muscles in his chest and arms. He had on a white lab coat and carried the morning's newspaper in his right hand.

"Good morning, Dr. Battle," I greeted. "Same thing as always?"

He stopped just inches before the counter then looked around as if he expected to see someone.

The corner of his upper lip twitched a bit before he turned his golden eyes to me. "Good morning, Elisa. Yes, I'll have the same."

His voice chilled me to the bone. I felt the goosebumps rise on my skin. It was different this morning, almost as if he was talking without moving his lips. It was as if I could hear him in my head. I tried to stave off a shiver at the fervid gaze he sent my way. I couldn't. And his stare didn't waver. He didn't look away, and for some reason, I refused to. I felt my breathing deepen as he got closer to the counter. The wind howled just outside the window and suddenly I felt faint. It wasn't lost on me that it had started pouring again and he was as dry as could be even though he'd walked in from the pouring rain.

"Um...your...your brother stopped by this morning," I said in an attempt to get my wits about me.

"I'm aware," was all he said.

I watched as he sniffed the air, turned his lips into a scowl and then...by God, I could have sworn the man growled low in his throat.

"Your reaction tells me you two don't get along very well?" I asked.

His golden eyes trained on me. "We get along just fine...when he respects my boundaries and actually tells me when he's showing up to wreak havoc on my life." Dr. Battle picked up his coffee, cookies, and croissant. "Good day, Elisa." He nodded once then headed out.

I was left standing there trying to figure out what that was all about. Could there be a rift between the

brothers? Was that why Dr. Battle had never mentioned Octavian? While Octavian had seemed excited to see Dr. Battle, his sour mood held no such delight.

I sighed and went back to making the box for Ms. Noreen's niece. I knew it would be a while before any more customers showed up. I picked up the box and my umbrella before locking my café door and heading next door. The rain was not nice to me. It seemed the moment I stepped outside, it started raining even harder. I walked as briskly as possible, scolding myself for forgetting to grab my coat.

I made it to the door, expecting to have to knock, but was surprised to see she had already opened the door, waving me in. I rushed inside, shivering and thankful.

"My goodness," she said. "What on earth possessed you to come out in this?" she asked.

She handed me the small hand towel she'd been holding and took the umbrella from me. She dropped in the apparatus sitting by the door then led me over to the fireplace. That was the one thing I loved about Ms. Noreen's bookstore. The fireplace was always welcomed in the fall and winter.

The walls were lined with floor-to-ceiling bookcases which required ladders to reach the uppermost books. I was going to miss seeing Ms.

Noreen glide the ladders to and froe as she cleaned or restocked books. There were several rectangle shaped tables with chairs spread throughout the store for those who wanted to sit and read or do other tasks. There were comfortable nooks with plush cushions and more private areas with desks and plugs for electronic devices. On the side where the open space looked like a loft with four fireplaces spread throughout, the exposed brick gave it a modern chic feel that the high schoolers and college students loved.

There were pictures of historic Black women throughout the place and pictures of the founders of Salix Pointe behind the front desk. I didn't want to think about this place not being open to the town anymore.

"Thank you," I said. "I saw you were over here and wanted to bring you hot chocolate and pastries. There are a few sandwiches as well. I didn't expect it to start pouring as such."

I handed her the box and the hot chocolate then used the towel to wipe my face, hands and neck.

"Here, sit down and warm up," she said. "I remember you from when I used to visit, and my aunt talked about your café often."

I smiled over at her. "She did?"

Tasmin nodded with a smile. "She was very fond of you and your grandmother. And this hot chocolate smells divine."

"My secret recipe. I figured you'd be a bit hungry."

She nodded. "I am. I had planned on coming over, but then I saw—" She stopped abruptly then darted her eyes around the room before they settled on me again.

"Saw what?" I asked.

She waved a hand. "Never mind. It was nothing. Thank you again for this."

"It's no problem at all. Your aunt was a staple in this community. It won't be the same without her."

"I can see that. As soon as I got here, the town embraced me like I'd never left."

"Do you plan to stay and keep the bookstore open?"

Tasmin was shaking her head before I even finished the question. "Ohhh no. I am not built for a life in Salix Pointe," she said then laughed. "I plan to sell this place and then be on the first plane smoking out of here."

My smile faltered. I couldn't imagine the bookstore not being here anymore. I could only hope she sold it to someone with roots here so that they could keep it up and running. However, I knew that was a long shot. No one here possessed the kind of capital or funding needed to outright buy the place.

"Oh no… the town will be so sad to see it go. It's been here for generations. Did you know it was founded in 1867? By one of your great aunts?"

Tasmin quirked a brow. "No, no… I can't say that I did. I mean I'd known it was an ancestor but not an aunt."

I nodded, eager to tell her just in case it made her second guess selling. "Yes, she was one of the first freedwomen to own property here as well. There is so much history in this place," I said, looking around.

I smiled recalling fond memories. Ms. Noreen used to give high school kids summer jobs. I remember being a cashier during the summer months when Tasmin stopped visiting, and once I was senior, she even allowed me to run the store some weekends.

"I can't imagine this place not being here anymore," I said, sadness settling within me.

"Just because I'm selling it doesn't mean the bookstore won't be here anymore," Tasmin said.

"Yeah, well, unless you sell it to one of us, an outsider won't care about the history and importance of this place."

"So this place is for sale?" sounded behind us.

Tasmin and I darn near jumped out of our skin as another rumbling clap of thunder shook the grounds, a violent flash of lightning knocked the electricity out. We didn't have time to register being in the dark as Dr. Battle's brother was standing behind us.

We jumped up and grabbed the other's hands like two frightened old ladies in a horror movie. Later we would laugh at how pathetic we looked.

"How-how did you get in here and who are you?" Tasmin asked, her body trembling as hard as mine.

Octavian stood almost statue still. In the dark shadows of the bookstore, he looked like a solider as he stood with his hands clasped in front of him, feet planted shoulder length apart, and shoulders squared. He studied Tasmin like she was a rare artifact. It reminded me of the way Dr. Battle had studied me earlier.

"This… is Dr. Battle's brother," I told Tasmin.

"That doesn't explain how he got into the store," she said.

"The front door was unlocked," Octavian said. "I assumed you were open for business. Was I mistaken?"

I frowned as I watched him rub his hands together then tug at his ears. The front door couldn't have been unlocked. I could have sworn I watched Tasmin lock it back as soon as she'd let me in.

"No, no. That can't be right. I loc—"

"Is there a reason you two are holding on to one another? Do I frighten you?" Octavian asked, his voice as smooth as silk, honeyed even.

Tasmin and I looked at our locked hands then one another. We dropped them. I was sure embarrassment washed over my features the same as hers.

"Well, yes, you did frighten us," Tasmin said. "May I help you?"

"I came in to purchase books, but if you're not open for business, I can come back," he said.

Tasmin and I had been so startled at the sight of him being in the store that we completely forgot the lights had gone out.

I said, "Before we can do anything, we need to get the lights back on. Do you know where the breaker box is around here?"

Tasmin shook her head as she looked around. "Not really, but I'm going to assume it's in the basement."

"That seems like a logical pla—"

Octavian waved his hand then said. "This place was built in the late 1800s. It's more likely that the breaker box would be someplace else. I'd surmise that by the 1920s a 60 Amp electrical system was the norm. I'd suggest you look for the building's blueprint to see if by the 1940s your aunt had any rewiring done. That way you'll know if you have knob and tube wiring. By itself, that kind of wiring is not a problem, but if it has been modified by an unqualified electrician then you're in for problem, a dangerous one at that…"

As Octavian spoke, his British accent became more prominent. His knowledge of electrical wiring notwithstanding, Tasmin and I stared at him in wide-eyed shock. Tasmin looked at me as I gawked at her. I already knew we were thinking the same thing.

Did he just wave his hand and the lights magically come back on? I knew I had to be crazy to be thinking such a thing, but—

"Oh look, the lights have come back on," Octavian said as an afterthought, as if he hadn't noticed it until now.

I shook my head. I was letting the weird things that had happened earlier make me irrational. There was no way that man had waved his hand and turned the electricity on. I was tripping and clearly needed to get my head in the game.

I watched as Tasmin went to the front door. She checked to make sure it was locked—it was—then she looked out at the rest of the street. She turned her head left and right and then looked back at me.

"There are no other lights on. Even your lights are out, Elisa," she said.

"Perhaps that can be explained by your generator," Octavian said then tilted his head just enough to look as if he was listening to something in the distance.

Then I heard the low murmur of a machine.

I let out a nervous laugh then breathed a sigh of relief. "That's right, Tasmin. I forgot that Ms. Noreen had a generator put in about five years ago because of the bad storms we get during hurricane season. Of course it would kick in."

I chuckled when I saw Tasmin look as if she was relieved as well. No one could blame either of us for thinking something crazy was going on. That was Salix Pointe; something weird was always happening, especially at the bookstore.

"I can take a look at your electrical circuit if needed. I'm quite handy in that department," Octavian said. "The surge could have fried a few wires…"

He said all of that and then strutted over to a bookshelf before Tasmin could answer him. I would say that he was a strange man, but knowing his brother… I'd say his actions were par the course. I looked outside and saw that some people in the town were milling about.

I asked, "Are you going to be okay if I leave you alone with him?"

I motioned to Octavian who browsed the book section on witchcraft. He seemed harmless enough and he was Dr. Battle's brother. I suppose if he had been up to no good, Dr. Battle would have warned me.

Tasmin nodded. "Seems as if he just wants to buy some books. I can figure out how to work the new cash register to make that happen if it will get him to leave faster."

I looked at my watch. "I have to get back to the shop, but if you want, you can join me for dinner later?"

"I really need to get this paperwork in order so I can contact the realtor about selling this place," she said.

I nodded. "I understand. I really wish there was a way to talk you out of selling this place…"

"There isn't," she said. "I have to get back home to my work and my life. I have no way of keeping up with this place. I think Aunt Noreen would rather I sell it than let it go to waste."

I didn't say that Aunt Noreen would rather it not be sold to an outsider who would more than likely shutter the bookstore all together, but I kept that to myself.

CHAPTER 5: TASMIN

"See you later," I said to Elisa, locking the door behind her. The same door I swore had been locked prior to Dr. Battle's brother arriving.

But I digress. I truly appreciated Elisa stopping by, especially since, now that Aunt Noreen was gone, I didn't know anyone in town. I hoped she didn't feel slighted because couldn't have dinner with her. I really did want to, but I needed to get the bookstore fully inventoried, and get all the paperwork in order, before I called the realtor in the morning. She had mentioned that she'd heard from the mayor of Salix Pointe several times regarding purchasing the property. While I knew I wanted to sell the place, I wasn't sure I wanted to sell it to that character. I digress...

I thought about how I never interacted with Elisa, or any of the other kids for that matter, when I visited Salix Pointe. It wasn't for lack of trying, but Auntie always kept me busy. If I wasn't picking herbs from her voluminous garden; memorizing the names of trees, plants, flowers, and spices; or learning how to prepare a variety of home remedies, Aunt Noreen would send me to the library with a laundry list of reading assignments. She said it was because she wanted me to be prepared for anything life threw at me. I thought that was a lot of pressure to put on a child, but I never questioned it, or her. Truth be told, if it wasn't for Auntie and her teachings, I probably never would have studied complimentary medicine. Still, at the time, I was just a kid, and I would have preferred to be playing with other kids; hence, a large part of my distain for Salix Pointe.

Back then, the other children probably thought I was some highfalutin, uptight, anti-social city girl who thought she was too good to play with them. That couldn't have been further from the truth. I'm just glad Elisa didn't hold that against me. I'd try to make that dinner up to her before I left in a few days.

"Is there something in particular I can help you find, Mr. Battle?" I asked, turning my attention to the well-dressed stranger who was intently looking over some very old books. I didn't know him to like him one way or the other but, just like Dr. Battle, his brother left me with a strange feeling that I could not explain. And yet, unlike Dr. Battle, I didn't find him threatening in any way.

He turned away from the bookshelf, taking a few steps in my direction, towering over my petite five-three frame. He was at the very least a foot taller that

I was. "Not Battle. Jerrod. Octavian Jerrod, but you may call me Octavian. Chuffed to bits to make your acquaintance," he said with a smile broad enough to show his pearly white teeth.

With his British accent, I was guessing that chuffed meant pleased. "My apologies, Octavian. I just assumed that you and Dr. Battle had the same last name," I replied, a bit embarrassed by my error. I extended my hand for him to shake. "Tasmin Pettiford. Nice to meet you."

"Tasmin. A lovely name for an enchanting maiden," he said taking my hand, kissing the back of it. Talk about laying it on thick. "No apology is necessary. My brother and I have different fathers," he remarked matter-of-factly. "It appears that it's my turn to apologize. It seems I've interrupted you from getting your work done. Had I known you were in the middle of something, I would have come back later."

When he first shook my hand, I thought it felt warm; perhaps a bit too much considering how cold it was outside. Now, the longer he held my hand, it became uncomfortably warm, forcing me to quickly pull away. It was then that I noticed that he seemed to wince in pain. "Octavian, are you okay?"

"Yes, it's just a mild headache," he replied, rubbing his temples. "I suffer with them from time to time."

The way he was squinting his eyes and rubbing his temples even more vigorously with his balled-up fists, I could tell that he was in more pain than he was willing to admit. "Can I make a suggestion?" The doctor in me couldn't help but try to make him feel better.

"Please do," he replied.

"If you give me a few minutes, I can whip up something for that headache," I answered, heading toward the breakroom in the back of the shop.

"Oh no, please, don't trouble yourself. I'll be fine. I don't want keep you from finishing your work."

"It's no trouble at all. I'm going to be here all day regardless. A few more minutes won't make a big difference."

"If you insist, Tasmin," he responded, slightly bowing his head.

I smiled at him. "I do. Feel free to keep looking around, and I'll be back shortly."

After I stopped coming to Salix Pointe for the summer, Aunt Noreen had the entire bookstore renovated, including the addition of a breakroom for the small staff of high schoolers who worked for her. Complete with a stove, refrigerator, and two microwaves, it had everything I needed to make a tea to cure Octavian's headache.

Auntie didn't believe in conventional medicine, and knowing her like I did, I figured she had a stash of homemade teas lying around. I searched the cabinets until I found what I was looking for. It was a tea that contained white and purple willow barks and ginger, all known headache remedies. I took a teabag out of the glass container and dropped it into an oversized mug. I didn't want to keep Octavian waiting too long, so instead of boiling water on the stove, I filled the mug with tap water and placed it in the microwave. While the brew was heating, I again rummaged through the cabinets until I found some raw honey. Luckily, there was also an unopened bottle of lemon juice that was still within the expiration date. Once the concoction was done, I flavored it with the honey and lemon, then carried it out to Octavian.

When I returned, he was sitting at a long table, thumbing through a book, with several others sitting off to the side. "Your bookstore is a treasure trove of riches," he pronounced, excitement in his voice.

I placed the hot tea on the table in front of him. "Glad you like it, but the bookstore is not mine," I responded. "Well technically it is since my aunt willed it to me. But, as you overheard earlier, I plan to sell it."

"Thank you," he replied, picking up the large cup. "Why would you want to sell such a gem?" He looked at me intently, waiting for an answer, as he breathed in the aroma of the savory blend before taking a long sip.

"I don't want the bookstore. Considering how long it's been since I've visited, I'm shocked that Aunt Noreen left it to me in the first place. Now that she's passed on, the last link I had to Salix Pointe is gone, which means once my business here wraps up, I'll have no reason to ever come back. Besides, I have my own business to get back to. I already feel like I've been gone from it for too long."

Octavian continued to sip from the mug, seeming to enjoy the flavorful mixture. "And what business is that, if you don't mind me asking?"

"Complementary medicine. I'm a doctor."

"Ah, a healer. A noble profession indeed. No wonder the fervent need to heal my ills."

"It's a character flaw for sure." I laughed.

"And what an exquisite character flaw it is."

I blushed despite myself. Sitting at the table across from him, I looked at the titles for two of the books in front of him, reading them out loud. *"The Oxford Illustrated History of Witchcraft and Magic. Angels, Demons, and the New World."* I looked at him, raising an eyebrow. "Interesting subject matter."

"Allow me to explain. I am a professor in the department of Mythology and Occultism at Bircham International University. These books are exactly what I've been looking for as complements to the courses I teach. While the university has its own course material, I like for my students to explore other, more esoteric resources."

"You seem very passionate about your work."

"I find the subject matter absolutely riveting. I take it you've never perused any of these tomes before."

I silently read the titles of the other two books on the table, the first being *Spiritual Cleansing: Handbook of Psychic Protection*, and the second *Plant Witchery: Discover the Sacred Language, Wisdom, and Magic of 200 Plants.* "I can't say that I have. Things unknown are unnerving to me. I like to go with tried and true proven science, like that tea you're drinking. Speaking of, how's your head?"

"Much better thank you," he answered. "Tasmin, let me posit this to you; while your home remedy can be seen as science, in a way, herbal remedies can be viewed as a form of magick."

"How do you figure?" I placed my elbows on the table, resting my chin on my folded hands. Intrigued by his logic, I was curious to hear his answer.

"Ponder this; how did you know this tea would cure my headache?"

"Well, I didn't. I just know that willow bark and ginger have been scientifically shown to relieve headaches in some people. But that's centuries old trial and error *science*. Homegrown science, but science, nonetheless. I still don't get how magick has anything to do with it."

"Magick has much to do with it. Your desired intention was to cure my headache, although you weren't sure it was going to work, correct?"

"Yes, but—"

"And you put that desired intention into action by making this tea," he continued his argument enthusiastically.

"Okay, but I still don't get—"

"Please indulge me for one more moment."

I reluctantly relented. "The floor is yours, Professor," I said, spreading my hands as if in surrender.

"It's your thoughts and beliefs that create your intention, and it's your intention that creates action. You infused your desire to heal me with the creation of this wonderful tea. You believed that it was going to work, and so it did."

I couldn't help but laugh out loud. "So you're telling me that because I wished for you to get better, magick made it happen? Not because of the proven science behind it? Nice try, Octavian, but I don't think so."

"I am not disputing science. I am, however, trying to open your eyes to the possibility that other forces could be at play," he said, a serious tone in his voice.

I stood up from the table, getting ready to walk toward the front counter. "Maybe your students fall for that hocus pocus mumbo jumbo, but I'm not buying it. Besides, I don't believe in magick. I believe in science; in the tangible, not the intangible."

"Really now?" he asked, picking up the books and following me to the counter.

"Really," I replied, fumbling with at the electronic cash register, trying to figure out how to ring up Octavian's purchases. "Unless you can prove it to me, then it's not real."

He flashed a sly smile. "I'll remember you said that, Tasmin. I'll enjoy proving you wrong."

I had no idea what he meant by that, but one thing I knew for sure was that I wouldn't be in town long enough for him to prove anything to me. Time was going and I didn't have the energy to further debate with him. It was time to wrap things up.

"I'm sorry, but I'm still learning how this machine works. Can you come back tomorrow? I should be able to get you squared away by then."

"I would be delighted. However, before I take my leave of you, my offer to examine your electrical circuitry stands. The storms are predicted to go on throughout the rest of the day, and I would be remiss if I allowed you to be in the dark again."

I gathered Octavian's books, putting them on a shelf behind me. "While I appreciate your generous offer, and while you appear to be quite skilled, I think I can handle it. But thank you anyway."

"Are you certain, because a job of this magnitude is definitely more in keeping with a man's bailiwick. I would hate to see a fair damsel caught off guard," he casually replied.

Fair damsel? Who even talks like that? You'd think Octavian was from the dark ages.

"You do realize that some women can do the same job just a well as, if not better than, some men."

"Perhaps, but in simpler times, men historically did the building and repairing, while women took care of the home and children. Roles were more clearly defined," he retorted.

What just happened? I felt as if I had been thrust into a backwards time warp. I leaned on the counter, tilting my head to the side, taking a deep breath before answering. "Well aren't you a throwback to the eighteenth century? Men also created chastity belts for women, but those are a relic of the past, aren't they? Slide on over to the twenty-first century. You'll see that women are quite capable nowadays."

"My, you're a cheeky little wench for such a small slip of a woman."

Oh he did *not* just call me a wench. That was one of the words that, in my book, was akin to calling a woman out her name. It took everything I had in me not to jump over the counter and punch him in his chiseled jaw.

Looking him squarely in the eyes, I replied, "Professor Jerrod, I'm going to say this one time and one time only. Call me a wench again and it'll be the last time you call me anything."

"I meant no disrespect," he stated.

"What planet are you from? Calling a woman *that* speaks of nothing but disrespect," I shot back.

"Tasmin, I sincerely apologize." He appeared remorseful, but the damage was already done.

I walked from around the desk to the front door, unlocking it, holding it open for Octavian. "That's Dr. Pettiford to you. And I don't want your apology, I just want you to leave. Once I get everything in order, I'll let Dr. Battle know. He can pick up the books for you. Good day."

"Good day, and again, I meant no harm. I truly hope you can forgive me," he replied, stepping outside.

"Maybe, but it won't be today, Professor." With that, I closed and lock the door behind him, intent on getting some more work done before heading back to Aunt Noreen's house.

Unfortunately, the more I tried to distract myself with the inventory, the more my thoughts drifted back to Octavian. Why was I letting someone I had just met get under my skin like that?

I had dealt with a lot of male supremacy over the years, but he was arguably one of the most infuriatingly misogynistic men I had ever met. It wouldn't surprise me if he thought that a woman's place should be in the home, making sure dinner was on the table when her husband arrived home from work, waiting for him at the door with a cognac in hand. I was hoping that my dealings with the professor were done after today, but I had this nagging feeling that we would very soon cross paths again.

CHAPTER 6:

DAFARI

"That couldn't have gone better, Casanova," I remarked sarcastically as Octavian exited the bookstore. I decided to close up shop early to keep an eye on my intrusive little brother.

He bristled when he realized I was standing there. "How long have been spying on me?"

"Long enough to see you make a complete clod of yourself. And you were doing so well. Remember when I called you archaic?" I chided, walking toward my Mercedes Benz S-class sedan. Yes, I lived in a sleepy little town, but that didn't mean I couldn't enjoy life's luxuries.

"How could I forget?" he sneered.

"Thank you for once again proving me right. Are you that old that you didn't realize that, in this age, calling a woman a wench can be akin to calling her a prostitute? Women have not taken kindly to being called that for centuries, my clueless brother," I chastised, unlocking the car. "Get in."

"Still prone to excess, I see. Some things will never change," he uttered, climbing into the passenger side. "And you damn well know it was not my intention to insult Tasmin, you insufferable arse." His annoyance amused me so.

"Hmmmm. Earlier, I was just an arse; now I'm an insufferable arse. I must have touched a nerve," I replied, a smirk crossing my lips.

"So glad you find my plight amusing, Dafari. I obviously dropped a clanger when I called her a wench. My linguistic gaffe really threw a spanner in the works. She gave me quite the ear-bashing."

"And rightfully so. A word of advice, my younger, and, clearly, less wise brother. I haven't been physically intimate in seven years by choice. With your anachronistic attitudes toward women that choice will be made for you. You will never get into Tasmin's, or probably any woman's, pants. At the rate you're going, I see years of celibacy in your future. Or perhaps, what's a good word? Ah yes, wanking."

I pulled out of the parking spot, anxious to get home. Elisa would be retiring around seven tonight, and I wanted to make sure I gave her the pleasant evening she desired. From what little Octavian told me, I gathered we had much to discuss, which could take a while. I wanted to make sure we had more than enough time to talk so I could be well-rested for what I had planned for Elisa later. I felt the need to make her night extra special since I was so brusque with her earlier.

"Get stuffed, Dafari!" Octavian rebuked. My brother had naturally dark eyes, but when he was angry, they glowed a bright white. "I am no tosser. Besides, that's rich coming from you. You've existed for three centuries, bedded a multitude of women, taking advantage of their free will. Now you have the nerve, the unmitigated gall, to chastise me about the complexities of the fairer sex? Although, I must admit that exchange between Tasmin and I went pear-shaped rather abruptly. As you heard, she wants nothing further to do with me," he said, calming down.

Octavian's temper was only rivaled by my own; unlike me, he was quick to let a cooler head prevail.

"That it did. Just so you're aware, I have no plans of being your messenger boy. What do you intend to do about Tasmin?"

"What do you intend to do about Elisa, besides continue to satisfy her carnally? They are *both* in danger, and we need to figure out a way to let them know without them thinking we're nutters."

"Don't you worry, dear brother. I will make sure Elisa knows when the time is right. You just concern yourself with getting back in Tasmin's good graces. She won't be as easy to convince as Elisa, and, at the moment, she despises you. I see much groveling in your future," I taunted.

"Dafari, I fear we don't have much time." His voice held a serious, almost urgent tone. "Your father can strike at any moment. He's very adept at cloaking his presence. Those women are virtually sitting ducks."

"I see your point, but while my father is a master at avoiding detection, he must be losing his touch if you were able to detect his energy trail."

Octavian let out a heavy sigh. "I'm not so sure, Brother. It almost seems like he purposefully left that trail; as if he wanted me to find you, Elisa, and Tasmin. No matter how much I try to push this feeling to the side, I can't shake it."

My brother's words gave me pause. Despite the fact that he was an annoying, egotistically competitive blowhard, I had learned eons ago to never dismiss his hunches. Whenever he had a sense of foreboding, he was rarely ever wrong. Of course, I would never let him know that. We drove the rest of the short distance home in complete silence.

Minutes later, I pulled into one of the garage bays of my palatial home. Octavian was right about one thing; I was prone to excess and held no apologies for it. I had lived all over the world like a king for centuries, and I had no intention of living otherwise, whether I was in hiding or not. My home, which was five thousand square feet, was built shortly after my arrival in Salix Pointe. Situated on the outskirts of town, it stood on three very private acres of land; perfect for someone like me who didn't want to be disturbed.

"Nice gaff you have here," Octavian remarked.

"Would you expect any less?" I retorted.

We had walked through the door that led from the garage to the enormous kitchen which boasted stainless steel appliances, granite countertops, a large island with seating, and a sizeable pantry. Octavian followed me to the opulent living room which flaunted deep cherry wood walls and ceilings, two ceiling fans, a double-sided glass and marble fireplace, a wet bar, two recliners, and a sectional. Walking behind the wet bar, I took two bourbon snifters from the shelf along with a bottle of fifty-year-old bourbon. Poured each of us a dram.

"Like I said, excess," Octavian voiced, taking the snifter off the bar, consuming the brown liquid in one gulp.

"If you're really that bothered by my extravagance, such as it is, I can take you back to town and you can stay at the local bed and breakfast," I shot back, sipping my own libation.

"And deprive you of my resplendent company? Dear brother, I wouldn't dream of it," he said then chuckled.

"Vexing is more like it," I replied, as I finished the last bit of my bourbon then poured myself another. "I'm only allowing you to stay here because our powers are vastly amplified the closer we are to each other. As much as it irks me to admit it, we're stronger together than apart. If what you say is in fact true, we need to concentrate our efforts on locating my father as soon as possible. If he killed Noreen, and is seeking to kill the witches, he needs to be stopped."

"*If* he killed Ms. Chadwick? There's no if about it, Dafari. Your father escapes captivity, Ms. Chadwick is murdered, and his energy trail leads to the very same town where the incident occurred. Why is it so difficult for you to believe that he's culpable?"

"You don't know for sure that—" Furious with Octavian's accusations leveled against my father, I couldn't control my fury. My eyes turned red and I bulked up in size.

In a rare loss of self-control, Octavian, feeding off of my rage, also grew in size, his white eyes looking directly into mine. "Wake up, man! Who else could have done it? A demon will *always* be a demon. Evil to the core."

"Then what does that make me?" I threw my glass of bourbon against a wall in frustration.

"It makes you the son of a demon." Octavian put his hands on my shoulders. "It also makes you the son of an angel, my brother. The better part of you."

In spite of myself, I felt a sense of calm overtake me, my eyes and body returning to normal, as did Octavian's.

"Dafari, we need to work together in order to keep the witches safe," Octavian replied. "But we can continue this later. Right now, I'm extremely knackered. Veil jetlag and all. I'm still on London time," he continued. "Where can I retreat so I may catch a kip?"

"Take one of the bedrooms upstairs."

"I'll be taking my leave now. No worries, Brother. I'll stay out of your way for the duration. Wouldn't want to interrupt you while you're astrally stuffing Elisa later."

While I was quick to anger, my brother was quick at attempting to defuse a situation with humor. I felt it was best to respond in kind.

"Don't be jealous, Brother. If your acts of contrition work, you may still get to stuff the good doctor yet," I replied mockingly. "Now leave me," I said, with a wave of my hand.

With a nod, Octavian departed. Waiting until I heard his footfalls on the stairs, I walked a few short steps to a closed door, the door that led to my sanctuary. While the rest of my home was opulence personified, my sanctuary, in contrast, epitomized minimalism, being reminiscent of a Japanese Zen garden. Complete with rhododendron and hydrangea shrubs, a circular island of moss, Imperial bonsai trees, a small bridge, white sand, a stream, stones, and a waterfall, it was the one place where I found some semblance of peace.

I stepped inside the dark room. The double-sided fireplace, visible from the living room, was also observable from the Zen garden. I snapped my fingers, the flames lighting up the area. Closing the door behind me, I surveyed the room, appreciating the duality of the space. To me, the part in front of the bridge represented the chaos and madness of everyday life, while the area over the bridge symbolized peace and serenity. Because the house was built near a creek, I was able to have pipes constructed for an indoor waterfall which cascaded down the wall on the far side of the room, the water flowing as a small stream under the bridge.

I crossed the bridge to the other side of the room. Rocks surrounded the rectangular space, enclosing the shrubs, trees, and soft white sand, which had etchings throughout to simulate rippling water. The moss island was positioned in the middle of the sand. I sat on the island, crossing my legs, palms face up resting on my knees.

It was still very early, and Elisa usually retired for the evening around seven. I used the time I had to focus on what Octavian had relayed to me so far; my father escaping and his assumption that he was responsible for Noreen's death, his parents parting ways, the witches being in danger. It was a substantial amount of information to sift through with no substantial evidence to speak of.

Notwithstanding the location where my father had been imprisoned, per natural law, he should not have been able to escape his confines, no matter how stong a demon he was. And why would he kill Noreen? Those in themselves were mysteries that needed deciphering.

And Mother and my stepfather splitting up; one would have thought theirs was a love story for the eternal ages. From what I recall as young child, after my parents divorced, Octavian's father appeared at what some would consider just the right time to pick up the pieces of my mother's broken heart. I found it a little too convenient.

And lastly, the witches. Why would someone want to harm them? Noreen was dead, never revealing to Tasmin what she or her niece were. Elisa was also unaware of her powers. They had been de facto effectively harmless.

I had ruminated on all I had learned for so many hours that I was almost negligent in preparing myself for my time with Elisa. I closed my eyes, taking some time to center myself, clearing my mind of all distractions, aiming for peace, tranquility, calmness. I focused on only Elisa, intent on hearing her call, but nothing happened. She usually reached out to me around the same time each night, but tonight was different, as if she was resisting me. That had never happened before, and I found it a bit…unsettling. I gave her a little coaxing, slightly reaching into her mind. Still nothing. I decided to wait a bit longer before making another attempt, instead deciding to focus on completing the environs.

I always allowed Elisa to set the scene to her liking, but tonight, I had something else, something special, in mind. While she has never ventured out of the continental United States, Elisa did have the desire to travel internationally. Her thoughts conveyed a longing to travel to YS Falls in Jamaica.

In lieu of taking her there physically, I planned to bring her there on the astral realm, where I could take artistic liberties.

The venue was already breathtaking; majestic waterfalls sat above the Black River with its seven river pools, lush gardens, and jungle foliage. I could see why it was a favorite in Elisa's mind. I added my own touches of a round king-sized bed with gold satin bedding and rose petals. Tiki torches surrounded the bed. The moon shone brightly in the sky, adding to the illumination.

Once I had constructed everything to my liking, I once again listened intently for Elisa's call. There was none. I was going to give it one last attempt, one last gentle nudge, lest I cause harm to her mind. That finally did the trick. Elisa appeared directly in front of me, wearing a peach silk gown that hugged her plentiful hips and ample bosom. Her cocoa brown skin smelled of her jasmine and lavender body wash. Her short afro glistened in the moonlight, scented with almond and coconut oil.

Her eyes were cast downward. "You didn't call on me tonight," I noted, lifting her chin with my finger, bringing her eyes up to meet mine.

"You seemed…angry earlier. I didn't think you wanted to see me."

I did something that I rarely, if ever, did. "I…apologize. It wasn't you. My brother has a way of…incurring my wrath. Forgive me?"

"I do," she quietly replied.

Looking into her eyes, I saw something that I recognized in myself; the tendency to withdraw. We differed in that she never, ever showed it in public. In our astral world, she was truly free to be whom she was; bubbly and vibrant one minute, quiet and reserved the next. But tonight, quiet and reserved would not do.

I leaned down, kissing her full, lush lips, my tongue meeting hers. Grabbing her round backside, I pulled her closer to me. She melted in my arms. In the astral plane, I had complete control. I transported us over to the bed and, with nothing more than a thought, removed our clothing, kiss unbroken. My lips moved down to her neck, then to her large breasts. I sucked on each nipple as she writhed and moaned beneath me.

I had done this astral dance with Elisa for three years, knew all her sexual proclivities. I knew how she loved when my tongue flicked back and forth against her flowering bud while I slowly fingered her at the same time.

"Yes, don't stop," she said breathlessly.

I pleasured her until I knew she was ready for more. Flipping her onto her stomach, I gave her what she really wanted; long, slow strokes that made her insides quiver. Her fingers tightly gripped the sheets while she bit into the pillow, pushing her derriere back to meet my every deep, powerful thrust. I loved it when a woman took all I had to offer.

"That's right, Elisa, take what you want. It'll be our little secret," I whispered in her ear.

She pushed back harder and faster, the change in the pitch of her melodic moans foretold of her imminent climax. I drove into her harder, her muscles clamping down on me. She cried out as she released, completely satisfied.

I was close, so close to my own gratification. I grabbed her hips, my pace accelerating. Just…a…few…more…seconds. All of a sudden, I felt a vigorous tapping on my shoulder from none other than my immensely annoying brother, causing me to experience a severe case of coitus interruptus.

"So sorry to intrude on your otherworldly rumpy-pumpy, but we need to have a chinwag posthaste."

"Damn you, Octavian!" I shouted, pinning him against the wall in anger.

Our astral link broken, I didn't have time to wipe Elisa's mind. Unless I quickly reestablished our connection, this would not end well.

CHAPTER 7:
OCTAVIAN

"Unass me, you heathen," I yelled at my brother as he held me against the bloody wall like I was the enemy.

I knew I'd risk his wrath if I interrupted his sleep—which meant he was probably in a bit of a pickle with Elisa—however, his father was near. It was imperative he knew that.

"You dare interrupt me while—"

I yanked out of his hold. "You insufferable prat! Don't you think I knew interrupting you now could get my bloody skull cracked? Thus, you should know I only did it because it's a dire emergency? Your father is near—"

Before the words could leave my mouth, an alarming cry of, "Help me," caught our attention.

Dafari's heated gaze darted around the room. "It's Elisa. Something's wrong. I left her in that dream state without getting her out safely which means I left the door open for any other entity to get to her," he said, alarm in his voice.

I noticed he had bulked in size once more. Anymore and he would be in battle mode and that would not fare well for anyone in his path.

I laid a hand on his shoulder. "Calm yourself lest you bring down hellfire and red skies. You may be half demon, but do not forget we come from a line of high-ranking battle archangels. You get any angrier, and you know what could happen, Brother."

He turned fire red eyes to me. "I don't care. I need to get back to Elisa!"

"Well she has to invite you—"

"She's terrified! Can't you feel it? She won't be cognizant of the fact she has to invite me back into her dreams," he snapped.

The unmitigated look of terror on my brother's face rattled me. I wouldn't say he was afraid of his demon daddy, but more so afraid of what his father could do to Elisa. In dreams was where his father was most powerful. That wasn't to say he wasn't just as ghastly on the earthly plane; however, he was a full blooded demon, an incubus. He was nothing to be trifled with on a plane that was his playground.

I touched Dafari's shoulder, and even though he didn't give me permission, I did something that he would normally hate me for. I placed a hand on his shoulder and shut down his neurotransmitters needed to produce wakefulness. His body slumped to the floor. Because I expended so much energy putting him to sleep as opposed to calming him, I found myself dragged onto the astral plane right along with him when my body fell to the floor.

When I came to, the echoes of a protection chant serenaded me. The fact that the voices behind the chant were Elisa's and Tasmin's weren't lost on me either. However, seeing Dafari's father in full-blown demon form with his hand drawn back, ready to strike Elisa sent me scrambling to my feet. I felt Dafari next to me as we lurched forward and tackled his father to the ground.

I heard his father growl then roar out in anger. While my dear old brother and I were powerful in our own right, there was no way I wanted to fight his father on the astral plane. He was a demon of ungodly power and strength. He was one of the first Fallen and one of the most powerful. He'd been around since inception which meant he knew how to fight in ways which neither my brother nor I could compete. At least not until we figured out how to protect Tasmin and Elisa.

The angry dog-faced scowl on Dafari's father's face showed he was not pleased. He charged at us only to stop, while shaking his head and spitting on the ground. The chants were working, and we could have taken advantage of that. However, being part demon, the chants were having an adverse effect on Dafari as well. He'd fallen to his knees, hands pressed against his skull as he ground his teeth.

I reached down to lift Dafari, keeping my eyes on Demon Daddy. "Brother, I think it's time you got us out of here, don't you think?"

Panting, he said, "Elisa…has to…wake up…"

"Oh, that's right. This is her dream. You can't give her a boost?" I asked when his father turned blood red eyes to us once more. "Being a full-blooded angel doesn't bode me well on this plane…" I looked at him. "And it's not doing you any favors at the moment, either."

His father charged at us again, fangs and talons lengthening to ways that told me he was not in the mood for a father-son reunion. As soon as the thought crossed my mind, the pit of my stomach bottomed out as we were yanked back to reality. We landed with a thud back into Dafari's sanctuary.

I moaned as I sat up. "Your father has never been very…fatherly has he?" I asked Dafari, the sarcasm dripping.

"Elisa and Tasmin have joined powers. I thought they wouldn't be able to until their powers were revealed to them, but—"

I nodded. "Yes, yes. I know. Their protection chant was powerful. How is it that Elisa was able to connect to Tasmin and call her for help...while on the astral plane? I didn't think it was possible for humans to pull other humans into their dreams."

Thinking of Tasmin made me remember how peeved she'd been when I'd called her a wench. She was a short little brown skinned spitfire whose burgundy locs hung down her back. Her trim, athletic build made me wonder if she was just as svelte and lithe while in bed. While it looked as if she had wanted to slap me into my afterlife, her feistiness called out to all things primal and male within me. I'd wanted to kiss her smart mouth to see if that would shut her up long enough to see that I meant no harm. While I understood that intent didn't change impact, I found it was important to me that she knew I wasn't a complete horse's arse. Besides, I needed to apologize so she would hear me out when I tried to explain who and what she was.

Dafari laid out on his back, right arm thrown over his forehead. "It is, but these aren't regular humans. They're witches, and perhaps they're more powerful together than we'd thought."

"Bloody hell," I said then stood. "Was Noreen aware of this?"

"I assume so since she went out of her way to protect them."

I frowned as I paced the floor. "That doesn't make sense."

"What doesn't?"

"Why Noreen wouldn't tell them that they're witches at least. Something's not adding up. Noreen, one the most powerful witches in the world, refused to tell her niece and her best friend's granddaughter the truth? Why?"

"For the same reason Elisa's grandmother, Mama Nall, didn't tell her either I suppose. We're missing something."

Dafari sat up then stood. Silence enveloped us a few moments before he said, "She called out to me."

"Huh? Who?"

"Elisa. When she was in trouble, she called to me."

I looked at him, waiting for him to tell me why it was a big deal. "Well, it was a dream so…"

"Use your noggin, Brother. If she willingly consents to have me in her dreams for the purpose of erotic pleasure, that's different. However, there was no intent or consent to sex when she *telepathically* called me…"

He left the end of his sentence trail off. It wasn't until he put emphasis on the word *telepathically* that it hit me.

"Blimey, are you telling me she was in your head? That's not possible, is it? She's a human, albeit a powerful witch, but human. She isn't supposed to be able to do that lest she fries her own brain."

"No shit, Sherlock," he quipped.

"Bugger off. Do you think that means Tasmin is as powerful?"

"I'd be willing to bet my soul that she is. My father is here now. We have more than enough proof of that. He tried to hurt Elisa and for that he must pay."

"That also means he will go after Tasmin next."

Dafari nodded. "I can't help but wonder why he didn't try to rip us to shreds," he said then cut his eyes at me. "Well, try to get to you at least."

"Gee thanks, wanker. See the next time I try to save your bloody arse."

He walked out of his sanctuary. "We need to find a way to reveal the truth to them and make them believe it. We have to do it fast."

I followed. "How do you suggest we do that? Let out our angel wings and levitate?"

"If all else fails," he answered.

"You can't be serious. If we reveal ourselves, our true selves, they'd run away screaming bloody murder. You know as well as I do that humans think of us in their image and while you and I have taken on such forms, our true form is frightening. What human would be willing to look upon us in true form and not be nutters afterwards?"

He turned to look me. "Again, if all else fails, we must do what we have to do. Time is of the essence."

CHAPTER 8:
ELISA

My body jolted as if someone had yanked me out of my sleep…Only, I wasn't asleep, and I was no longer at home in my bed. I was on the island of my dreams in a bed that was foreign to me. My body's pressure points and erogenous zones hummed in synchronicity. Dr. Battle had been here with me, on top of me…inside of me…It had felt so good that I was delirious with pleasure. Out of my mind with sensations and eroticisms that I could have never imagined.

And then…just like that…he was gone. Something or someone had yanked him away. I heard waterfalls in the distance. Birds chirped and insects hummed. The place smelled of honeysuckle and lemon verbena, and I was as naked as the night was long. Hives sat up on my skin as I whipped my head left and right trying to get my senses about me.

"A shame for him to leave you here like this…all alone and vulnerable. Ripe for the picking…"

"Who's there? Where am I?" I screamed, wrapping the sheet around my body.

My skin prickled at the sound of his voice. It was low, modulated, and had a seductive undertone that made my pulse quicken. My breasts swelled and I felt my nipples get harder than they had been before. My core beat at a rhythm I didn't understand. My breathing deepened and I found it hard to catch my breath.

From beneath the waterfalls, I saw a shadow, more like the outline of a male body. Glowing red orbs made me pull myself from the bed. Naked or not, sheets be damned…my instincts told me to run, but my feet betrayed me. As soon as they touched the lush grass, it was as if something froze me in place.

"Normally, I like the chase, Elisa. Under any other circumstances, I'd let you run and chase you like the wonderful sensually seductive prey you are," he crooned. "However, time is of the essence."

The more he talked, the further he walked out of the shadows of the waterfall. The sheets of water parted like curtains. My eyes had to be playing tricks on me. The man looked like Dr. Battle, but older, wiser and more sinister. I did a doubletake as I wasn't sure who—better yet what—I was looking at. He was dressed in a gray suit that had clearly been tailored to fit his warrior-like frame. His feet clad in black Italian leather dress shoes. His shirt was black, and a blood red tie lay against his chiseled chest. The man was massive in size, the glowing orbs where eyes should have been alarmed me, but not more than the mouth full of jagged fangs.

I opened my mouth to scream, but nothing came out. I willed my feet to move, but they felt nailed to the ground. There was a buzzing in my head that threatened to overtake my senses. I heard drums and chanting in a language I didn't understand. My head swam, and my body screamed for orgasmic release. How was it that I was afraid and aroused at the same time? Something was wrong.

I saw Tasmin in my mind. She was leaving the bookstore. Something or someone in a cloak was near her. My attention was thwarted. The thing…the man was closer to me now. He was right in front of me, hands cupping my chin to bring my eyes up to his. He then dropped his hand and brought his face close to mine. He used his head to knock my chin to the side. My body went limp. Hands dropped to my sides as if my body was no longer mine to control. The sheet slid from my naked body.

As if he was whispering in my mind, he said, "Tell my son I've missed him…However, that won't stop me from ripping him and his brother limb from limb if they try to stop me…"

I watched in horror as the man's jagged fangs got longer, deadlier. I knew without a doubt that if he bit me, it would be fatal. The man…thing licked my neck then chuckled. Then, I saw Tasmin again. Her things had been thrown around the floor. She was home at Ms. Noreen's now, pacing the front room floor, holding her head.

My mind screamed, "Help me!"

Tasmin's eyes shot open. They glowed as white as snow. My head fell back and the chant I'd heard in my mind earlier flowed from mine and Tasmin's lips in sync. The thing dropped its hold on me. He hissed and spat like my taste repulsed him.

The man transformed into something my mental state couldn't comprehend. His clothes shredded as his body bulked into unnatural proportions. His nails elongated to the point they looked like mangled talons. He drew back his meaty hand as if he was about to strike me.

My mind called to the only other person I could think of…Dr. Battle.

I shot up in bed. My racing heart beating as if I'd run a four-minute mile. I was drenched in sweat and my body shivered as if I were cold. I whipped my head around like it was on a swivel. It was only when I realized I was at home, in my own bed that I breathed a sigh of a relief. It had all been a dream, just a bad night terror. I clutched imaginary pearls on my neck and fell back. I needed to get my wits about me.

What an awful, alarming dream. The last part of it replayed in my mind. Once I'd called out to Dr. Battle in the dream, he, and his brother, had come charging after the demon. I shook my head. I shouldn't have had that nightcap before bed. I had even dreamed Tasmin was being followed by someone in a cloak and then her eyes had glowed white. *Never* again will I drink rum before bed.

I looked at the clock to see it was five in the morning. "I may as well get up," I mumbled.

I swung my feet over the side of the bed and blanched at the feel of the cold wood underneath my feet. I searched for my slippers on the side of my queen-sized bed then slipped into the furry warmness. I would have to get to the café shortly. I'd already showered before bed so the only thing to do would be to get breakfast and coffee.

I grabbed my white sage bundle by rote and went in search of my black tourmaline crystals. I'd charged them under the last full moon and knew they helped to ward off bad dreams. I'd come from a family of women and men who knew how to use herbs, stones, teas, and prayer chants among other things to fight off ailments, bad dreams, evil spirits, ghosts…and a host of other things people deemed superstitious.

My family had roots from the Low Country—Gullah-Geechee people. We came from the deep south where superstition ruled the roost. We couldn't step over another child lest they stopped growing. We couldn't sweep an adult's feet, or they had to spit on the broom, lest they go to jail. If a black cat crossed a person's path, it meant bad luck was coming unless they went back to where they'd come from and start over. If all the dogs were howling in the same neighborhood, it was a sign that death was walking the streets. Don't rock an empty rocking chair or it would invite spirits. Never walk under a ladder.

Never open an umbrella indoors. By all that was good and righteous, do not break a mirror or the person would have seven years bad luck.

I grew up hearing and believing all of those things. While some of them seemed outright ridiculous…I had enough experience to know that some held weight. I missed Ms. Noreen. After my grandmother had died, Ms. Noreen had been the only one I could be open and honest with. If she had been alive, I could have told her about my dream when she came into the café. I could have told her I thought an incubus had visited me in my dreams and she wouldn't have deemed me a nut…I shivered at how real the dream had seemed.

I'd waken up many mornings over the past three years sweaty and panting. My body would feel as if it had been taken on the wickedest rides of sexual encounters… I shook my head to stave off the silliness of it all. Incubi weren't real…right? It had been just a bad dream, a nightmare. The rum had to be the culprit…right?

I lit the sage bundle and walked through my house. I let up a window in every other room so I could invite good intentions in and let the bad mojo out. Hey, I did say some of the superstitions I still lived by. It was hard to break such traditions when there had been proof in the pudding that some of them worked.

I shook my head, trying to get the images of Dr. Battle out of my mind. Thinking of how he'd had his way with me in that dream made me shudder. I couldn't deny that being with him had been…sensual, seductive, and downright satisfying. My body still hummed from the things he'd done to me in my dreams. From the way he kissed and touched me to the way his body connected to mine when he eased inside of me…If incubi were indeed real, Dr. Battle would be the kind I wanted to visit me more often.

Good grief! I shook my head as I pulled my crystal from its bowl then slid it in my robe's pocket. I needed to get a hold of my raging hormones. It had been seven long years since I'd been intimate with any man. The last man I dated wanted me to tie him to a whipping post and make him bleed as I whipped him. That was over before it started.

I doused my sage bundle, making sure all embers were completely gone. My mind traveled back to the dream. Why would Tasmin be in my dreams being chased by a cloaked figure? And why would I see her pacing her front room…chanting the same things I was with glowing white eyes? I couldn't make sense of any of it.

I shook my head to clear my thoughts as I prepared to make my morning coffee. I was going to miss looking out my kitchen window and seeing Ms. Noreen in her herb garden. She had several on her property and always welcomed me when I needed or just wanted some fresh herbs. She often made me teas and talked about the ways in which she and my grandmother used to run the streets together.

I'd lost my grandmother, Mama Nall, five years ago when old age took her home. She had been what us Southerners called a root worker. Being from the Low Country, my grandmother could trace her roots all the way back to West Africa and she made sure we knew where we came from as well. Some of my family still lived in Georgia but not in Salix Pointe. Although we'd come from a family who practiced vodou, root work, conjuring and the like, some of my family thought Salix Pointe was too weird even for them.

My parents had died in a car crash when I was ten. While losing them had hurt in ways I was too young to express or understand, Mama Nall taking me into her home was the best thing to happen for me. She taught me to use herbs, roots, and elixirs to help with prayers and healings. Some even claimed Mama Nall did root work that could be considered black magic, but I always laughed that off. There was no such thing as magic…Was there? Living in Salix Pointe had taught me to question things that shouldn't even be possible.

I opened my kitchen window, set to let some fresh air in when I noticed Ms. Noreen's porch light on…That wouldn't have been a problem except her front door was wide open. I knew Tasmin had planned to stay there while she was visiting so the fact that the door was ajar after five in the morning raised my hackles.

I quickly raced to change my clothes and slid on a pair of boots. I grabbed my steel bat that sat near my front door and raced toward Ms. Noreen's. I waded through the small brook that separated our properties, hopped over a thatch of peppers in one of her gardens and raced up the small stone steps. I gasped. There, on the front room floor lay Tasmin.

I hurried inside, closed the door behind me just in case some mad man was around and then knelt beside Tasmin. I laid the bat down. Just like in my dreams, her bags had been strewn about on the floor and she was still dressed in the clothing she'd had on earlier.

I tapped her cheek with my open palm. "Tasmin? Tasmin, are you okay?" I asked.

I could see her chest rising and falling so I knew she was alive.

"Tasmin," I called to her again. "Wake up."

Her eyes fluttered as she stirred and moaned. I gave her a few moments. If she didn't fully wake, I would call Doc Benu and have him come see about her. Luckily, she opened her eyes and gazed up at me.

"What happened and what are you doing here, Elisa?" she asked, trying to sit up.

I urged her to keep her head on my thigh. "No, no, you lay still for a few seconds more. You have a knot on the side of your head. You tell me what happened. Did someone attack you?"

She took a deep breath as her eyes watered. "I've had the craziest day since being here thus far. First, Octavian called me a cheeky wench then I thought someone in a cloak was following me. Once here, I got a phone call telling me my practice had burned to the ground and that was on top of already feeling as if I was going to pass out. I won't even attempt to explain anything else, because I don't quite remember…and I don't want to come off like a lunatic."

I helped her to stand then guided her to the sofa. I wouldn't let on that what she had said about someone in a cloak following her had alarmed me. It was the same as in my dreams. However, just like she didn't want to be seen as a nut, neither did I.

"You just lie back. Let me get you something for that knot on your head," I said.

I hurried to Ms. Noreen's kitchen. I grabbed a clean towel from her laundry room then put ice in it. I grabbed a tea pot to boil water for ginger root tea. I knew Tasmin would have a headache based on the size of the knot on her head.

"Here you go," I said passing her the towel with ice once I walked back to the front room.

She took it and placed it on the side of her head.

"I've got water going for some ginger root tea. That should help with the headache."

"Thank you, but you don't have to stay. I know you have to get to your café," she said.

I waved her off. "I have a few minutes to spare."

She sighed then laid back. "I can't believe my practice has burned down," she said, her voice a bit shaky. "Now I have to worry about selling the bookstore and figuring out what happened to cause the fire. Not to mention rebuilding and filing an insurance claim. How much worse can this visit get?"

"I'd be careful saying things like that. Salix Pointe has a way of answering those kinds of questions in ways in which you won't like," I said then chuckled.

"Please don't remind me of how weird this place is. I remember from when I used to visit," she said.

"Did you see who was following you?" I asked.

She tried to shake her head then winced. "That's the thing; I'm not sure anyone was actually following me or if I imagined it all."

"What do you mean?"

"It could have been a shadow, my own, that I got afraid of. I left the bookstore, walking to my car and all of a sudden from the reflection on my car's window, I thought I saw someone in a cloak following me. Then I turn around and no one's there. I only see my darn shadow," she said, letting out a breath as if she was exasperated. "And is there a waterfall around here that I don't know about?"

The hair on the back of my neck rose as I sat forward. "No, why? We only have that brook that separates the two houses."

"I could have sworn before I passed out, I heard a waterfall," she said.

I stared at her with wide eyes. My hands shook as I thought back to my dream. There was just no way…It couldn't have been possible…

CHAPTER 9:
TASMIN

My head was hurting from hitting it on the hardwood floor when I passed out, and I most likely had a concussion. I was in such bad shape that I didn't realize it was the next day. Had it not been for Elisa finding me, who knows when I would have come to? Then there was the mind fog I was experiencing from everything else that had happened.

"Here you go," said Elisa, handing me a cup of ginger root tea. "How's your head?"

I placed the towel with the mostly melted ice on the floor, taking the tea from her. "Throbbing. The dizziness just makes it worse. Thank you for this, and for the save earlier." I took a slow sip of the tea, not sure how it would taste. She had added just the right amount of honey and lemon, as if she already knew how I liked it. "Elisa, I know you have to get to work. You go ahead. I'll be fine."

"Doesn't look like it from where I'm sitting," she replied, matter-of-factly. "Besides, I have an in with the owner," she said with a laugh.

"I really appreciate it, but I don't want to—"

"Look, you were out cold when I found you. You, of all people, know that you should watch someone after a head injury. I just want to make sure you're okay."

As much as I didn't want to impose on her time, I found her presence comforting. "Okay, how about we do this; if you're not in too much of a rush, I'll take a quick shower and ride with you to work. That way, you can keep an eye on me while we chow down on some of those excellent pastries of yours," I said, managing a weak smile.

She looked at me skeptically, but eventually relented. "Fine, but I'm timing you, just in case. Don't need you passing out again."

Elisa, carrying my empty cup and the wet towel, headed back toward the kitchen, I assumed to wash the cup and put the towel in the laundry room. I made my way upstairs, intent on taking a quick shower, but the dizziness slowed me down.

As I gathered a fresh set of clothes, I tried to wrap my head around all that had transpired in less than twenty-four hours' time. First, there was the eerie feeling that I was being followed by some cloaked figure. It could have all been in my head, but then again…Then there was that urgent call from my parents telling me that my beloved practice, a business that I had owned for just over a year and had put my heart and soul into, was destroyed. That call hurt me to my core. I had just walked through the door to Aunt Noreen's house when I looked at my buzzing phone and saw Mom's name on the screen.

"Tasmin, sweetie," my mom began, not even giving me a chance to say hello. "We have some bad news."

"We got a call from the alarm company for your office," I heard my dad chime in. I thought he was going to say there was a break-in, but what he said next was so much worse. "There was a fire and an explosion. The building's gone, Tazzy." Tazzy was my childhood nickname. I hadn't heard Dad call me that in a long time.

"When? How?" was all I could get out. I was in utter shock.

"Honey, it was about three hours ago. We drove to the office as soon as we got the call," my mom continued. "The fire had been put out by then, but the fire investigator had just started looking things over. She said she would contact us once she had anything concrete to share. The strange thing is your building was the only one destroyed. The attached buildings on either side are just fine; no damage at all. The inspector couldn't explain it."

That was strange. I knew very little about the nature of fires, but I did know that if there was one, anything attached should have sustained at least some damage. With an explosion, I would have expected that damage to be major. What was really going on?

My dad, very much attuned to what I was thinking, replied, "Tazzy, don't you worry. We'll get to the bottom of this; I can promise you that." Dad was himself an investigator, albeit with the Brooklyn District Attorney's office. Even though I felt my entire life's work had imploded, I felt slightly better knowing that my dad was on the case. He was an amazing investigator, and I knew he would do everything in his power to figure out what had happened.

"Thank you, Daddy," I said. I felt hot tears welling up in my eyes.

"Sweetie, we are so sorry," Mommy added. "I know this is a lot for you to take in right now, especially with you taking care of Aunt Noreen's final wishes. Something told me we should have stayed in Salix Pointe after her home-going. I should have listened to my gut."

The entire family was in attendance for Aunt Noreen's home-going ceremony, with most leaving shortly afterwards. My parents had offered to stay to help me get Auntie's affairs in order, but I wouldn't hear of it. I knew they both had jobs to get back to and figured I could handle things on my own. In hindsight, I wished I had taken them up on their offer. Then again, had they been down here, no one would have been in Brooklyn to deal with the aftermath of the fire.

"Mommy, it's okay. Right now, I just need to know what happened to my business. Daddy, I know you're on it."

"You know I am, Tazzy. I've got you," he acknowledged.

"Tasmin, everything will be fine. Don't worry; we'll get through this together, as a family." Mom always knew what to say.

"Thank you, Mommy and Daddy. I love you both."

"We love you, too," they replied in concert. That was the last thing that was said before we disconnected our call.

I walked into the bathroom, closed the door, and turned on the shower. I took off the one piece of wrist jewelry I always wore; my black tourmaline and selenite bracelet. One of the many things Auntie had me study was crystals and their properties. I had grown to appreciate that as I got older.

As a hobby, I liked to make jewelry for myself, mainly earrings, waist beads, rings, and bracelets. Shortly before coming to Salix Pointe, I made my black tourmaline and selenite bracelet. While history has associated the color black with something bad or evil, in many instances, it had a good meaning. For example, many of the black crystals had protective properties. I chose black tourmaline because it was considered the bodyguard stone, offering protection, acting as a psychic shield, and eliminating negative energy. Selenite, my other chosen crystal, also eliminated negative energy. Additionally, it was able to open channels to other worlds, communicate with spirits, and had the ability to cleanse and charge other crystals, including itself. They also provided good contrast since tourmaline was black and selenite was white. I added the ankh pendant to the bracelet, because it symbolized life. I asked for my Ancestors to bless and protect me after the bracelet was completed.

I took off all my clothes, tossing them in the clothes hamper. Put on a shower cap then tested the water, making sure it was warm enough before climbing into the shower. I washed my face first, being careful around the knot on my right temple. It still smarted. I couldn't believe that I passed out. I had never passed out in my life. As I washed the rest of my body, I thought back to the events leading up to it, as much as I could remember, anyway.

Right after I hung up with my parents, the strangest thing happened. I noticed a feeling of warmth and tingling around my left wrist where my bracelet sat. The stones appeared to be glowing. Then I heard these words echoing in my head: 'I call on The One Most High, I call on my Ancestors, I call on my Warrior Angels. Surround us in white light, protect us from all evil'. Funny thing was, I had never heard those words before, and they weren't in English. Yet, I understood them perfectly. Accompanied by rhythmic tribal drum beats, on and on went the entreaty.

I had no idea why I was hearing those words. I wasn't in any danger, at least I didn't think so. Then I felt it; an undeniable, overwhelming sensation of fear so intense it caused my heart to feel like it was beating out of my chest.

Suddenly, a woman appeared, and she looked remarkably like Elisa. She was naked and looked petrified. In an instant, the point of view changed, as if I was looking through her eyes. There, directly in front of her, appeared some hideous beast. Its mouth, full of dripping fangs, was dangerously close to her neck, and appeared as if it was about to strike. That was when she let out a bloodcurdling scream for help. Her plea was so deafening, it made my head pound. I dropped all my belongings on the floor, clutching my head in pain.

The invocation and tribal drums became even louder, drowning out all other sounds. The woman and I began speaking the words in unison. "I call on The One Most High, I call on my Ancestors, I call on my Warrior Angels. Surround us in white light, protect us from all evil."

The chant only seemed to anger the creature. It became a mammoth hulking figure over her, raising its appendage, ready to trounce, only for the woman to vanish at the last possible moment. I must have passed out right after she disappeared because that was the last thing I remembered.

I shook my head, as if to clear it of the cobwebs that were residing there. All of it sounded incredibly implausible, and yet, it all seemed so real. I knew if I told anyone about it, they would send me back to

New York and have me locked up in the psych ward at Bellevue Hospital with a quickness.

I got out of the shower, slathered my body with some vanilla shea butter with coconut oil, and quickly got dressed in a crop top, jeans, and a pair of black high-top sneakers. I remembered to put my bracelet back on my wrist. After grabbing my crossbody bag, keys, and jacket, I went back downstairs, only to see Elisa standing by the front door, purse and keys in hand. I noticed she had traded in her wading boots for some black suede high heel boots.

"Sorry I took so long," I said apologetically, opening the front door and walking outside.

Elisa followed me. She had pulled her SUV around so it was on Aunt Noreen's side of the brook. "No worries. Are you feeling any better?"

"Some," I replied. "I probably just need some food in me." I locked the front door then followed Elisa down the stairs.

"We can grab something at the café," answered Elisa, as we climbed into her vehicle. When we were comfortably inside, she asked, "Earlier, you said something about Octavian calling you a wench. How and when did that happen?" she asked, a smirk on her face.

I rolled my eyes. "Girl, it was when he was still at the bookstore. That man is strange, if you ask me."

"Why do you say that?" she inquired.

"For one, he was looking for books about magick and witches. Then he seriously tried to convince me that magick is real," I remarked incredulously.

"Did he really?" Elisa asked with a chuckle. "Why would he do that?"

"Elisa, I have no idea, but it all started when I made him some ginger root tea because he had a headache. That's when he started trying to convince me that the tea was magical, saying that because I wanted to cure his headache so badly, I had somehow infused the tea with my own magical mojo in order to heal him."

"Stop it!" Elisa said, laughing harder. "He really said that?"

"Okay, so those weren't his exact words, but that was the gist of it," I remarked jokingly. "Of course you know I wasn't buying anything he was selling," I asserted.

Elisa pulled up in front of the café, quickly jumping out the SUV. "How could someone so fine be…" As she unlocked the door, she appeared to be searching for something tactful to say. I, on the other hand, didn't care about diplomacy.

"How could someone so fine be a kook, a weirdo, an oddball? And you think he's fine?" I asked with a frown.

After switching on the lights and washing her hands, Elisa got behind the counter of the coffee bar, pulling out bags of coffee and tea, turning on the appliances. She then walked over to the pastry counter, sliding open the glass doors. "I was going to say eccentric, but I reckon those work, too," she said with a giggle. "And yes, he is fine. You don't think so?"

"He's a'ight, if you like that pompous, uppity, sexist type," I declared. I quickly changed the subject. "Can I help?" I felt guilty about her being late for work and felt the need to help her get up to speed.

"Sure. The kitchen is just through that door. Can you turn on the ovens for me then start bringing out the baked goods on the top two shelves in the refrigerator? I'll heat the ones on the bottom shelves after the ovens warm up."

"No problem," I remarked, washing my hands as she had done.

When I walked to the back, I noticed the two large gourmet ovens and one smaller oven, as well as the oversized stainless-steel refrigerator. I set the ovens to pre-heat then started grabbing the pastries from the top shelves. They smelled so good my stomach started to growl. I needed to eat and soon. I systematically ran back and forth, handing Elisa trays while she filled the shelves with the pastries she had baked last night. Once we were done with that task, she set about warming up the other pastries. While she did that, I took all the chairs off the tables, spread out the tablecloths, and put the pumpkins outside.

"So how did it go from you two discussing magick to him calling you a wench?" she asked once we had a break.

She had made a cup of hot apple cider with cinnamon and whipped cream for me, and a white chocolate mocha with steamed coconut milk and whipped cream for herself. We sat at one of the small tables sipping on our drinks and eating the warmed-up apple pecan muffins she brought out.

"Well, the professor —" I started.

"Wait, he's a professor?" she interrupted.

"So he told me. He said he was a professor of mythology and occultism at some university across the pond," I noted.

Elisa laughed. "That probably explains his fascination with magick. Sounds like he *really* believes what he teaches."

"Clearly," I said with a shrug. "Anyway, he was going to buy some books, but I couldn't get the cash register to work. I asked him if he could give me time to figure out how it worked and if he could come by later today. He said yes, but that's when everything went sideways. Just as he was about to leave, he asks me if I wanted him to check out the electrical circuitry."

"You mean the same circuitry he asked about when he scared the bejesus out of us?" Elisa asked, consuming the rest of her muffin and white chocolate mocha.

"Exactly like that, except he added that a job like that was man's work. Once he said that, it was all downhill from there. I felt as if I was talking to a British caveman. I half expected him to try to club me over the head and drag me by my locs. Long story short, we were verbally sparing back and forth, he made a sexist comment, I made a snarky one, and he called me 'a cheeky little wench'," I said with distain, imitating his British accent.

"Nooooooooo!" Elisa was almost on the floor she was laughing so hard. "Why, Professor, why?"

"Girl, at that point, he was persona non grata. He tried to apologize, but it was too little, too late. I told him he could have his brother pick up his books and I kicked him out." I finished the rest of my apple cider and muffin, tossing my refuse in the trash bin. "And speaking of Dr. Battle, that one gives me the heebie jeebies. From the time he arrived in Salix

Pointe, Aunt Noreen took a liking to him. I never understood why she was so fond of him. From the way he talked about her at the home-going, it seemed like the feeling was mutual."

"Well, he does have a certain appeal," Elisa noted, her voice drifting far away.

"He's got that Prince of Darkness vibe going on. Whenever I'm around him, I have this disquieting feeling. I can't explain it, but it's very unsettling. You've known him for just as long as my aunt did. What do you think of him?"

"Well, I can't say I really know him, but, for the most part, he's always been kind to me. Sure he's quiet, mysterious, and kind of broody, but I think that's part of his charm. He seems to be a creature of habit. He's always my first customer and buys the same thing every morning; a large white chocolate mocha, an almond filled croissant, and two chocolate chip cookies. He's single, but it appears to be by choice. Trust me when I say plenty of women, and some of the men, would gladly shoot their shot if he showed any interest."

I raised an eyebrow. "For someone who doesn't 'really know him'," I stated, making air quotes, "You seem to have him pegged. Does that include you?"

"Does that include me what?" she inquired.

"Does that include you amongst his many admirers? If you had the chance, would you shoot your shot?"

"Me, no…no, I-I couldn't," she replied, clearly flustered. "I'm not that forward. Besides, he's never shown any interest in me. He just likes my cookies."

I couldn't help but laugh at what she had just said. I knew she wasn't trying to be funny, but her Freudian slip thoroughly amused me.

She must have caught on, because she began to laugh too. "That came out all wrong," she said giggling like a little schoolgirl. I just meant—"

"I know exactly what you meant, but it seems to me that the lady doth protest too much. Seems to me you fancy Dr. Dark." I said, chuckling.

"Whatever," she retorted, heading toward the counter.

I stood up, knowing she would be opening soon. "Anyway, thanks again for watching out for me. I'll be at the bookstore if you need me. Have fun with your first customer. I'm sure he'll be here soon. Buh-bye," I teased.

She just smiled and, dare I say, blushed, when I mentioned Dr. Battle. Yeah, me thinks the lady doth protest too much.

CHAPTER 10: DAFARI

The morning came upon us faster than expected. Both Octavian and I were still reeling from last night's dust-up. Had we not had help from the witches, my younger brother and I could have easily met our untimely ends. Novices though they may be, completely unaware of whom and what they were, Elisa and Tasmin were far more formidable than we could have ever imagined. But how? Why? Even with my father's attack on Elisa, there was no way they should have been able to emanate that much power, and so quickly. While I was still recovering this morning after being bested by their combined efforts, I was at least half angel. My father, on the other hand, was a full demon; I can only imagine how he was faring after receiving the full brunt of their powers. A blow like that, even on the plane where he was the most formidable, should have had him recovering for at least several more hours. That would be to our advantage.

I knew my impetuous little brother believed my father killed the heart and soul, the matriarch of this town, but something within me disagreed with his rash jump to judgement. Yes, my father was no pillar of goodness and light. The fact that he was a Fallen spoke to his villainous reputation. And yes, he had committed many cruel and despicable acts over the centuries, which eventually led to him being chained to a mountain, but the one thing he was not was reckless. His moves were always calculated, deliberate, and purposeful.

There was no discernible motive for him to murder Noreen. Had he been lurking in the shadows for any length of time, he would have observed that Noreen only practiced basic magick these days; healing townsfolk with reiki, creating healing potions, designing crystal jewelry, and other cursory tasks. Her days of leading a coven seemed to be over. Since there were no other relatives of the Bloodline Tituba living in Salix Pointe, and the witch heiress-apparent, her grand-niece Tasmin, had no interest in residing in Salix Pointe, Noreen had more or less settled into a mundane existence. Why kill her when that action had the potential to unleash Tasmin's latent powers? While the prodigal niece was no fan of Salix Pointe, as Noreen had told me during several of our talks, my father would be keenly aware that Noreen's death would bring Tasmin back to her bloodline's magical epicenter, even if for a short time.

I wish I knew who had killed Noreen. I would tear him limb from limb. While I didn't make a habit of befriending humans or making any lasting relationships, there was something special about Noreen Chadwick, her status as a formidable witch notwithstanding. For the last one hundred years, I had been running; running from family, running from the ghosts of my past, running from family duties. I would relocate to someplace new; someplace where I could work in professions that afforded me the luxury of avoiding people as much as humanly possible. Then, seven years ago, I found Salix Pointe, a town that was not only capable of concealing my location from those who would seek to unearth my whereabouts, but was also home to an extremely powerful witch, a verified descendent of Tituba. There was also a verified descent of Marie Laveaux, none other than Elisa's grandmother, Mama Nall.

When I first arrived in town, I knew I had to establish myself. As luck would have it, the town was in desperate need of a veterinarian, as the previous one had disappeared under mysterious circumstances. I thought this would work in my favor. However, from the outset I quickly came to realize no one was able to settle in Salix Pointe without the explicit approval of the town's Council of Elders lead by Noreen Chadwick, Mama Nall,

Mayor Ephraim Lovett, and Doc Benu. While I easily swayed the mayor, the medical examiner, and the other two council members, Mama Nall, a puissant witch in her own right, was a bit harder to sway, but eventually gave her blessing of her own accord. Noreen seemed to be immune to my charms altogether, something I attributed to her substantial abilities. While she never outwardly expressed it, I had the feeling that she knew I was something…otherworldly. Despite that, or maybe because of it, she had welcomed me with open arms.

No one knew of our regular Saturday afternoons together, where she would regale me with stories of the early days of Salix Pointe, and how the locals managed to keep the small town thriving despite it being so isolated. I found solace in the time we spent together. In hindsight, I now realize that I was drawn to Noreen on an emotional level. With her, I experienced something I hadn't with my own mother, absolute acceptance. My mother and I had a strained relationship, one reason being that when she looked at me, deep down I knew she saw my father. She tried to hide it, but her emotional distance was palpable, especially when compared to the discernible bond she had with my baby brother, her little angel…literally.

Speaking of the bane of my existence, Octavian was already up and dressed at the ungodly crack of dawn when I made my way down to the kitchen. Sitting at the kitchen island, he was intently studying an article online.

"Good morrow, Brother," he spoke, bright-eyed and bushy-tailed, to my extreme annoyance.

"Easy for you to say. You weren't bludgeoned by the protective chant of two witches," I retorted with a scowl.

"My, you're quite mardy, I see; but understandable. Tasmin and Elisa were quite impressive. The question is why. How is it their powers were able to manifest so quickly, without any training?"

"You're the professor. I'll leave that for you to ponder. I, on the other hand, need to figure out how Elisa was able to call to me telepathically. She called out to me for help, as if she knew I would be there in her time of need. How would she know that?"

Octavian looked up from his laptop. "Just one more mystery for us to ruminate on, brother of mine. And here's another. Take a gander at this," he said, tuning his computer screen toward me. The article's headline read 'PARK SLOPE PHYSICIAN'S OFFICE BURNS TO THE GROUND IN LATE NIGHT BLAZE', with Tasmin named as the doctor of the practice within the article. "It appears that Tasmin's practice was destroyed last night. From what I've read, the fire is being considered dodgy due to the nature of blaze. There was an explosion, but, so far, the fire investigator has yet to determine the cause of the blast. And get this; her office was the only building destroyed."

Although I was still feeling some slight disorientation from last night's events, my curiosity surrounding the building's destruction overshadowed that. "You're suspecting something unnatural, aren't you, Octavian? But why would someone want to demolish her practice?' I inquired.

"Perhaps to keep her in Salix Pointe. Consider this, Dafari; with the destruction of Tasmin's business, she has no need to rush back to New York. She would have ample time to finish up her affairs here."

I raised an eyebrow. "So you're thinking that keeping her here could possibly —"

"Make her easy prey," Octavian said, finishing my thought. "She's only now coming into her powers, and I'm sure she has no idea what's happening. That would make her ripe for the picking. Dafari, I suspect this is your father's work."

I let out a heavy sigh. "Are you insinuating that he set that fire, because if you are, that's highly doubtful. According to the article, the fire occurred around the same time we were battling him in Elisa's dream. While he is virtually omnipotent, even he can't be in two places at once."

Octavian dubiously countered, "He does have minions."

I was not in the mood to belabor the point with Octavian, so I left it alone, and deflected the conversation. "I wonder how Tasmin is managing."

Octavian closed his laptop, focusing his full attention on me. "I'm sure she's gutted, man. That was her life's work. Healing is her calling."

"You seem to care quite a bit about someone you just met; someone who came very close to cuffing you in the face yesterday," I said in jest.

"Ah, my dear brother, with the trepidation you exhibited regarding Elisa last night, I could say the same about you. She appears to be more than just an astral plane, what's that term, booty call?"

I pulled out a chair, sitting at the counter. "You disgust me. Besides, I've known Elisa for years."

"And yet, all you've done is bought coffee and biscuits from her eatery and shagged her on the astral plane. Those are the foundations for a marvelous relationship."

"You're a fine one to talk. But enough of this; we need to figure out a way to track my father before he actually hurts Elisa or Tasmin."

Octavian rose from his seat, only to begin pacing back and forth. "I fear there is so much more going on, Brother. There are too many variables that don't add up. You won't want to hear this, but at this juncture I believe we need to contact the one person who knows your father better than anyone. We have to call Mother."

I looked at him hard, my steely gaze saying more than words ever could. While she did know Father very well, and while we did need to explore every possible avenue regarding his agenda and possible whereabouts, our mother was the last person I wanted to speak to.

"Dafari, at some point, you are going to have to get over this rift you have with Mother. It's gone on for far too long, and she's the only mother you have."

"To my chagrin," I retorted.

"You don't mean—"

"Don't you dare profess to tell me what I mean or do not mean, little Brother!" I yelled, my anger welling up inside me. It was then that I realized that if I was to truly help Elisa, I must let a cooler head prevail. "You can call Mother if you like. I'm going to get dressed. Let me know what you find out."

Octavian opened his mouth to speak but changed his mind. I left him there as he prepared to call our mother. While I didn't care to speak with her, I hoped Octavian's conversation would reveal some information that could help us locate my enigmatic father. He was a master of concealment, the shadows his ultimate lair. If we had some idea as to where he may have been hiding, we could possibly get one step ahead of him.

As I got showered and dressed, I thought about Elisa and last night's happenings; thought about how at first she appeared to be blocking me from reaching her mind, then called out to me telepathically, a feat no ordinary human should be able to do. Then again, Elisa was far from ordinary, and I wasn't just referring to her powers. She was unique. She had the uncanny ability to brighten anyone's day, even when hers was filled with gloom. I had come to rely on her cheerful greetings as a source of comfort. In contrast to some of the inhabitants of Salix Pointe, like Noreen, Elisa possessed an incontestable genuineness that caused me to gravitate toward her in a way that I found extremely alluring. My daily jaunt to her café was less about enjoying the tasty delicacies, and more about seeing her smiling face. I hoped that wouldn't change after last night. I hoped she didn't remember anything that happened, and if she did, I hoped she thought it was all a bad dream, save for our time together. I would only know for sure once I arrived at her shop later this morning.

Ready for the day, I walked back downstairs, prepared to hear whatever information Octavian had gathered. Instead, I was met by an anxious angel, nothing but worry in his tone.

"I was unable to reach Mother. It's unlike her to not answer my calls."

She always answers his calls. Not surprising, I thought, but didn't vocalize. "Maybe she's out and about. You know she likes her nature walks." I tried to sound reassuring.

"While that's true, Mother *always* takes her daily constitutional early in the day. It's mid-morning in London. I fear something is amiss."

Mother was, if nothing else, predictable. I had to agree with my little brother; something possibly was amiss. "Perhaps you should go check on her."

"You were reading my mind, Brother. I can go through the veil, make sure Mother is well, then come back in short order."

"I'll accompany you, just in case." There was no love lost between Mother and me, but she was still my mother.

"Have you lost the plot, Dafari? That would be sheer folly. Tasmin and Elisa would be left alone and vulnerable without protection, no matter how brief our departure. You would do well to spend your time keeping an eye on the fair witches. Besides, as a full angel, I could leg it faster traversing the veil should any problems arise."

Much as I hated to admit it, Octavian's points held water. "Fine, we'll do things your way. Just be careful."

Octavian spread his hands, creating a portal between earth and the spirit realm, poised to check on our mother. "Why dear brother, it almost sounds like you care."

"Almost," I retorted. "I'll be waiting at my office."

"I'll return straightaway. Go check on Elisa and Tasmin," he replied, and in instant, he was gone.

Taking his advice, I drove the short distance to town, parking my car in front of my office. I watched as Tasmin departed Elisa's shop, walking to the bookstore. Once she entered, I made my way to the café, unsure of what to expect. Elisa was behind the counter, brewing her gourmet coffees.

She hadn't even turned around when I heard her say, "Good morning, Dr. Battle. The usual for you this morning?"

When she did turn to face me, I observed that her smile had a little less shine than usual. She looked a bit worn and haggard. "Good morning, Elisa. Yes, I'll have the same."

"Coming right up," she replied, working on my order. *You really should try something new every now and then*, I heard her say, or rather project, to my mind.

Maybe I will, one day, I projected back, uncertain if she could 'hear' me.

I assumed she couldn't when she handed me my order without responding to my comment. "Here you go," she said.

Usually, I kept the conversation to a minimum, but today something within me wouldn't allow it. As I paid for my order, I asked, "Are you alright, Elisa? You seem…unwell."

"I'm just tired. I didn't sleep well at all last night."

I didn't get the impression that she remembered anything from our tryst. For that I was grateful. As for my father's attack, if she remembered any of it, one could chalk that up to being one horrific nightmare.

"You need to get some rest. Your presence would be missed by many if you weren't here."

Elisa leaned on the counter, her pretty smile returning. "Does that include you, Dr. Battle?"

I simply gave her a half-smile and bowed my head. "Good day, Elisa." I was relieved to see that, aside from fatigue, she had suffered no ill effects from last night.

I was about to walk to my office when I saw Tasmin hauling several garbage bags from the bookstore. I figured now was as good a time as any to pick up Octavian's books.

"Dr. Pettiford," I said, getting her attention.

"Morning, Dr. Battle," she replied. "Let me guess; you're here to pick up your brother's books."

"If it's not too much trouble."

"No trouble at all. Follow me." She opened the door, holding it ajar for me. There were books strewn all over the tables. "Sorry for mess," she replied. "I'm trying to finish up this inventory before the realtor comes by." She reached over to the shelf behind her for a bag filled with books.

I placed my items from the café on counter. "It's a shame you're selling this place. Your aunt truly wanted you to have it."

"I'm guessing she told you as much," she stated, placing the bag on the counter.

"Your aunt and I conversed occasionally. She was very fond of you. To her, you were the only relative worthy enough to have this part of her legacy."

"I don't know why she left it to me. Auntie knew how much I didn't like it down here. I never wanted this bookstore. I had no idea she left it me. And for the record, she was very fond of you, too."

"And I, her. Noreen Chadwick was a remarkable woman. Her passing was a great loss to us all."

Tasmin had since figured out how to use the cash register and was ringing up Octavian's purchase. "Thank you for that. I loved my aunt very much," she said, pausing for a few seconds. Once she composed herself, she continued, "That'll be seventy-seven dollars, please."

I took out my wallet and handed her the cash inside. "I heard about your practice. I'm sorry."

"How did you—" she queried, handing me my change and the bag of books.

"My brother read about it online this morning. He was…concerned for you."

The look on her face showed her apathy toward Octavian. "Please tell him thank you, but there's no need for concern. I'll be fine."

My brother had a lot of work to do with this one if he was to ever get in her good graces, let alone her pants. "For what it's worth, my brother may think like a relic from a long dead era; however, at heart, he means well." *You're welcome, Brother*, I thought.

"I'll take your word for it," she remarked with a smirk. "Thank you for picking up his books," she said, adding, "And thank you for being so kind to my aunt."

"You're welcome. I was just returning what she gave me," I replied, picking up my items. "I'm sorry for your loss, on both counts."

My hands were full. Seeing this, Tasmin darted around the counter to open the door for me. "Thank you, Dr. Battle. I appreciate it."

As we parted ways, I thought of how that was the longest conversation we ever had since we first met. I actually did sympathize with all the challenges she was experiencing. I anticipated she would endure many more before this was all said and done.

I walked to my clinic, intent on waiting for Octavian to return. Instead, as I walked into my office, I saw he was already there, leaning on my desk and breathing hard, as if he had just run a marathon.

I quickly walked over to him, a feeling of consternation overtaking me. "Octavian, what happened?"

"Brother," he said between pants. "This situation is far worse than we could have ever imagined."

CHAPTER II:
OCTAVIAN

"Mother is gone," I said.

"Gone? What do you mean gone?" Dafari asked, a frown etched across his features.

"I mean her entire flat is in shambles and she's nowhere to be found and it smelled of burned cinnamon." Dafari's head tilted to the side and he frowned. I kept talking. "The energy around her home can't be read. It's the oddest thing," I said, pacing. "Normally when I walk into a place, I can read and see the energy present and those left behind. In Mother's flat…there was nothing. Just static."

"Static?"

"Yes, like radio static, but for angels it's just silence."

Being half demon, sometimes Dafari's gifts were a bit different than my own. While he couldn't read or see energy, he could feel it. That meant if he had gone to Mother's he would have felt something was off. His gift was like intuition, but with instant confirmation.

"Did it feel like foul play?" he asked.

"It looked that way. Why else would her home be ramshackled as such?"

"Let me guess, you're going to assume my father had something to do with it?"

"By all that's good and holy, man, yes. It has him written all over it. Not to mention he paid her a visit soon after he escaped. Perhaps he doubled back…"

Dafari stood and was about to say something else until the bell on his front door rang.

"Dr. Battle," a sing song feminine voice rang out.

Dafari groaned low in his throat. "I do not have time for this right now," he mumbled then headed toward the front of his practice.

I followed pursuit, curious as to whom the voice belonged. My curiosity was satiated the moment we rounded the corner. I couldn't say I knew what to make of the pair standing before me. The man was dressed in all black minus the gold tie lying against his chest. The suit had been tailored to fit his tall lean frame. He had on boots that had been made of alligator hide. His skin was tanned golden and his blue eyes were startling even on him. He had a smile that said he was nickel slick. Or at least he thought he was the smartest person in the room. He had on a black top hat and a white cane was in the crook of his arm. He was so Cajun I could smell the andouille sausage on him.

The woman, who was the owner of the voice I assumed, was of an ethnicity I couldn't readily identify. It was hard to when the aura around them had been tampered with. I wondered if my brother could pick up on that. Someone had tried to hide the stench of black magic wafting off them. The hairs on the back of my neck stood. I gave her a quick once over. I saw she was an octoroon and had come from some of the first settlers of *Gens de Colours* in Louisiana. She was also dressed like she was about to go to a ball or cotillion of some sort. Her slim, curvy frame looked well put together but that was where the compliments stopped.

I chuckled while sliding my hands in the pockets of my slacks. Who in God's name wore a gown in the middle of fall just to walk around in? She had on far too much rouge. I assumed she was trying to hide her true age. Too bad I could see right through her getup. She even had one of those fancy hand fans with the frills and lace gloves. If she had come with one of those parasols women used to carry to keep away the sun back in the day, I believe I would have guffawed at the outrageousness of it all.

"Mrs. Lovett, Mayor, to what do I owe the pleasure?" Dafari greeted them.

The mayor smiled and my flesh felt as if maggots were crawling underneath.

"We came to introduce ourselves to your brother of course," Mrs. Lovett all but squealed. She unwrapped herself from her husband's right arm and walked over to me. "*Comment ca va?*" she said as she extended her hand, not for me to shake, but she bent her wrist as if she expected me to kiss the back of her hand.

I'd have rather kissed a rattlesnake. I grabbed her hand and shook it. The icy chill that settled at the base of my spine was telling. "Top of the morning to you. I'm Professor Octavian Jerrod. Pleased to make your acquaintance." My palms burned and ears rang so loud, the animals started up again.

"Ah, from the UK, are you?" the mayor asked.

His voice had a deep drawl so southern it would make the most southern of men jealous.

"Yes," I answered.

Dafari looked toward the room where he kept the animals then back at us. "If you would excuse me a moment," he said then headed off to quiet the animals.

"What brings you to our neck of the woods, O? May I call you O?" Mrs. Lovett asked.

"No. You may call me Professor Jerrod. I'm here to fellowship with my brother."

She looked taken aback, even clutched the pearls around her neck at my frankness. She cleared her throat then said, "You know, Dr. Battle never mentioned he had a brother and he's been here for seven years."

I didn't respond to that. I wasn't even sure what she expected me to say. What I did know, was that I didn't like the pair. There was something sinister lurking just beneath the surface of who they were, and it alarmed me.

Mayor Lovett stepped forward when he saw his wife had placed herself in an awkward position. "Now, now, *cherie*. Let's not crowd the man. He may not be used to such a beautiful woman giving him the time of day. We did hear he was at the café and bookstore. Perhaps Elisa and Tasmin are more of his speed if you know what I mean," he said to her then kissed her neck before urging her to step behind him.

My eyes dimmed as soon as the insult to Tasmin and Elisa had been leveled. I was taller than the man by at least four inches. Still, he stood as if he was the tallest man in the room. Dare I say the man had a bit of an ego problem? He was a tosser and his wife was a bit of a muppet. Perfect coupling if you asked me.

"Octavian, let me welcome you to our quaint little town. What you put in is what you get out of it," he said, but he didn't bother to extend his hand.

I wished he would have. I'd have loved to see if I could feel his real aura.

"Like my lovely wife here said, Dafari has never mentioned you. Had he, would have lain out the welcome mat. Boy was I *honte* to know you'd come to town and we hadn't welcomed your arrival."

I held up a hand. "No need to be embarrassed or ashamed. It was a spur of the moment trip. I wouldn't have cared for all the bells and whistles anyway."

The man studied me as if he was trying to read me. That gave me pause. I tilted my head to study him just as he tilted his to give me a once over.

He chuckled low in his throat then said, "How long do you plan to be in town? We're having a jubilee on All Hallows Eve. Would love if you would be in attendance."

I was all set to decline when Dafari walked up behind me. "We'd love to attend."

I glanced back at him with a quirked brow. "We would?" I asked him.

Mrs. Lovett clapped. "Oh, that would be wonderful, Dafari. This is the first year you've ever accepted the invitation."

"Since it's possible my brother may be here for a while, it will do him some good to meet a few people," Dafari said.

I was going to kill him. No. I'd tie him down and strip him of his wings. That would learn him. I turned on him fully, set to chew him a new pair of knickers when I noticed a black cat in his hand.

Mayor Lovett said, "Ilene Suzanne, grab the *minou, mon cher.*"

Mrs. Lovett gently took the cat from Dafari's arms as she said, "*Pauvre ti bête…*"

Poor little thing my arse. The way the cat was hissing told me it was anything but a poor little thing.

Mayor Lovett turned back to me and my brother. "We look forward to having you around. *Bienvenue* to Salix Pointe, *mon ami.*" He held his hand out for his wife. "*Allons, mon cher.*"

"Did you have to be so standoffish?" Dafari asked when they'd left.

"Asks the man who has never even mentioned me or been to a jubilee since he's been living here? You leave me with a tanned vampire and the octoroon version of Scarlett O'Hara, with no warning, and expect me to behave? I think not," I snapped. "Something's off about that pair."

"Yes, there is. There always has been and up until now, it was of no concern to me."

"And now?"

"Now, we're trying to solve a murder and a few mysteries to boot, everything and everyone is of interest. They throw that bourgeois of a jubilee every year. I'd say it would be perfect timing to vet the people of Salix Pointe, wouldn't you?"

"Are you so vexed by the notion your demon daddy killed Noreen and went after Mother that you would suspect mere humans in this town of murdering such a powerful woman?" I asked.

"If you hadn't notice, little brother, mere humans would not be the words I'd use to describe the people of Salix Pointe."

CHAPTER 12:
ELISA

I have to be losing my mind, I thought as I handed a hot mug of coffee to Cara Lee Newsam.

She was one of three women waiting for me to serve them. She and her two sisters, whom the town had dubbed the Three Merry Widows, frequented my café. However, on Fridays they normally sat in and had their coffee and pastries while in the café as opposed to taking them to go.

Anyway, call me crazy, but I could have sworn Dr. Battle had responded to me when he was in my shop earlier. Once again, he'd ordered the same thing as he normally did. When I mentally suggested that he order something different from time-to-time, I heard him, clear as day, respond, "*Maybe I will, one day…*" If I hadn't had my wits about me, I'd have freaked out. But I was in my right mind. That was why it was easy for me to chalk it up as me imagining things. It was either I was imagining things or losing my darn mind.

"Thank you, sweetheart," Cara Lee said with a warm smile.

She was dressed in a purple sweater that had small orange pumpkins all over it and black corduroy pants. On her feet were little black boots that matched the black scarf around her neck. She had a clear quartz stone necklace that had been fashioned with copper wire. Her dark skin had aged gracefully, and although she carried her sixty-five years well, the age and wisdom could be seen on her face.

As I handed her youngest sister, Mary Ann Howard, her mug of apple cider, I noticed a black jade crystal sitting by her on the table. They're oldest sister, Martha Lee Singleton, smiled up at me when I set a mug of spiced hot chocolate in front of her. I noticed the stone sitting by her. I'd never seen that stone before but, somehow, I knew what it was.

"Where'd you find blue kyanite around these parts?" I asked her.

She glanced at her sisters before turning her green eyes back to me. "Oh I found it one day while my sisters and I were out walking back near the old caves."

The Three Merry Widows were known for their excursions. For them to be up in age, they sure never let it stop them from living life on their own terms. I nodded at her answer, but there was something about the stone that seemed out of place, and I didn't know why.

"You know about stones, Elisa?" Cara Lee asked.

"Of course she does, Sister. She's Mama Nall's granddaughter. She had the perfect teacher," Martha Lee said.

I smiled at both women. "Yes, ma'am, I do. Mama Nall taught me all she knew."

Cara laid a hand on mine. "*All*...she knew?"

There was a question in her eyes. I felt as if she was asking me something else without outright asking. Her violet eyes gazed into mine and I felt a tug in my gut, but before I could dig deeper into what was happening, the bell on my front door rang. In walked Mayor Lovett and his wife, Ilene Suzanne. Dressed as if they were going to a ball, they looked every bit of pretentious as they were.

"Look what the wind blew in," Mary Ann muttered.

"Wished it would have blown them in another direction," Martha Lee quipped.

"We're not that lucky," Cara Lee put in.

I smiled to keep from laughing at the widows' disdain for the mayor and his wife. "Good day, Mayor Lovett and Ilene. What can I get for you today?" I asked. The quicker they ordered, the quicker they could leave.

Mayor Lovett removed his top hat and nodded at me then turned his cold blue eyes to the Merry Widows. “Aren’t you three late for a doctor’s appointment or something, *tantes*? I know with old age comes different, dare I say, ailments, *shaa*?” His deep southern baritone was offensive as he spat those words.

The Widows set their mugs on the table then set their eyes on the mayor. Alone, one of their looks had the power to intimidate full grown men. Together, their glare even caused me to recoil. The intense gaze in their eyes radiated tension in the room that could be cut with a scythe.

“If I were you, thaumaturge, I’d take my *salop* of a wife, order what I came for and get,” Martha Lee spat.

There was no need for shock at her words. The Widows had never been women to cower. However, I was curious about what she had called him… Thaumaturge? What on earth was that? The Merry Widows had never been fond of the mayor. During his campaign, they did everything in their power to keep him from getting elected. Rumor had it, he had come from a bloodline of slave owners in Louisiana. His forefathers had been feared slave owners and slave catchers. There had been bad blood between the widows and the Lovetts since I could remember.

Ilene smiled, but it was venomous. "Old woman, I'd watch what you say lest…the cat get your tongue."

It was only when her bag mewled and something moved inside that I noticed her cat, Disemspi. Yes, that was the cat's name.

"Ilene, you know you can't have that cat in here," I said as nicely as my nerves would allow.

Ilene's laced hands went to her bag. "Well, why not? He's a service animal," she hissed.

"He's not a service animal and you have to get it out of here," I said.

That highfaluting hussy turned to her husband and whined, "*Bébé*, do something. I can't leave poor little Disemspi in the car."

I shook my head and headed behind the counter. I didn't care what the mayor said, that cat had to get out of here. Not only was it unsanitary, the cat itself was a weird little thing. It stared at people as if it could understand what was being said. It was creepy.

"*Cherie*, don't you think you can accommodate my wife just this once?" Mayor Lovett crooned, smiling and looking at me as if he was trying to dazzle me.

It didn't work. "My name is Elisa and no. We've had this conversation before—"

"Might I remind you whose town this is...Ee-lis-ah?"

He spoke my name slowly, letting each syllable roll off his tongue as if it left a bad taste in his mouth.

"I don't give two hoots about you being the mayor in this town, Ee-frum," I said, intentionally saying his name in a way I knew chapped his ass. "This is my cafe. My rules. Either the cat goes or all three of you do."

"You ungrateful little witch," Ilene spat in my direction just as Tasmin walked into the café. "It was my husband who convinced the town we needed this little two-bit café and you dare threaten to put him out?"

Mayor Lovett said nothing as his wife insulted me. Those blue eyes of his twinkled with delight and made me want to blow powdered cow manure in his face.

I took a deep breath. "Ilene, if you call me anything other than my name again, I will throw salt in your eyes."

The Merry Widows howled with laughter. I didn't readily know why but assumed it was because of the stunned look on Ilene's face while she clutched the pearls around her neck.

“Mama Nall really did teach her well,” Cara Lee said while holding her hand to her chest as she laughed.

“You wouldn’t dare,” Ilene squealed.

I set the tray I’d been holding down and pick up the pink Himalayan salt on my counter. “Try me,” I said.

“Should I come back later?” Tasmin asked, holding up a hand with an unsure look on her face.

“No,” I said. “The mayor, his wife, and *their cat* were just leaving.”

Mayor Lovett chuckled and then walked closer to the counter. “Why don’t you like me, Elisa?” Mayor Lovett asked.

I had a good mind to tell him that he was a forked-tongued arrogant, pompous jackass, but I figured I’d been plenty unmannerly after threatening to throw salt in his wife’s eyes.

“Ephraim, I never said I didn’t like you. However, your wife seems to think that because you are mayor you can tell me how to run my café. That will not happen. I don’t allow animals in here. If she can respect that, you’re both welcomed here anytime.”

He gave that cool smile again. His eyes raked me over as if he was undressing me. The palms of my hands tingled, and my fingertips burned.

"I'm happy to hear that, *shaa* I wanted to invite you to the jubilee we're having this year. I'd love to see you there. In fact, I'm going to insist you come." Before I could tell him that it would be a cold day in hell before I stepped foot in that creepy manor he called home, he turned to Tasmin. "Good day, little lady." His greeting sounded like something straight out of Gone with the Wind.

"Good afternoon," Tasmin said. I noticed she kept her distance. I knew she was smart.

"I'm Mayor Lovett and this is my wife—"

"I know who you are. We met at my aunt's repast."

"That's right. Anyhoo, we hope your stay in town has been pleasant thus far," he crooned.

Ilene cut in. "Judging by the company she keeps, I wouldn't count on it."

Tasmin looked at the woman from head to toe and then casted a quick glance at me. *What on earth is she wearing?* I heard in my mind, but in Tasmin's voice. I went statue still. That was the same thing that had happened with Dr. Battle that morning.

"I assure you my stay has been pleasant. Elisa and Dr. Battle have been very gracious in hospitality," Tasmin said.

"Now, now, Ilene, put your claws away. We want the good lady here to come to the jubilee on All Hallows Eve. She won't feel welcomed if you—"

As he was talking, I turned to look at the Merry Widows and got the shock of my life. Martha's and Mary's stones were levitating just above the table, Cara Lee's stone was lifting from her neck, and I could have sworn their eyes glowed. I screamed. The stones dropped. The widows looked at me. Ilene's cat screeched, jumped from her bag and ran through the legs of a customer walking in.

"Now look what you've done," Ilene screeched at me. "Disemspi, come back, sweet cat." She took off after it. Mayor Lovett put his hat on, tipped it, and then strutted out after her.

"Are you all right?" Cara Lee asked as she and her sisters walked over to the counter.

"Yeah, why'd you scream like that?" Tasmin asked. "Did something happen?"

I stared at the Widows. They looked to be just as concerned as Tasmin did, which made me believe that I must have been seeing things. I *was* losing my mind.

"Ah, it was nothing really. I saw the cat getting ready to jump from the bag Ilene was carrying and didn't know if it was about to jump on the counter is all," I lied.

The Widows looked at me skeptically, as if they knew I was fibbing.

Tasmin nodded and looked through the window at the mayor and his wife who were chasing their cat into another shop on Main Street. "That is one strange couple," she said.

"Don't we know it," Martha Lee said. "We're sorry to run out on you ladies, but we must get back to the Gourd."

Tasmin's brows furrowed. "The Gourd?"

I said, "Yeah, I'm not sure if you remember the pond that sits out near the Ross Farm? The one that's shaped like a drinking gourd?"

"Oh yeah. Aunt Noreen took me there a few times to pick wild herbs and gather stones," Tasmin said.

Cara Lee said, "Yes, we meet there daily to do readings and such."

As she talked, the sisters pulled on their coats and picked up their belongings. They ordered coffee and muffins to go and then they were gone. After they left, there was quite a rush, and once again, I asked Tasmin to help me.

"You know," I said once the crowd was gone, "I probably should think about hiring some help."

Tasmin nodded. "You should. I would have never thought this small town could get so busy."

"Oh yes. It's the holiday season. It will get a lot worse with tourist season and all." I wiped down the display case with the pastries while Tasmin sat at a booth, sipping tea.

"I'm surprised there are tourist since this place isn't even on a map," she said.

"Word of mouth has been our best marketing tool." I blew out steam then tossed the towel in the soapy water behind the counter.

"My initial reason for coming over is to ask you where I could go clothes shopping. I hadn't planned on being here this long, so I didn't bring nearly enough clothes."

"Yeah. Sharon's on the other side of town. As a matter of fact, I'm taking a lunch break now. So I can go with you."

No one would bat a lash about the café being closed since the whole town knew I took an hour and half for lunch every day. Tasmin and I hopped in my SUV and trucked it over to Sharon's. It was the only clothing store that carried decent inventory that didn't look like it came from the set of The Mod Squad or Scooby-Doo.

Traffic was light as the wind blew the trees in a sultry sway. It was cool enough for a jacket, but not cold enough to wish we'd stayed inside. Fall could be seen all around as the leaves were colors of pinks, oranges, reds, and browns. Wind blew dead leaves around as we watched a gaggle of kids be ushered across the street. I waved and blew my horn at a few of my neighbors as I passed them. We passed the library where Gloria Wilson, the town's librarian, and her husband, Lynn, were hanging banners announcing an All Hallows Eve dance for the children. Houses had been decorated in Halloween décor and some had even gone as far as to decorate for Thanksgiving. Yes, Salix Pointe had an eclectic group of citizens.

Sharon's was situated on Butler Drive, nestled between other craftsman style houses that had been turned into businesses. It was a simple sunflower yellow establishment with white windowpanes and a wooden brown door. The grass held oversized pumpkins, bales of hay, and colorful scarecrows. That was the gist of Sharon's décor for the season. The inside was small and cozy with the register sitting in the back of the room to the left. The whole right side was fitted with racks of clothing while the wall had built-in shelves holding different styles of shoes. In the next room was a fitting area where women were entering to try on their latest bounties.

Tasmin was pretty quick with her shopping. We were in and out of Sharon's with time to spare. Tasmin was a jeans kind of girl. She bought six pair of jeans—some to take home with her she'd said—seven shirts, a pair of black boots, and a new teapot. We chatted about different things while I browsed and she shopped. I reminded her of some of the town's history. Like when the town had been used to help with the Underground Railroad, how some of the houses still had hidden underground bunkers, and how a few abolitionists had hidden out here to escape prosecution. I did end up purchasing a few candles and new house slippers along with a black night slip that called to me.

On our way out of Sharon's, I decided to go into an old shop that Mama Nall used to always visit. For some reason, my gut pulled me in that direction.

I studied the old building that looked similar to an old Victorian style home. "Hey, Tasmin," I said.

She walked up next to me. "Yeah?"

"Let's go into this shop right quick."

"Tarot Readings, Charms & Runes?" she asked.

I nodded.

"Please don't tell me this is some spooky old woman who claims she can read palms and use her inner eye to see into the future…"

I laughed. "Something like that," I said then walked ahead.

"Elisa, you have got to be kidding me," she quipped behind me as she rushed to catch up.

"No, I'm not. For some reason, my gut is telling me to go to this place."

"Your gut?"

"Yes, my instincts. Intuition if you will."

"O…kay, but why?"

"I don't quite know," I said as we jogged up the fourteen stone steps of the house.

We paused once we got to the porch. The Halloween decorations there were, dare I say, overboard. There was a life-like reaper with glowing red lights for eyes on the left side of the door. It came with the proverbial scythe and black hooded cloak.

"Okay, that's just creepy," Tasmin said.

On a wooden swing, that had seen better days, sat a witch with locs, a pointed hat, and a purple cloak. The way she was placed made it so her eyes appeared to be looking directly at us.

"That's even creepier," I said.

There was a cauldron with something bubbling on the inside. We had no desire to see what. Scattered about the porch were plastic rats, a few snakes—which weren't real, thank goodness—spiderwebs, skeletons and other Halloween décor that showed the owner of the place had way too much time on her hands. I looked up to see she even had bats hanging overhead. I thought I'd seen something moving but couldn't be sure.

As I got ready to knock, the door opened on its own. The inside looked like mist was floating just off the floor. Strings of lights decorated the baseboards while it smelled of burned cinnamon. That was an odd smell.

"Please come in," a smooth feminine voice said. "But enter at your own risk…"

I quirked a brow then looked at Tasmin.

She shrugged and then said, "You wanted to come to this spook shop…"

I got ready to step inside when I heard, "Good day, ladies."

I didn't have to look behind me to know it was Octavian. He was the only one in town with a British accent. Tasmin took a deep annoyed breath, rolled her eyes, and then sucked her teeth.

I turned with a chuckle then waved. "Hello, Professor," I greeted with a smile.

He gave a gallant nod in my direction then turned his black eyes to Tasmin. He gave her a slow, easy and charming smile. One that I was sure had melted panties from here to the UK. However, Tasmin gave a look so deadpan, I had to pretend to be looking at something in one of my shopping bags to keep from outright cackling.

"Not this insufferable jackass again," Tasmin said.

I snapped my head in her direction. "Tasmin!" I couldn't believe she'd said that and so loudly!

"What?" she said, looking at me with confusion.

"You really called him that out loud," I whispered.

Tasmin's brows furrowed. "Called him…what?" she asked as if she didn't know what I was talking about.

"You called the man an insufferable jackass."

"No, I didn't. I mean… I did, but not out loud"

I gave a slow blink and looked at her as if she had lost her marbles. She was looking at me in just the same manner.

"Ah, ladies," Octavian called.

Tasmin and I ignored him because we were still staring at one another like we'd each grown an extra head or three.

"Ladies," Octavian called again. "If you would look above your heads, please."

She and I looked up at the same time. The scream that erupted from us at the sight of a snake so big and bright yellow was loud enough to shatter glass. Before I knew it, Tasmin grabbed my arm and pulled me back as both our hands shot forward. In a move that neither of us would be able to explain, something akin to electricity shot from our hands and the snake flew from the rafters into bushes several shops down the road.

I gasped. Tasmin darn near screamed but caught herself. We looked at Octavian. He didn't appear to be shocked or stunned.

He actually smiled wider then said, "I can explain that."

Octavian stood in my front room, holding a mug of coffee that he kept staring at. "What kind of magick did you put in this?" he asked. "It's far too delicious to be a common blend."

"Thank you," I replied, looking at him as if he were daft.

After the snake incident, Tasmin and I rushed down the steps of the establishment and hightailed it back to my truck. I'd never moved so fast a day in my life. Once back at shop, I made plans to close early while the professor tried, unsuccessfully I might add, to engage Tasmin. The woman wanted nothing to do with him. She rushed back to her aunt's bookstore where she had a line, much to her dismay. I hated to say it, but Octavian was going to have to eat a butt-load of crow before Tasmin even breathed in his direction.

However, he insisted time was of the essence, and it was imperative she and I found out and understood what we were. He asked me to get Tasmin to my home long enough for him to explain what we needed to know. And here we were.

Tasmin said, "You've lost your ever-loving mind if you think we're supposed to believe this tale of us being witches!"

"For as long as I've been on this plane, being out of mind has only happened once," he said.

"So you…let me see if I understand you…She and I are witches?" I said.

He nodded.

"Ms. Noreen was murdered by a demon?"

He nodded once more.

"And you are what exactly?"

"I'm an archangel, son of—"

"Get the heck out of here," Tasmin spat then looked at me. "Please don't tell me you actually believe this basket case?"

"To be honest—"

"To be honest, you should probably listen to what my brother is trying to convey to you as we don't have much time to hold your hands or coddle you." His voice echoed around the room like surround sound. It bounced off the walls then reverberated, but…he was nowhere to be seen.

"Ah! Nice of you to show up, Brother," Octavian said. He nodded once toward a dark corner in my foyer.

As if out of thin air, Dr. Battle walked from the shadows. He had a walk that would put mere men to shame. He walked as if he had somewhere important to be but all the time in the world to get there.

"How did you get in my house? Where…did you come from?" I asked, my raised voice showing my anxiety.

"You saw exactly where I came from, Elisa," he said.

His hair curtained his shoulders as his eyes gazed into mine. He was dressed in black slacks, a black collarless shirt, and black loafers. I almost couldn't keep my head on straight. In all my life I'd never seen a man who looked like him.

"And you never will," he replied with an arrogance I hadn't readily seen in him before… only his mouth didn't move.

"You are correct in your assumptions. I'm in your mind, Elisa, as you were in mine this morning."

"Please get the heck out of my way," I heard Tasmin say behind me.

"It would be in your best interest to stick around," Octavian told her.

As my eyes widened at the sight of Dr. Battle's golden eyes glowing, I heard a snap-crackle and then saw Octavian fly clear across my front room.

Tasmin yelled. I whipped around to look at her. She was staring at her hands as if they were foreign to her. She looked from me to her hands then to Octavian, who was pulling himself from the shambles of my bookcase. Tasmin took one last look at me, snatched my front door open then hightailed it out of my house.

CHAPTER 13: TASMIN

What did I just see? What did I just *do?* One minute Professor Jerrod was in front of me, the next someone else…*something* else was. Something that I could only describe as ethereal, not of this world. A being of pure light energy with the head of a lion, seven eyes, and massive white wings. That could *not* be real! He…it scared me to no end. And then there was that burst of energy coming from my hands that sent that thing smack dab into Elisa's bookcase. That was the second time today I blasted something, although the first time was with Elisa.

Could Professor Jerrod actually be telling the truth? Could we really be, dare I say it, witches? How was that even possible? How was it that both he *and* Dr. Battle knew this, while Elisa and I were totally clueless? Then there was the most unbelievably devastating part of it all; my aunt, my beloved Aunt Noreen was murdered by a *demon?* I couldn't wrap my head around it. It was too much to take in all at once. I needed to shake it off, at least for the time being.

The moon was finally in its waning phase, and I could at long last perform the ceremony to release

Aunt Noreen, allowing her to sit amongst our ancestors. Once this ritual was completed, I thought I would be free to leave Salix Pointe, leave all the weirdness behind me. But after hearing Auntie was murdered, I wasn't so sure. Run from the possibility that I may be witch? Definitely. Run from the supernatural creepy brothers? Without a doubt. But run without finding out who stole my aunt from me; I just didn't know.

I pushed all the madness to the back of my mind; pulled myself together in preparation to properly honor Aunt Noreen. Once I was back in the house, I gathered everything I needed in a duffle bag and headed out back to the largest white willow tree on the property. Since the moon was waning, it allowed only a very small sliver of light to shine through. I set up several battery-powered lanterns, allowing me to be able to see better in the dim moonlight. In her will, Auntie left detailed instructions for her letting go ceremony, including a caveat that I create the ritual myself. My guess was that she wanted it to come from my heart. She knew I wouldn't let her down. One thing I knew about her was that she would want all five elements of nature as part of the ceremony; air, earth, fire, water, and Spirit, the Spirit being hers. She would also want both of us to be protected, me in this world, her in the next; I used that as the focal point for the ritual.

She once told me that seven was the most spiritual of all numbers. Following that principle, I gathered everything I needed in sevens. Starting with a ring of protection around me and the white willow tree, I formed a large circle with seven different tealight candles, representing the fire element; black, white, blue, purple, yellow, pink, and green. In between each candle sat some Palo Santo incense, symbolizing the air element.

Then I started the manual labor part of the ceremony, digging a shallow trench around the tree. Luckily, the earth was mildly soft due to the recent rains and the cool temperatures. Once that was done I began to add all my earth elements into the trench. I started with flower petals from wind flowers, snap dragons, false indigo, St. John's wort, mallow, oenothera, and mullein. I followed that by adding seven drops each of sage, frankincense, myrrh, lavender, sweet orange, lemon, and peppermint oils. Lastly, I added black protection crystals; tourmaline, obsidian, Apache tears, staurolite, jet, kyanite, and jade.

For my water element, I poured water from the creek into the trench. Now for the hard part, spreading Aunt Noreen's ashes. I was hesitant

because once this part was done, it really would mean letting her go, and I just wasn't ready to do that yet, especially after what I had been told. But if she was to be free, truly free, I had to. With tears in my eyes, I took the lid off the urn, slowly walking around the tree, releasing her ashes into the trench.

Once her ashes were spread, I placed the urn on the ground. Wiping the hot tears from my eyes, I recited words that I hoped would release Aunt Noreen from this world and carry her on to the next. "Noreen Chadwick, beloved aunt and family matriarch, I free you from your earthly confines, and release you from the ties that bind. Ascend to live amongst our ancestors divine, may your light always and forever shine." I paused for a few seconds, adding at the last minute, "If what Professor Jerrod said was true, then best believe I will avenge you."

I waited a few minutes, taking it all in then gathered up the lanterns to head back to the house. As I started walking, I saw light reflecting off the windows of the house. I turned around and couldn't believe my eyes. The tree was…glowing. From the roots on up, that white willow tree was illuminated with a lavender radiance. I tried to back up, wanted to turn around and run away as fast as I could, but it was as if my feet had grown roots that had affixed me to where I stood. I was afraid, and yet fascinated, by the sight in front of me. Since I couldn't move, I did what some would consider crazy; heck, I thought it was crazy. I pulled my cell phone out of my pocket and started recording. Why? Because I knew if I told anyone about it, they would think I was categorically insane.

The lavender luminescence became more dazzling by the moment, the tree having a mystical glow. The color changed from lavender to bright blue, then gleaming white. Despite the unnatural circumstances, it was a beautiful sight. I watched and recorded until the lights finally faded back to normal. Then, when the hold on me was finally released, I ran back to the house like I'd stolen something.

That clinched it; it was definitely time for me to leave this unnatural burg. Although I wanted to find out who, or what, killed my aunt, I couldn't stay here any longer. I packed up what few belongings I had and threw everything in the car. After I made sure the house was locked up tight, I headed back to the garage. When the garage door opened, I looked across the brook toward Elisa's house. I felt a twinge of guilt because I was leaving without saying goodbye. I had only been in town for a few days, and we hadn't known each other long, but we had developed some sort of bond, a comradery that I had come to appreciate. I drove out of the garage, intent on never looking back. After I had traveled for a good ten to fifteen minutes, I slowed down, pulling off to the side of the road. I took out my cell phone, dialed Elisa's number then hit the road again, gunning my car as fast as I could.

"Tasmin?" I heard Elisa say when she finally answered. "I saw the lights from my house. What happened over there? Are you okay?"

At least I knew I wasn't crazy. Elisa also saw the tree light up, albeit from a distance. "I'm so sorry, Elisa. I told you I wasn't cut out for Salix Pointe. Between everything that happened at your place, my aunt being murdered, and that tree lighting up—"

"Wait, Tasmin, slow down. That was a tree?"

"I can't explain right now, Elisa. I just want to tell you how sorry I am for running out on you. I'm on my way to the airport—"

Before I could finish my sentence, I heard a pop, then my car started to spin out. I screamed, attempting to turn into the spinout. I saw my life flash before my eyes. The car felt like it had spun at least five times before stopping on the other side of the road.

"Tasmin! Tasmin, answer me!" Elisa yelled frantically. "Are you okay? Tasmin!"

I took a few deep breaths, trying to calm my rapidly beating heart. "Yeah…yes…I'm okay, Elisa. A tire blew and my car spun out, but I'm unhurt."

"Oh, thank goodness," she said, letting out a sigh of relief. "Where are you?"

I looked around, realizing this definitely wasn't New York. There were no street signs or mile markers to use as a point of reference. The only thing I knew was that I was on the main road. "I'm about fifteen minutes out on the main road."

"Okay, I'm coming to get you," she quickly replied.

I would have refused her kind offer, so as not to put her out, but I knew getting Triple A out here wasn't an option. "Okay, thank you, Elisa. There's an emergency car kit in the trunk. I'll get it out and light the emergency flare so you can find me."

"Good idea. You're welcome, Tasmin. Now sit tight. I'll be there as soon as I can," she replied reassuringly, disconnecting the call.

I pressed the lever to open the trunk then climbed out of the car. Opening the emergency car kit, I removed the single flare then closed the trunk. Using the flashlight on my keychain, I read the instructions for how to light the flare. Once I did, I set it on the ground where I knew Elisa would see it. Only thing to do now was wait. I started to walk back to the driver's side, prepared to get back in the car, when out of nowhere a man appeared in front of me blocking my entry, startling me to no end.

"What the...where the heck did you come from?" I asked, looking around.

The way this man was dressed, and looking fresh as a daisy, he clearly hadn't walk here, but there was no car or any other vehicle within eyeshot. Wearing a crisp, well-fitting red suit with a black dress shirt, and designer black leather shoes, the man looked remarkably like an older version of Dr. Battle, apart from his olive colored skin tone. Like Dr. Battle, his long, wavy hair was jet black, save for the streaks of gray at the temples. His imposing muscular frame towered well over six feet.

"Don't be concerned where I came from, Tasmin. If I were you, I'd be more concerned about myself," a silky smooth, yet sinister, voice replied.

"Who are you? How do you know my name?" I queried, slowly backing away from him.

"Who I am is not important. Why I'm here is."

He inched his way toward me, his walk authoritative and self-assured. I turned, intent on running, but once again, he appeared in front of me. I smelled the distinctively nauseating odor of sulfur. What was he? I tried to run in different directions, but he blocked me at every turn, eventually backing me up against the car.

"Mmmmm," he muttered in a low tone, appearing to be sniffing me. That was just gross. "You smell divine, Tasmin."

"Sorry I can't say the same," I retorted, mustering up as much bravado as I could.

He let out a laugh so menacing it made my blood run cold. "Beautiful, feisty, and a wicked sense of humor. What a delectable combination. No wonder the angel whelp is so taken with you. I wonder how he would feel if I…took you first."

Angel whelp? Was he talking about the professor? He was the only angel I knew, or so he claimed to be. And there was no way I was going to let this freak of nature violate me. I always carried pepper spray. Although I've never had to use it, I never felt so grateful for having it on me.

"Look, I don't know who…or what you are, or why you're messing with me, but I've got people on the way, so if you know what's good for you, you'll get up off me," I said, trying to divert his attention while pulling the pepper spray out my jacket pocket.

He looked me dead in the eyes, a sneer on his face. "That's what I'm counting on, my sweet."

Wait, he was expecting Elisa? What was really going on? I wasn't going to give him the chance to get at her. I pulled out my pepper spray, a heavy stream of the liquid hitting its mark. Only, I didn't get the reaction I anticipated. Sure, I expected the whites of his eyes to turn red, but I what I didn't foresee were bright red glowing eyes to be staring back at me.

He laughed again, amusement in his tone. The more he laughed, the more I saw his teeth change, changed from normal human teeth to grotesque, elongated fangs, fangs that were too close for comfort. His hands were no longer those of a pampered man, but of some repulsive creature. His strong masculine frame bulked tremendously in size.

I'd admit it; I was absolutely terrified. He pressed his hard body against mine, forcing one of his legs between my thighs. "Don't worry, Tasmin, I'll be gentle. I want this to be just as special for you as I know it will be for me," he taunted.

Oh, heck no. I wasn't going out like that. It was then that I gathered all my strength, in an attempt to shove him off me. "Get away from me!" I yelled.

I figured I'd only manage to push him back a few inches, but instead, I managed to hit him with an energy blast, sending him sprawling several feet away of me. While he only appeared to be stunned, it afforded me the opportunity to hit him a few more times, keeping him off balance.

I was about to hit him again when, in my periphery, a sliver of white light caught my eye, followed by an irradiant silhouette flying at lightning speed toward my attacker. The figure struck him with the full force of its weight, knocking him to the ground. When it briefly turned in my direction, I realized that it was the form Professor Jerrod revealed to me earlier at Elisa's home.

A darker, more ominous figure materialized next to him, one that I assumed was Dr. Battle. His appearance was nightmarish. With features similar to that of the creature who attacked me, he had red glowing eyes, massive fangs, sharp claws, and an enormous physical frame. Unlike my attacker, he had large angel wings, except his feathers were an equal mixture of black and white.

Both Professor Jerrod and Dr. Battle had what looked like swords, one pure white, the other dark, respectively. Taking a battle stance, they flanked the creature. Professor Jerrod attacked first, swinging his sword wildly, as if in anger. The creature, on the other hand, fought in a more polished, thoughtful manner, easily parrying each of the professor's swings. The same occurred when Dr. Battle attacked; frenzied moves on his part, calculated, well-planned strikes from their opponent. All of a sudden, the beast found an opening, swinging his sharp claws, gouging them into Professor Jerrod's abdomen. Blood spewed rapidly from the deep gashes. The professor collapsed on the ground. Dr. Battle, letting out a terrifying blood-curdling roar, went after his look-alike as if possessed.

My bracelet began to feel warm and glowed, like it did the night I passed out. Then I saw headlights in the distance and realized it was Elisa's SUV. She pulled up close to my rental, quickly running to my side. I began to hear the same chant in my head that I heard before.

"Do you hear it, too?" Elisa asked.

I nodded, showing Elisa the glowing bracelet on my left wrist. What I didn't know was that she had an identical one on her right wrist. I had never seen her wear it until tonight. I grabbed her right hand with my left, both of us loudly speaking the protection chant in unison. Immediately both combatants dropped to their knees, my attacker being affected significantly more than Dr. Battle. Elisa and I used the opportunity to further go on the offensive, sending energy blasts directly at the creature. He screamed as if in pain before disappearing, leaving the stench of sulfur behind him.

I promptly ran over to Professor Jerrod, while Elisa ran to check on Dr. Battle. The professor had lost a lot of blood, his wounds still oozing. I checked to see if he was breathing or had a pulse. There was nothing.

"I need some help over here!" I yelled.

Dr. Battle, with Elisa's help, staggered over to where we were. He appeared a bit disoriented but had mostly recovered. "What do you need, Tasmin?" he asked.

I took off my jacket, tossing it to Elisa. "Elisa, I need you to apply pressure to his wounds."

"Got it," she replied, folding the jacket then pressing it firmly over his lacerations.

"Dr. Battle—"

"Dafari," he said, quickly correcting me.

"Dafari, he's not breathing and doesn't have a pulse."

Naturally he understood what that meant. He positioned his hands on his brother's chest… and waited. We started CPR, with me giving two initial breaths and Dafari starting chest compressions. Back and forth we went, two breaths, thirty compressions, trying to bring Professor Jerrod back to life.

"You are not going to die on me," I affirmed, as Dafari continued compressing his brother's chest.

As he completed his last set, I gave one breath, then another. All of sudden, just as I was lifting my head, a hand grabbed the back of my neck, pulling me back down. I felt Professor Jerrod stir, his lips meeting mine in a kiss, his tongue entering my mouth. I was so surprised I sprang up, looking at him in disbelief.

A weak smile on his face, he uttered, "So you do like me."

CHAPTER 14:
DAFARI

"I was trying to save your life, you jerk," Tasmin yelled in response to my recently resurrected brother's glib comment, punching him in the arm. "I thought you were dead. You are unbelievable," she continued angrily, standing up and walking toward her car.

For several seconds I knelt beside Octavian in shock. By rights, my brother should be dead and should have remained dead, but there he was, talking, making light of the very dire situation he had just survived. I removed Elisa's hands from covering Tasmin's jacket, lifting it up. To my and Elisa's astonishment, Octavian's wounds were completely healed, no trace left of the enormous lacerations inflicted by my father. Elisa quickly ran to Tasmin to relay the news.

The fact that Octavian was alive was a miracle unto itself. As a Fallen, my father's talons were laced with a lethal poison that was essentially fatal to a pure-blood angel. Octavian had sustained mortal wounds with overwhelming blood loss. Tasmin confirmed that he had no signs of life, and yet, he was breathing and had a heartbeat. It appeared Octavian was right; Tasmin was indeed a healer. She had literally breathed life back into him.

"How are you feeling after returning from the dead, little brother?" I asked, still somewhat in disbelief.

"I feel incredible," he replied, still lying on the ground.

"Well, you have Tasmin to thank for that." I stood up, reaching out an arm for my brother to grab. "Come, Sleeping Beauty. You can thank Princess Charming for your miraculous recovery later. Right now, we need to make our leave. While I doubt it, my father may be bold enough to return."

"Agreed. And you're right; I will have to thank Tasmin later, in my own special way," Octavian concurred, a sly grin on his face. Even after a near-death experience, my brother still couldn't help being a pretentious arse. He took my arm, standing up slowly, still a bit unsteady from our encounter. After he regained his footing, he pulled me to the side, saying, "I believe it would be unwise for Tasmin and Elisa to return to their homes tonight, considering the circumstances. Perhaps, dear older brother, you can provide them with refuge for the evening."

I looked at him, annoyed at his suggestion. "Oh goody, a pajama party," I replied sardonically. My home was decidedly much larger than I required, but I cherished my privacy. Nevertheless, the witches were still in grave danger, and it would afford me the opportunity to have a much-needed conversation with Elisa. "Fine, baby brother. Maybe now you can explain things to Tasmin without getting blasted again."

"Oh, bugger off, Dafari," he shot back, looking in Tasmin's direction. "I have the feeling she doesn't believe I had truly perished. Hell, I'm having a hard time coming to grips with it myself."

I watched as Elisa helped Tasmin transfer her belongings to Elisa's vehicle. "Octavian, with all that's transpired in the last few days, can you blame her? They've both had a lot thrown at them, and while I still believe we don't have time for coddling or hand holding, perhaps a subtler approach would best serve us."

"You may have a point, Brother. But I must ask; does your subtler approach include not divulging who their attacker was?"

"No, Octavian. They need to know who, and what, they are up against. However," I countered, "I still don't necessarily believe he was responsible for Noreen's death."

Throwing up his hands, Octavian decried, "Dafari, are you mad as a bag of ferrets? He's already attempted to kill Elisa in her dreams, Tasmin tonight, and, for all intents and purposes, he *did* slay me. For you to be so blinded by the obvious is sheer bollocks."

Our squabble would have surely continued were it not for Tasmin and Elisa walking over to us. "Hey, we're ready to head back," Tasmin said. "I'm not really comfortable staying by myself tonight, so Elisa volunteered to crash at Aunt Noreen's house with me."

"Actually, ladies, my very magnanimous brother feels that, in light of what has transpired, it would behoove you both to be guests at his home tonight. Isn't that right, Brother?" Octavian queried, looking very self-satisfied.

While I suggested no such thing, I instinctively knew that Tasmin would more readily accept the offer if it came from me, as opposed to my irritating little brother. "Yes, what he said," I replied, unenthused. "Elisa, I suggest a brief stop to your home so you may gather some belongings for this evening."

The women looked at each other then at us. "I'm not so sure about that. I appreciate you saving my life and all, but going to your place, I'm not necessarily comfortable with that," Tasmin replied.

"Tasmin, I totally get where you're coming from, but after what just happened, I'd much rather go with them than run the risk of getting attacked again. You know what they say; the devil you know. No offense," said Elisa, looking directly at me.

"None taken," I said.

Still apprehensive, Tasmin asked, "Are you absolutely sure about this, Elisa, because if you are, then I'll trust your judgement on this one."

"I'm not sure of anything right now, but my gut is telling me that they'll keep us safe; at least for tonight."

"Okay, but just for tonight," Tasmin noted, walking to the driver's side of the SUV, climbing into the back seat. Following Tasmin's lead, we all climbed into Elisa's vehicle, with Octavian sitting in the back with Tasmin. I, of course, sat up front with Elisa. We drove in silence until we reached her home.

"Elisa, one of us should accompany you inside, just to be safe."

"You'll get no argument from me," she quickly replied, exiting the automobile.

I looked back at Octavian. "Go help her, little brother," I ordered. The last thing I needed was to leave him with Tasmin and return to the two of them verbally assaulting each other, or worse. Although he shot daggers at me with his gaze, he nonetheless relented.

Once he and Elisa entered her home, I seized the opportunity to clear up a misconception, but I wanted to break the ice first. Turning around to look at Tasmin, I asked, "How are you getting on?"

She took a deep breath before answering. "I'm okay. I'm just still trying to figure all this out. It's a lot to take in."

"Indeed, it is. Just know that Octavian and I will do our best to assist you and Elisa to better understand the situation at hand."

"Thank you, Dafari. I have so many questions that need answers," she responded, looking out the window.

"As to be expected." I needed to address the proverbial elephant in the room before my brother and Elisa returned. "Tasmin, I know you're skeptical, and at times my brother can be a complete horse's arse, but trust me when I say Octavian had indeed perished," I replied.

She looked at me, studying my expression. "I know he was badly wounded and had no signs of life, because I checked, but he's totally healed; walking and talking as if nothing happened. How is that even possible? Can…archangels heal themselves?" She said archangel with an air of disbelief.

I was hesitant to discuss Octavian's and my assumption as to her abilities so abruptly, but, considering her question, I felt there was no other choice. "Yes, archangels can heal themselves. However, the…demon —"

"So that thing that attacked us was a demon?" she interrupted.

"Yes, it was," I continued. "As I was saying, the demon had the ability to mortally wound Octavian with a lethal poison. My brother was deceased, Tasmin, and should not have been able to recover. It appears that you brought him back to life."

"Me?" she questioned, the trepidation in her voice apparent. "How?"

"Most likely, you've always had this gift, but it was probably dormant or blunted. All signs point to your powers evolving."

She let out a heavy sigh. "Great, just great. If this is the case, and I'm not saying that it is, you do realize that this means your brother was right."

"Yes, and if he is, he'll probably never let you forget it," I replied. Speaking to Tasmin, I realized how much she reminded me of her aunt Noreen, her strength and wit being very much like hers. I felt as if we had reached a new level of understanding. Just then, Elisa and Octavian emerged from the house.

"To be continued," I finished, tabling the conversation.

Elisa opened the trunk, placing her belongings in the back. "Sorry I took so long," she said, while getting into the driver's seat.

"No worries," I replied. I wasn't sure if Elisa knew my address, but I did know that her telepathy was becoming stronger by the day. "Elisa, do you know where I live?" I relayed to her telepathically.

A look of shock and awe crossed her face. "So I can really hear you in my mind?" she sent back.

"Yes, you can. You're a telepath, Elisa. But we can discuss your powers later. Right now, we need to get home. If you would allow me, I can direct you."

"Please do," she communicated. It was remarkable how quickly she had caught on.

"Dr. Pettiford," I heard Octavian say, still in keeping with the formalities since she banned him from calling her Tasmin.

"Yes, Professor?" she replied.

"I've been told that you brought me back to life. I would just like to thank you from the bottom of my heart for reviving me."

"I'm still not sure about this healing thing, but if I did, you're welcome."

That was the most affable Tasmin had been toward Octavian since my brother's fatal faux pas. It seemed those two actually had a moment of civility.

"I must admit your method of resuscitation was quite...enjoyable. It made dying all worth it." Although I wasn't looking at him, I knew Octavian well enough to know that he had a puffed-up grin on his face.

Tasmin took in a deep breath then exhaled. "How is it that someone could die, come back from the brink of death, and still be such a jackass?" she asked, showing her disgust.

And just that quickly the moment was gone. *Way to go, Brother.* "That, Tasmin, will be a question for the ages," I answered. "My little brother has a knack for jackassery," I noted.

Elisa and I shot each other sidelong glances during Tasmin and Octavian's verbal exchange. "He just can't get it right, can he?" she asked with a giggle, continuing our telepathic chat.

"Apparently not," I replied, clearly at a loss for words.

All the while, I was giving Elisa directions telepathically. She had reached my home in good time. Despite everyone being battle-weary from tonight's skirmish, questions still needed to be answered. Once we were all inside, I showed Elisa and Tasmin to the bedroom suites they would be staying in. With all that was going on, I had the feeling they would be here for longer than one night. We all proceeded to our respective rooms to shower and change clothes. I definitely felt the need to wash off the battle grime.

While the others were still tending to their own needs, I started doing one of the few things that truly relaxed my mind; cooking. As immortal beings, neither I nor Octavian required sustenance, although we could eat if we chose to; however, Elisa and Tasmin did need to eat. Being centuries old, I had been around the world several times over, and knew how to prepare dishes of all kinds. When I moved to Salix Pointe, spending time with Noreen also meant her teaching me new recipes. Before tonight, other than Octavian, she was the only person I had ever allowed into my home. I remember her telling me that if I ever wanted to find a nice, respectable young lady, I should know how to cook, because women liked to eat, too.

One of Noreen's signature dishes was her Gullah red rice. Derived from West African Jollof rice, it contained rice, onions, peppers, tomato paste, sugar, salt, pepper, garlic salt, and turkey sausage. I had come to love it just as much as she did. I prepared a large pot for Tasmin, Elisa, and myself, making a smaller one sans sausage for Octavian, as he was pescatarian.

I heard Elisa's footfalls before she even spoke. "Is that what I think it is?" she asked, taking in a deep inhale.

"And what would that be?" I questioned.

She took another deep breath. "It smells like Ms. Noreen's Gullah red rice," she replied, sitting at the kitchen island.

"You would be correct," I affirmed as I presented her with a large bowl of the hot dish along with a glass of red wine.

"Thank you, Dr. Battle," she said, taking a bite of the food. "This tastes just like Ms. Noreen's recipe. It's delicious."

"Thank you, and please call me Dafari. I think we've gone way beyond formalities."

"Okay, Dafari," she replied, blushing as she said it.

I placed a bowl of rice and a glass of wine for Tasmin on the counter, and rice bowls and snifters of bourbon for Octavian and me. Tasmin arrived first.

Seeing the food, she sat next to Elisa saying, "That's not —"

"Yes, it is," interrupted Elisa, taking a sip of wine. "Dafari cooked. Try it. It tastes wonderful."

Tasmin looked at me dubiously, raising an eyebrow. "I'll be the judge of that." Elisa and I watched as she took a heaping forkful into her mouth. She savored it for a moment then looked at me with a smile saying, "Auntie would be so proud."

I wasn't one who cared for praise, but I had to admit, I was pleased by the women's approval, especially Elisa's. "Thank you, ladies. Noreen taught me well."

Octavian arrived, fashionably late. "Started without me, I see," he quipped, tearing into his food.

"You're lucky I made you anything, plant eater," I retorted.

"I believe, Dafari, the correct term you're looking for is pescatarian. My diet consists of entirely fruit, vegetable, and fish."

"I believe the term I'm looking for is blowhard," I countered before moving on to important matters. "Since we're all here, I think we should discuss all that's occurred. Ladies, I know you both have numerous questions, so feel free to ask."

"Well, before we start with the Q and A session," Tasmin began, "I need to show you guys something." Setting up her cellphone on the counter, she showed us a video of a tree illuminating for several minutes before finally dimming.

"Was that what happened during your ceremony for Ms. Noreen?" Elisa asked.

"Yes, it was. I tried to run when it started, but I literally could not move from where I was standing. I recorded it because I almost couldn't believe it myself."

"Hmmmm," Octavian started. "You know what that looks like to me?" he asked with that smug air of his.

"Enlighten us, baby brother."

"Dare I say magick?"

Tasmin sneered at him. "Anyway. That's why I took off so abruptly. I'd had enough of this town and all its weirdness. Then the tire blew out on my car, I spun out, and you know the rest. By the way, how did you guys even know that I was in trouble, and how did you get to me so fast?" she asked, addressing Octavian and me.

"We were still with Elisa when you called," I replied. "As to how we arrived so quickly, we can traverse something called the veil, a connection between heaven and earth. Being a full-blooded angel, Octavian, can travel without issue. I, on the other hand, have to proceed a bit more cautiously, since I am half angel, half demon." Unlike Octavian, I didn't have the opportunity to reveal my true form to Elisa or Tasmin. I felt it was best to just rip off the bandage.

"You're a what?" Elisa and Tasmin asked in unison, shocked by the revelation.

"Maybe that's why I always had an uneasy feeling around you," added Tasmin.

"Most likely," I replied. "Like your aunt, we believe you are an empath."

"Did my aunt know about you?"

"I suspect she did, but she never voiced it."

Tasmin rubbed her palms down her face. "Honestly, at this point, I really don't care what you are. I'm just grateful you two showed up when you did. Thank you."

"So are you saying you owe us your life?" Octavian chimed in.

Elisa and I shook our heads while Tasmin replied, "Don't push it, Professor. I might still owe Dafari, but as far as you're concerned, I brought you back from the dead, so the way I see it, we're even."

"She does have point, dear brother. I say cut your losses while you can," I teased, as he shot a cutting look at me.

"Okay, so I have a question," Elisa chimed in. First looking at me then Octavian she continued, "You're half angel and half demon, and you're a full angel. You're brothers and you somewhat resemble each other, so…"

"Same mother, different father," Octavian and I uttered at the same time.

"Our mother is African. Dafari's father is Mediterranean, mine is African-American," Octavian clarified.

"But you're British," Elisa noted.

"Yes, well, my parents and Dafari migrated to London sometime before my birth. I was born and raised there."

Turning to Octavian, Tasmin remarked, "From the first day we met, you tried to convince me that I had magick, which leads me to believe that you either suspected I was a witch, or you already knew for sure."

"Truth be told, I was aware that you were a witch. I was alerted by our…superiors once your aunt crossed to the other side. That was when your powers started to manifest, although, it wasn't until you arrived in Salix Pointe that you noticed anything. Elisa, on the other hand, has had her powers since childhood, but she chose to never fully explore them."

Filling her and Tasmin's glasses with more wine, Elisa countered, "There are enough oddities in this town without me being one of them."

"I hear that," Tasmin noted in agreement, clinking her glass to Elisa's. "So riddle me this; why us? Why are Elisa and I being targeted?"

"That we're still trying to figure out, but after some thought, Octavian and I suspect that Noreen wasn't the only one murdered. We believe that Dr. Ange-Diable was removed in order to make it easier to eliminate her."

"Why would someone want to get rid of Doc and kill my aunt?" questioned Tasmin. "Neither of them would hurt a fly."

"Apparently, your aunt was seen a threat. She was an extremely powerful witch; one of *the* most powerful in the world." Octavian pointed out. "As far as Dr. Ange-Diable was concerned, he, like my dear older brother, was half angel, half demon. As you know, he was Ms. Chadwick's loyal companion. He was also her protector; hence, in order to get to her, he needed to be taken out of the picture."

"Wow, the things you don't know," Tasmin remarked, taking a long sip of her wine.

I picked up the story from there. "She also knew you were a witch, Tasmin. In my opinion, I feel she didn't tell you because she didn't want you to be saddled with a burden that you clearly didn't want."

Tasmin stared into what remained of her wine, swirling it around. “She was right. I didn’t want it. I still don’t, but it looks like I have no choice.”

I stopped, pausing briefly to look at Elisa. “We also speculate that Noreen wasn’t the only target. I’m sorry, Elisa, but it appears that your grandmother, and your parents before her, were taken prematurely. They all were aware of your burgeoning abilities. And, in her own right, Mama Nall was also a formidable witch.

Elisa and Tasmin looked at one another then back at me. “Why wouldn’t they tell me?” Elisa questioned.

I gave her the best explanation I could for the information I had at the moment. “I can’t speak to why Mama Nall never told you, but as for your parents, they probably felt you were too young to handle such responsibility.”

Tasmin shook her head as if clearing out cobwebs. “So, let me see if I have this straight; over several years, five people were eliminated in order to keep Elisa and me from finding out we’re witches, and two of those said people were themselves witches. Despite that, we found out anyway, and now we’re being targeted as a result. Am I correct so far?”

“That would be an accurate assessment,” Octavian confirmed.

"And the demon that attacked me?'

"*I* believe he is the murderer we seek. My brother, on the other hand, begs to differ."

If looks could kill, the one I was giving Octavian would have incinerated him. Both women looked at me quizzically, waiting for my response. The moment I was dreading was upon us. "There is no proof to speak of that he is the one who committed any of the murders. Save for Noreen's murder, we don't even know if he was in Salix Pointe at the time."

"On all that is Holy, Dafari, are you completely gormless? He attacked Tasmin and killed me right before your eyes only a few short hours ago, man! Not to mention going after Elisa in her dream. All roads lead to him. What more do you need?"

"Wait, that wasn't just a night terror? It was actually a full-blown attack?" Elisa asked, visibly taken aback.

Octavian responded before I could get a word out. "Yes, Elisa, it was indeed an attack. Had you not pulled Tasmin into your dream, and had we not arrived when we did, you quite possibly could have been another causality of that demon."

"Hold up," Tasmin started, "When he first was all up in my face, before he turned into that hideous creature, I remember thinking how much he resembled Dafari, just older."

Elisa turned to Tasmin, completely caught off guard by what she said. "You, too? I remembered thinking the *exact* same thing."

All eyes were on me. There was no avoiding it now. "He resembled me because…he's my father."

CHAPTER 15:
ELISA

"Excuse me?" Tasmin said.

With wide eyes I leaned forward. "As in your biological father?"

Dafari nodded once. "Yes. The demon who attacked both of you is my father."

Tasmin threw her hands up. "That's it. I don't think I can handle any more reveals tonight."

I said, "But…he was fighting you just as he was Octavian. One would have thought you three were enemies as opposed to—"

"Yes, Demon Daddy has a tendency to not care about familial relations one way or the other when he's on a bender," Octavian said.

"A bender?" Tasmin asked.

"A killing spree," Octavian clarified.

"This is too much. It's all too much," Tasmin said as she stood. "Thank you, Dafari, for the meal and the wine, but I need to go lie down and wrap my head around all of this. I hate to be a rude guest, but I'm truly spent right now."

"It's completely understandable, Tasmin," Dafari said.

"It is, but please keep in mind, we have to discuss these things and more as it's apparent that his father isn't going to relent until he gets what he wants," Octavian said. "You two have to realize that the sooner you learn, not only more about your powers, but how to use them, the sooner you'll be able to better protect yourself from threats seen and unseen."

"We're aware of that," I said. "However, you can't expect us to automatically be okay with all of this. Give us a least the night to sleep on it. We just learned we're witches, that our loved ones were possibly murdered, on top of shooting orbs of energy blasts from our palms, and to make matters worse, Dafari's demon daddy wants to kill us."

Octavian chuckled then looked at his brother. "See, even she likes your father's sobriquet."

Dafari took a deep inhale then ignored Octavian. "Sleep on it tonight and we will revisit this first light of the day."

As I lay in the comfortable bed later that night, I couldn't help but think about all that had occurred. My eyes burned with unshed tears. All these years, I'd thought Mama Nall had died of old age only to find out that the only grandmother I'd had left had been taken away from me just like my parents. I missed them all so much, and hearing that they'd been killed in such a way made the grief fresh all over again.

I was glad the bed I was in was comfortable. The room itself was a spacious one and consisted of white ecru walls with a king-sized bed that had purple and lavender bedding. Against the white wall on the left side of the room sat a fancy desk and chair. Across from that was a chest of drawers and a matching dresser, both of which looked to be custom made judging by the intricate carvings.

The walk-in closet, which sat empty, looked to be as big as my whole bedroom back home. There was a sitting area that had a marble fireplace, a couch with a lounger and a 50-inch flatscreen television. The large en-suite bathroom with the walk-in shower, that had two shower heads, had called to me when I noticed it earlier. If we hadn't needed to discuss all that had happened, I'd have stayed in there a lot longer. The jet sprays massaged me almost as good as a skilled masseuse. There was also a glass bowl sink and a toilet with a bidet.

I turned on my side then looked at the moon through my window. It was a waning crescent moon which meant the illuminated part of the moon decreased from the visible semicircle until it disappeared from view entirely at new moon. At that very moment, I felt like my life was in such a phase and it was frightening. How would I go from being a simple café owner to a powerful witch? How was I supposed to figure all of this out when it was just laid at my feet?

I felt warm tears slide down my cheeks. I didn't know how I would handle this on top of trying to compartmentalize the fact that all my elders had been murdered. I'd been ten and orphaned for crying out loud. Then to lose Mama Nall? I put on a good act. I saved face, but it was crushing.

I turned on my back and sighed. I didn't remember much about the accident as I supposed my mind erased it in some way. I remembered us driving through the rain to get back to Salix Pointe. I remembered a flash of white and gold light, which I assumed was lightning. I remembered my mother screaming and my father—I shot straight up in bed. The chants! My father was chanting!

I slapped a hand over my mouth as if to stifle a scream. Could it have been possible my father was the witch and not my mother? Why I automatically assumed it would be her who was the powerful one and not him was beyond me, but I remembered now. Clear as day, my father's right arm went across my mother's chest as if to shield her, then his left hand shot forward as if to try to stop whatever it was that had shot the gold and white light at us. No matter what he'd done to try to save us, it hadn't worked. Not for them anyway.

I sighed heavily then fell back against the pillows. I needed to talk this through but knew Tasmin was going through a reckoning of her own. I didn't want to burden her further. Octavian was probably somewhere pacing, trying to figure out what was going on and come up with ways to annoy Tasmin more. Dafari…I wished I could talk to him. From the time he and I had met, he always seemed to be understanding and patient. I had so many questions, but my body was tired and my mind foggy because of the stress.

"The first thing you should work on is closing your mind and being careful what you wish for," I heard from the shadows of the sitting room.

I saw his glowing golden eyes before I actually saw him. Even though I recognized his voice, the hairs on the back of my neck still rose. The room chilled but my body felt as if it was on fire. It was an odd combination.

I slowly sat up in bed. "Are you going to come out of the shadows?" I asked.

He was silent for a moment. He blinked once, as I saw his golden eyes disappear then reemerge seconds later. I waited anxiously. My breath caught when he finally stepped from the darkness. I didn't know what I expected, but it hadn't been for him to only be clad in his boxer briefs. I sat in that bed staring at him as if I'd never seen a man before. A fly could have flown in my mouth and out again.

I swallowed. His hair was down, curtaining his shoulders and face. I'd known he was built like an African warrior, but by all the Orishas, I didn't know he was built like a living, breathing Shangò. His dark skin was moisturized to the point I wanted to reach out to touch him. The powerful stride of his thighs along with the ripple in his abs as he strode toward the bed touched everything woman within me.

"Everything about me is supposed to rattle your delicate sensibilities, Elisa," he said once standing at the foot of the bed.

The heated way in which he gazed upon me put me at sixes and sevens. I didn't know if I wanted to run away from him or run to jump around his waist. I didn't like that he had that kind of effect on me.

"I don't like the effect you have on me either, but here we are. You must learn how to close your mind and, again, be careful of what you wish for."

"Stop doing that," I said, suddenly annoyed. "Stop reading my thoughts!"

"Stop projecting them to me," he retorted, seemingly just as annoyed.

"I-I don't know how," I said, moving around uncomfortably.

My lady parts felt engorged and it felt as if I was going to have an orgasm where I sat. I could feel moisture pool between my thighs. I rolled my shoulders same as he did. I threw the covers back so I could get out of bed, but he held up his hand.

"Please...stop moving," he demanded in a voice that stilled me.

There was a threat somewhere in the undertones, but something told me the only harm he would cause would be carnally.

"You would be correct," he said through a snarl. "And your body would feel every thrust and dip of my hips. I can smell your arousal, and if you move another muscle, I cannot be held responsible for the ways in which I will take you."

I swallowed again. "Okay," was all I could say.

His shoulders, arms, and chest had bulked in size and his breathing was rugged. He closed his eyes as if he needed to catch his breath and gather his senses. When he opened them again, glowing red eyes bored a hole through me. The rise in his boxers caused my eyes to widen. He had been blessed in ways that mere men could only dream of, and to be honest, I wasn't sure I could handle it.

Good grief, I thought.

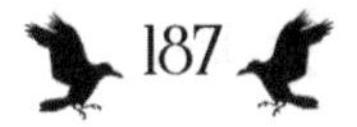

"Are you going to be okay?" I asked.

"No," he said.

Then he did something that made little sense. He walked around the bed then climbed inside with me. If my smell was causing him that much angst, why would he climb into bed with me?

"What are you doing?" I asked, alarm rising.

I liked him a helluva a lot, but I wasn't ready to explore sex with a man who had just told me he was half angel and half demon.

He said nothing as he eased me back. "Turn the way in which you sleep most comfortably," he said.

I turned on my left side. A few seconds later, he closed his arms around me and spooned me from behind. The move should have alarmed me, but it didn't, not in the way it should have. While I was nervous, being in his arms made me feel safe and secure. And he smelled so good that if I hadn't been lying down, I'd have swooned. Perhaps I was one of those women from old romance novels. I could feel the rise in his nature against my backside. It made me—I stopped my thoughts remembering he could hear them.

"Wise choice," he growled against my ear.

His voice made me shiver and made my insides quake. He slid a hand on the softness of my stomach then nuzzled my neck.

"Guard.Your.Thoughts, woman," he said, only this time his voice was thick with something I couldn't put a word to, but I could feel it.

It was an energy that I'd never experienced, but it was all consuming. I could feel him all over me. My heart beat faster. I squirmed. I couldn't help it. His grip tightened around me. I tried to move so I could turn and face him, he wouldn't allow it.

"Go to sleep, Elisa. For your own good, go to sleep," he said. He practically sounded as if he was begging.

But I couldn't go to sleep. How could I when he had me wired and open like a desert highway? I rubbed my thighs together.

He sighed then made a sound as if he was a wounded jungle cat. "Octavian," he called.

"Wh-why are you calling your brother?" I asked.

In the next blink, there was a knock at my door.

"Come in," Dafari said.

In walked Octavian wearing a robe that looked straight out of the 19th century. If I wasn't so, for a lack of better words, hot and bothered, I'd have cackled like a mad woman. That was how ridiculous the garment looked. The light from the hall illuminated his get up and only then did I see a smoking pipe.

"You rang, dear brother," he asked then pulled the pipe from his lips.

"Put her to sleep," Dafari demanded.

I said, "I don't want to go to sleep. Why do you want me to go to sleep?"

Octavian glanced down at me then over at his brother behind me. "Is she ill?"

"No. I am not ill," I said.

"No, but she's making me ill. Put her to sleep," Dafari growled.

Octavian sniffed the air then frowned before raising a brow. "What is that musky titillating scent—" he stopped then glanced back at me before quickly averting his eyes back to his brother. "Oh," Octavian whispered. "Say no more."

Before I could protest again, Octavian walked over to the bed then touched my temple.

In my dreams, Dafari and I practiced the art of coitus and held congress under a full moon in the middle of my backyard. There was some sort of ritual circle around us made of the most powerful crystals in the world. The wind howled and the rain washed over us. Trees rocked and swayed as if they were praising our tryst. It was wild. It was primal. It was passionate. It was all consuming. I wanted him to take me in ways that no well-raised woman should admit publicly, and he did. He gave me everything my body could hand and some things I couldn't. Yet, I still begged for more. He left trails of his saliva in places that only I or my future husband were supposed to have access to.

In my dreams, I acted so wanton that I knew I'd be ashamed to look him in the eyes the next morning…

CHAPTER 16:
OCTAVIAN

My dreams were a strange place for me last evening. I dreamt of a time I'd rather forget. It had been one of the most traumatic times of my life. That was neither here nor there because I refused to think on it any further.

I walked downstairs to find that I was the only one up. I put on a pot of water for my morning cuppa then pulled out eggs, grits, and fish. I knew my brother and Elisa wouldn't mind fish and grits for breakfast and was pretty sure Tasmin wouldn't mind either since she had deep southern roots. While I prepared breakfast, I thought about Elisa and Tasmin coming into their powers. There was much they needed to learn. I planned to speak with my brother about their training whenever he decided to crawl from between Elisa's thighs in the dream world.

They had a lot to learn in a short time. Despite my brother's protestations, I had no doubt that his father was at the center of all the madness, and I intended to prove it once and for all. Perhaps Dafari was distracted by his dilemma with Elisa and that was why he couldn't see that his father was clearly our culprit. He still hadn't told her he was an incubus. I'd love to be a fly on that wall when he did so.

After seasoning and battering the fish, I tested the grease and then stirred the grits. I didn't readily like cooking but found it calmed me just as reading and studying always had. I missed my class across the pond. Teaching had always been my chosen profession. Lecturing about myths, customs, occult wisdom, different beliefs and rituals from all over the world came second nature to me. Being alive for as many centuries as I had, had afforded me the luxury of having learned some things from firsthand knowledge.

"What in the world do you have on?" I heard behind me, interrupting my thoughts.

I turned to find Tasmin behind me dressed in gray sweats and a t-shirt. On another woman, it may have looked ill fitting, but on Tasmin, she wore it well. I studied her features. My gaze settled on her lush lips. Even though I was sure she didn't remember our kiss as fondly as I did, I wanted to do it again. However, I'd prefer she be a willing and ready participant the next time.

I looked down at my robe and then back to her. "Top of the morning to you, too, Dr. Pettiford. What's wrong with my banyan?"

"With your what?"

"My banyan. By the 18th and 19th centuries, us British gentlemen wore loose, informal gowns in the privacy of our own homes. The banyan, what I'm wearing, is made of Chinese silk that's quilted for warmth, and mine has a fitted cut," I explained as I spun around. "The banyan was an essential garment for fashionable men and suggested sophisticated, worldly masculinity."

"That may have been fine for the 18th and 19th centuries," she said, "but for the current times, you look like you just walked out of a dime store historical romance."

I chuckled then turned back to flip the fish. "You don't know style, Dr. Pettiford."

"If you say so, Professor Jerrod," she replied.

"Fancy a cuppa?" I asked, picking up the tea pot.

"Yes, but I'll pour it myself."

Though I would have loved to serve her, I set the honey and fresh lemons in front of her along with tea and a tea diffuser. I studied her as she readied her tea. She smelled heavenly at the first break of dawn and looked even better. While she had her locs pulled back into a ponytail, a couple of strands hung down her back and at her temples. It made her look alluring when mixed with the natural smolder of her eyes.

"How're you feeling after last evening?" I asked. "Has it all settled in for you?"

"Settled in? No. I'm still processing. It's a lot, but…something tells me that I have to process this while experiencing it at the same time."

"You would be correct."

"And no grits for me, please," she said.

I grabbed plates and silverware then served her before myself. I sat across from her at the kitchen island.

"Thank you," she said. "Are you always up so early?"

"Most days," I said.

I noticed she was still cool with me and wondered if she was still upset about my initial faux pas. I hoped not. Surely she would give me a second chance at a first impression. I hoped she wasn't one of those humans who held a grudge for so long it became a part of her personality. As an angel, my nature was to forgive. I suppose I couldn't expect a human to be the same, witch or not. Still, I didn't think it would do us any favors if she were to hold that slip of the tongue against me.

"If you have any questions, I'd be more than stoked to address them," I said, still trying to break the ice.

She glanced at me as she chewed her fish. "So…you're an angel here on earth, right?"

"Yes."

"How long have you been here?"

"Two-hundred and ninety-three years to be precise."

She choked on the spoon of eggs she'd put into her mouth. I jumped up to help, but she held out a hand to stop me. "No, no." She coughed again then took a sip of the cool water next to her tea. "I'm fine. I just—didn't expect that answer."

I smirked then ate a forkful of the fluffy eggs. "What were you expecting, poppet?"

She studied me for a moment as if she didn't know whether she wanted to be offended about being called poppet or not. Finally, her features softened.

"I don't know," she said. "How is it that you look so…young but are so…old?"

"Genetics, deary. After a certain human age, I stop aging in the human world. Although I can project an image of myself to make it appear as if I'm aging normally."

"That's feasible. But tell me, how is it possible you're that old but don't know not to call a woman things such as wench in this day and age?"

I chuckled. "Valid question. Sometimes, for us ethereal beings, the time in which the most traumatic thing happened to us is the language and verbiage we most use." The chuckle died when I got ready to say more. "For me, that year was in 1855." I cleared my throat and sat up straighter. The dream I'd had the night before flashed across my mind.

Tasmin studied me, looked at me as if she wanted to ask more but decided against it. I was sure the look on my face told her I wouldn't be amenable to discussing it further.

"So, even though you're still alive in current times, you're saying that in some kind of way, your verbiage hasn't caught up?" she asked.

I nodded once. "In laymen's terms."

I knew I should have explained it further but doing so required me to revisit a time in which the god upstairs was unkind to me.

"Do you normally get positive responses when calling women wenches?" she asked.

"I normally get positive reactions from women regardless of what I call them," I said.

She scoffed and shook her head. "The arrogance is astounding on you," she said, sarcasm evident. "Tell me more about Dafari's father."

"He's a formidable opponent, that's for sure. I would not take anything he does lightly. You and Elisa come from a strong bloodline of witches with ancestry that can be traced back to the cradle of civilization."

"Okay, but that doesn't explain why he's after us specifically. Aren't there other witches—"

"Sure, there are other witches he could go after, but we think he's after the both of you for other nefarious reasons. Like, perhaps he's trying to bring on the apocalypse or use your magic to release the Four Horsemen. It would be right up his alley to release pestilence and famine."

Tasmin's brows furrowed. "But why would he want to do that?"

"He's a Fallen, Dr. Pettiford. His kind has been at war with the Heavens since they were cast into the Valleys of the Earth."

"The what?"

"The Valleys of the Earth, where Dafari's father was supposed to imprisoned. He was supposed to be chained to the side of Mount Hermon, which is where demons of old used to gather. Once they were casted to the valley, the mountain was sent there with them."

"Should Elisa and I have some kind of…security detail? Weapons?"

"For now, my brother and I will be with each of you whenever and wherever you go outside this home."

She looked pensive. "And what about the bookstore? There are things I still need to do there."

"I'll be your shadow wherever you go, Dr. Pettiford."

"Why you and not Dafari?"

I smiled. "Just the way the cookie crumbles, my dear. Besides, I think you'd enjoy my company if you open yourself up to the possibility."

"I beg to differ," she said as she stood and grabbed her plate from the counter.

I watched as she sauntered over to the sink. She made quick work of washing her plate and tea mug. Then she did something that shocked me and scared the living daylights out of her. As she moved her hand toward the knives I'd used to cut the fish, they flew at her hand, sharp ends first. She yelped and jumped back quickly, but not fast enough to avoid a cut on her palm. The knives stuck into the wall behind her.

She hissed, swore under her breath, and then jerked her hand back as blood dripped from her palm to the floor. I hurried over then took her palm into my hands. She'd been shaking moments before, but I saw her visibly relax under my touch.

"What just happened?" she asked as she looked up at me.

"I can't quite call it," I said, holding her hand under cold water. "But if what I'm sensing is true, while Elisa is telepathic, you're telekinetic."

"I can move things…with my mind?" she asked, shock on her features and awe in her voice.

"That's the gist of it, yes. Here, hold your hand under the sunlight," I told her as I studied the gash. "It's not as bad as it should be…"

That puzzled me. I saw how much blood had spilled from her palm, but judging by the wound, it was just a simple slice; what one would call a flesh wound. The only way that could be possible was that she had the capabilities to heal herself. That shouldn't have been possible either. Sure, she could heal others. That was her gift. Not even the telekinesis gave me pause, because she wasn't the first in her line to have such abilities. However, the power to heal herself? I'd have to speak to my brother about that.

I held her palm up to examine it some more and she jerked back. I gazed down at her in surprise to find a stern finger from her left hand pointed at me. "If you kiss any other part of me without my permission again, I will…" She balled her lips and shook her head as if she was trying to find the right words to say. "I-I will hex you."

I threw my head back and laughed. "Now, now, poppet. Let's not get beside ourselves, shall we? And to think, I'd pegged you wrong. You couldn't be a wench. Wenches love my kisses."

Just then, I heard Elisa's chuckle as she came into the kitchen. "Good morning," she greeted behind us.

Tasmin scoffed then turned to reach for the tea pot. I turned to greet Elisa, only to see her smile falter as she stared wide eyed behind me. I turned back, thinking perhaps maybe Tasmin had injured herself once more only to see the tea pot flying across the room.

It slammed right into my eye, causing me to growl out in pain and curse in my parents' heavenly tongue. "God blind me!"

"Oh my God," Tasmin squealed as she slapped a hand over her mouth then reached toward me. "I didn't—I didn't know it would do that. I am so sorry," she said hastily as she tried to move my hand to look at my eye.

I was in so much pain, that I didn't care that she had apologized. The dagblasted tea pot was hotter than open fire in a hell pit and it had slammed into my skull like a meat mallet. I jerked away from Tasmin's touch, stormed past a stunned Elisa and then stalked up the stairs.

"Tasmin, I heard you wish you could hit him with the tea pot and then it came flying across the room. What the hell?" I heard Elisa say.

"I didn't mean to do that, I swear! I-I-I didn't even know I *could* do that," Tasmin explained, pleading her case.

"That thing clobbered the crap out of him!"

So Tasmin had wished to hit me with the apparatus, did she? I was starting the think the little hellion just got a kick out of being combative. No way should a forward-thinking woman still hold such a grudge when I had already vehemently apologized for not being more careful of my words. Sure I'd been a bit more antagonistic than would be recommended, but by God, was she going to hold that against me forever?

I passed my irritating brother along the way. He was dressed in slacks and a button-down shirt. His hair was pulled back into a ponytail and he looked to be as chipper as a harlot in a room full of drunk bankers.

"What in hell happened to your eye? Did you offend the good doctor again to the point she resorted to violence?"

"Piss off," I snapped at him.

"Well good morning to you, too," he said dryly. "I'm going to head out with Elisa—"

"I think it would be best if you shadowed Tasmin for today," I snarled. "I'm no longer in the mood to share her company."

Before he could respond, I went to my room and slammed the door.

When I came back downstairs twenty minutes later, Tasmin and Dafari were gone. Elisa was finishing the last of her breakfast.

She looked up when she saw me walk in. The expression on her face told me the knot and bruise just over my right eye was just as bad as I thought it was. "Are you okay?" she asked.

"It'll heal on its own in time," I said.

"Can archangels not heal themselves?" she asked.

"We can."

She looked as if she expected me to explain, then, why I wasn't healing. I had no desire to expose myself in such a way. I didn't want to explain how because I was connected to Tasmin in a way she wouldn't understand that she had the power to wound me in ways no other being, mortal or immortal—good or evil—could. If I had told Elisa that, then that would open a can of worms neither my brother nor I were ready to tackle.

Dressed similarly to Dafari, I decided on a black button-down dress shirt and jeans instead of slacks. I slid my feet into a pricy pair of loafers then checked my watch. I took in Elisa's attire and noticed she wore some variation of the same thing daily; tight fitting jeans that hugged her ample hips and derriere rather nicely, a simple tee-shirt of a different color daily, a black leather biker's jacket, and black calf-length combat boots. Her naturally kinky mane was pulled back into a ponytail that looked like a puff ball. It was good to see that my brother had wiped her mind so that she didn't remember me coming into her bedroom to put her to sleep, at his request, last evening.

"Elisa, if you don't mind, I'd like for us to get going on whatever you have to do today," I said. I sounded curt even to my own ears.

"She didn't mean for it to hit you," Elisa said as she grabbed her purse and keys.

"She wished to hit me with a hot teapot. So she said, so it was. I'd say the intent was there," I said.

"Yes, but she didn't know the dang thing would fly across the room, Octavian. We're just getting the hang of this stuff. You and your brother could be a little more patient," she said, edge to her tone that hadn't been there before.

Perhaps she was triggered. "She should be mindful of what she wishes for, especially when you're around."

Elisa rolled her eyes. "You are your brother's…brother. Good grief. How are we supposed to be mindful of these things when we don't even know we're doing them?" She yanked the front door open and strutted out.

It was safe to assume Dafari had ticked her off about the topic at some point. I wouldn't broach the subject around her again.

"I need to stop by my house to pick up a few things for the shop," she said once we were in her truck and on the way.

I nodded then asked, "Do human women of today always hold grudges as Tasmin does?"

"They do when you go around intentionally antagonizing them," she said.

I looked at her. She was chewing gum in a way that made me think she had a lot on her mind. Still, I asked, "What do you mean?"

She glanced at me, sighed and shook her head. "For example, the kiss while she was giving you mouth-to-mouth…"

"I couldn't let an opportunity like that pass me up."

She chuckled then popped her gum. "Keep that up, and I see more teapots in your future."

Even I had to chuckle at that. She wiggled her right arm to adjust the bracelet there and the move made me remember that she and Tasmin had

instinctively linked them to defend themselves the night before.

"Did Mama Nall give you that bracelet?" I asked her.

She shook her head. "No. My father did on my seventh birthday. It replaced the red yarn bracelet he said he'd placed there when I was born. He told me it was protection. I stopped wearing it when I was ten, after my parents were killed. I felt it hadn't protected me from the pain of losing them. I put it on again at sixteen because Mama Nall told me that to not wear it meant I was dishonoring his memory. Sad to say, I took it off again after she died five years ago. Again, I felt as if it did me little good when I kept losing the people who meant the most to me. Then, about three years ago, I put it back on."

"Did something happen to make you put it back on each time?" I asked.

Elisa's brows furrowed. "Not…really. I just felt the need to put it back on, you know? Like got this urge to do so. Mama Nall was big on trusting instinct. She used to tell me that no matter how big or small that feeling in my gut was, it was best to follow it as it wouldn't lead me wrong." She smiled a sad smile. "I miss her so much. I could really use her wisdom right now. She and Ms. Noreen were all I had left…"

I could have told her that the bracelet she wore was a talisman, meant to protect, guide, and hold magical powers from ancestors' past, but she looked to be genuinely grieving in the moment. So I pressed on. We kept up general conversation as she drove. Even though the sun the was shining, judging by the overcast, rain was eminent. I saw people out jogging, walking dogs and talking to their neighbors. From the looks of things, Salix Pointe looked like your average run of the mill small town. However, the energy portal in this place was like a magnetic pull to all things otherworldly. While there were non-magical folk in the town, I sensed, just as my brother had, that this town was filled with more than just witches.

"Just to make you aware, finding your grandmother's and Noreen's coven would be beneficial to you and Tasmin," I said as we passed a collective of school aged children.

She glanced at me with a raised brow. "Their coven? They had a coven?"

"Yes. They were too powerful to not have one. I suspect Mama Nall and Noreen were a part of the same coven to be exact. Alone they were powerful, but together they were even more dangerous to those meaning them harm."

"Then why were they killed? How were they killed?"

"The only beings who would have been powerful enough, strong enough to kill them would have had to get their powers straight from the heavens."

"But Dafari's father is a Fallen," she said as she turned into her driveway.

"Still got his powers from the heavens. Just because he is a Fallen doesn't mean his powers were stripped or are any less potent. If anything, being a Fallen makes him even more dangerous. He is an angel without boundaries. Without rules or control."

"So is there no higher being he has to answer to?" she asked.

"It's complicated," I answered. "On another note, you and Tasmin will have to start training to hone your powers."

"Training?"

"Yes, you have to learn to make your powers work with you and for you."

"I suppose that was why your brother was so adamant about me guarding my thoughts last evening," she said then sighed. "Will you be training me? If so, can we start with showing me how to do that so he can stop being a dick about it?"

I shook my head and laughed inwardly. "No, no. I can't do that. I mean I could, but it would be best that you allowed my brother to train you in that area as you and he already have a connection, and having that connection will make it much easier for you to learn how to control your thoughts. With that being said, you and Tasmin have a lot to learn. Finding the coven and your book will help you."

"What book?"

"Ever heard of the Book of Shadows?"

"What is this? Charmed?"

"Pardon?" I asked, confused as to what she was referencing.

"You've never heard of the show Charmed?"

"I'm sorry to say I haven't."

"It's a show about three sisters who're witches and they have a Book of Shadows."

"Child's play I'm sure. I digress, your grandmother and Tasmin's aunt would have such a book. It's where they kept all the spells, potions, elixirs, and instructions of how to use and make those things."

Elisa was about to say something else but did a doubletake, gasped then gawked. "Someone has been in my house!"

She parked and hopped out her truck. I was right behind her. Her front door had been splintered in half. It didn't take me long to pick up Demon Daddy's signature energy trail.

Elisa went to rush inside, but I grabbed her arm to stop her. "Let me go in just in case he's lying in wait or has left a trap."

Elisa nodded while wringing her hands. I could feel the fear and nervousness wafting from her. I sent a signal to my brother, alerting him to what we'd found. I also had to make it clear that he should stay with Tasmin and that I had it handled. I knew Dafari and knew he would trek through hell to keep Elisa safe.

I balked at the drops of blood leading up the stairs through the mangled doorway. The smell of the blood was acidic, most certainly sulfuric in nature. There was no doubt in my mind Demon Daddy had been behind the break-in, but the blood confused me. Had he injured himself to the point of bloodletting? Had something or someone else injured him? That couldn't have been possible since only another angel could injure or maim such a being so severely. That wasn't to say he couldn't be injured, but not life threateningly so.

I stepped over the threshold into a sea of chaos. Furniture had been overturned, pictures had been ripped from the walls, dishes lay broken about the front room as if someone went to the kitchen, grabbed them and then tossed them across the room for sport. The walls had cracks running up and down them like a chaotic maze. The foundation was uneven which made the floor feel as if I was walking over upturned earth. The stairs leading to the second floor were so damaged that physically getting to the second level would be impossible.

I read the energy of the room, and just like when I'd gone to my mother's flat, there was static. I couldn't read the room. I sniffed the air again just to be sure it was sulfur I smelled. That was when another smell, one I didn't pick up on the first time, assaulted my senses. It reminded me of…burned cinnamon. Again…just like at my mother's flat.

"Octavian," I heard Elisa call out to me, nervousness in her tone.

I turned around, set to answer her when I spotted something that gave me pause. In the center of all the madness lay a small blue piece of crystal. My heart raced as I hurried over to pick it up.

"Blue kyanite," I whispered as a chill crept up my spine. "What in the—"

"Octavian, are you okay?" came Elisa's concerned voice once more.

"Don't come in here," I said. "Stay back. I'm okay. I'm coming out."

I slid the stone in my pocket then exited Elisa's home. The look on her face said she was anxious.

"How bad is it?" she asked, walking up to me.

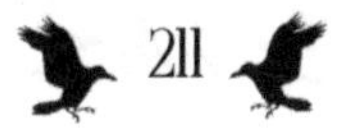

"It won't be habitable for a while, Elisa. I'm sorry."

She sighed hard and then slapped tears away from her face. "This was my parents' home. It's been in our family for generations."

I looked at the home and even with the mess inside, it looked up to date. "It looks fairly modern," I said.

"Renovations over the years, but the base, the foundation…This was my second great-grandmother's first home as a free woman," she said. "You sure it's that's bad?"

The dour look of sadness on her face pained me. "Perhaps once everything has calmed down, my brother and I will bring you back to examine the damages. As of now, you can't even traverse the stairs to get to the second floor," I explained.

Her shoulders slumped as she shook her head then headed back to her truck. I followed her. The stone in my pocket felt as heavy as an anvil. Perhaps it was my imagination of what the weight of it being present meant. I hadn't tried to contact my mother again since the first time. I sent out a mental 911 signal, hoping it would make her contact me soon and fast. Dafari and I didn't make a big deal of her home being in shambles before because we knew my father would move heaven and earth to protect her even if they had separated. Nevertheless, something was amiss.

Elisa and I rode the rest of the way to her shop in companionable silence. I did something I hadn't done since my brother and I were children, I connected to him telepathically.

"When I say blue kyanite, what comes to mind?" I asked him.

His immediate response made the bottom fall out of my stomach.

"Why do you ask?" he sent back.

I didn't respond then threw a black box back around my thoughts. I didn't want him to be privy to my thoughts at the moment. I couldn't even fathom what I was thinking to be true lest I drove myself mad with the possibility that Dafari had been right about his demon daddy after all. But…that was impossible. It had to be.

I was pulled from my thoughts when Elisa parked her truck. She was late to her café and already had a line of about twenty people. I was impressed with how she schooled her features before exiting the truck with a smile. She rushed to the front door, greeting her customers fondly.

"I'm sorry, everyone. I had a bit of an emergency this morning," she said while unlocking the door.

"Do you want us to give you a minute?" a pretty golden-skinned woman asked while holding the hand of a squirming little boy.

"No, Erica, it's fine to stay if you want. I know you only want coffee and a bagel," Elisa said.

Erica nodded with a smile. She looked relieved.

"Well, I'd like some of that spinach and artichoke quiche if you have some made," a man said.

My eyes widened at how big the man was. He was a Paul Bunyan type even down to the checkered red and black wool shirt he wore. He looked as if he pulled trees out the ground from the root for fun.

"I know, Marcus. I have some leftover from yesterday, but planned to make more today," she said. "And tell D'alyzza her sweet potatoes pies will be delivered day before Halloween along with Troy's cupcakes for his party."

The man named Marcus nodded with a smile. I watched on as she called each customer by name. I could see the familiarity with which she spoke to each person. It showed why her café had been so successful. I walked in and all eyes turned to me.

"Top of the morning, everyone," I said.

"This is Professor Jerrod, Dr. Battle's brother," she told everyone.

A chorus of *hellos* and *good mornings* rang out. Elisa rushed behind the counter and tied on an apron. She washed her hands before turning on coffee makers.

"Everyone who just wants coffee or tea and ready-made muffins or pastries please stand to your left. Everyone who wishes to wait for fresher bakery goods and more complicated orders please have a seat if you can, and I'll be with you shortly."

After a while, I could tell, that even though she worked proficiently, she needed help. I grabbed an apron and washed my hands.

"Show me what you want me to do," I told her, and she did.

While she told me what to put in the ovens, she served up different aromatic coffees and teas. To be honest, I'd do anything to take my mind off the blue kyanite found in her home. I greeted customers. I took orders. I wiped down tables. I swept the café's floor and made children smile when they came.

By one in the afternoon, she and I were able to take a breather.

"I don't know what I'm going to do about my house," she said as we sat and enjoyed coffee and tea. "I don't have anywhere to go. I mean Mama Nall's house is still out by the Gourd, but I haven't been there in months. There are so many things that need to be fixed… I could go to a B&B, but…And I don't want to impose on Dafari any more than I already have."

"Believe me, you're not imposing on him," I said. "If anything, he'd prefer you stay there with him, if only to better protect you."

"Yeah, but I can't stay there forever, and even if I could, I wouldn't want to. I like my own space. Who would have done such a thing?" she asked then her eyes widened. "You don't think Dafari's father would have—"

"He could have. He's capable of anything. I also smelled sulfur which is a telltale sign of a demon having been present."

"What could he have possibly been looking for that would cause him to tear up my home?" she asked.

"You, and when he didn't find you, he probably decided to leave a calling card. That's me just guessing, but it would be a safe bet."

I then explained to her everything I'd told Tasmin that morning. Azazel had an agenda and he would see it through by any means necessary. I just wish we knew for certain what that agenda was. On the flip side of that same coin, I had to deal with the fact that blue kyanite at the scene also meant something else entirely. Something I had no mind to tangle with.

Elisa's café got busy with a steady stream of customers again. When an exhausted mother came in with a screaming child, I asked Elisa to allow me to serve her. I knelt in front of the child then asked if I could shake her hand. She nodded. When I did, she calmed instantly, and her tears dried up. I stood and asked the same of her mother. When she extended her hand to me, I took it and watched as her whole aura calmed. She took a deep relaxing breath and I watched the weight of the world lift from her shoulders.

"Perhaps…if you looked out in the barn where your husband kept all his tools, you'll find what you need," I told her.

The woman tilted her head then gawked at me. She looked as if she wanted to say something, but her daughter was pulling her toward the door. Just as she exited, three older women walked in.

"Good afternoon," the shortest one sang out as she briskly walked to the counter.

She had on red corduroy pants, black boots, and a red sweater that had black bats all over it. On her head was a hat with the front flipped up to show small brooms adorning it.

"Good afternoon, Cara Lee," Elisa said. "I have your muffins ready."

"Forget those muffins. Who is this?" the older woman asked sauntering up to me.

I smiled down at her, getting a kick out of the twinkle in her eyes. "Professor Octavian Jerrod," I said.

"Ahhh, so you're Dr. Battle's brother," another one said.

She held a mega-watt smile on her wise face. Her brown skin reminded me of silk. She looked like a schoolteacher in a ruffled red shirt and black skirt. The penny loafers on her feet had actual pennies in the holes on top.

"I am," I said with a head nod.

She smiled, while still eyeing me, said to Elisa, "I know my sisters and I were hoping you and Dr. Battle would become an item, but the professor here just might do as well."

I chuckled. Elisa shook her head with a laugh.

"Mary Ann, stop trying to play matchmaker," Cara Lee said. "I can see clear as day who his one true love is, and it isn't our sweetheart Elisa."

"Dagnabbit," Mary Ann fussed. "Well, back to waiting on the doc to realize what we already know," she said then walked over to the counter.

Cara Lee was still smiling up at me. Her eyes twinkled with a mischief that told me she was a catch back in her time, a force to be reckoned with.

"Bet your husband had his hands full with you, didn't he?" I asked her.

"You'd better know it," she said, smile widening. "What…are you?" she asked in an awed whisper.

I noticed she was wearing a clear quartz stone ring while Mary Ann wore black jade earrings. That made me look up to see the other woman they'd walked in with them. While Mary Ann and Cara Lee had been all smiles and friendly, the third woman gawked at me as if she had seen a ghost.

With a puzzled look on her face, she gave a timid greeting. "Good-good afternoon," she said.

"Good afternoon," I returned, noting her nervousness.

"That's our eldest sister, Martha Lee," Cara Lee said. "Sometimes, she's as rude a wet cock."

If I hadn't been disturbed my Martha's apprehension toward me, Cara Lee's comment would have made me howl with laughter. However, I felt a familiar energy emanating from Martha that gave me pause. My smile faded. I stepped around Cara Lee as my eyes zoned in on the necklace around Martha Lee's neck.

"Where did you get that?" I asked in a tone so cool that the air in the room changed.

"Where'd I get what?" she asked, her voice distant.

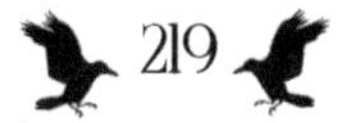

"That blue kyanite around your neck." My voice had hardened, causing the woman's sisters to come back to her side.

Martha Lee held her head high. "That's none of your business," she said, tone coolly disapproving of my questioning.

Mary Ann and Cara Lee glanced at one another then at their sister before turning back to look at me. They were curious as to why their sister and I seemed to be in some sort of mental tug of war.

"Has he been to see you?" I asked Martha.

"What's going on?" Elisa asked as she walked over. "Has who been to see her?"

"She knows exactly who I'm talking about," I answered Elisa then to Martha, "I can see and read his energy all over you. Why was he here and what did he want?"

"I don't have to tell you anything," Martha spat. "Come on, sisters. We should leave here."

"Wait a minute," Elisa said. "Please, someone tell me what's going on here?"

Cara and Mary look up at their sister, curious but also following her lead as she pivoted and headed to the door. I had a good mind to throw the locks from where I stood and barricade them in but had to remember…if who I suspected had visited the old woman then she was under his protection. While I was strong and powerful in my own right, I would never be more powerful than…him.

"What in God's name just happened?" Elisa yelled at me once the elder women had exited.

I looked at her. "I think there is more going on here than meets the eye."

CHAPTER 17:
DAFARI

I cannot recall ever seeing my brother so angry with any woman. Although he didn't overtly identify Tasmin as his attacker, the way that he basically ordered me to be her shadow for the day, told me that my assumption was correct. Even though Octavian could heal himself, the gargantuan burn to his eye must have smarted like the dickens.

When I reached the kitchen, Tasmin appeared to be quite agitated. "I really didn't mean to hit him, Elisa. You believe me, right?" her voice pleading, almost on the verge of tears.

"Of course I believe you, Tasmin. Besides, you can't readily be expected to control something you had no knowledge of just a few minutes ago." She was reassuring Tasmin, but Elisa was cutting her eyes directly at me, giving me a look that dared me to contradict her. At the moment, I wouldn't dream of it.

"So you did cuff my brother. With what, may I ask?"

"A hot tea kettle, but it was an accident. I really didn't mean to have it fly at him. I may have thought

I wanted it to, but I didn't really think it would happen," Tasmin rambled on.

"Wait, you *thought* it?" I asked incredulously.

Taking a deep breath, Tasmin continued. "Yes, but that wasn't the first thing that happened. I went to grab the knives that Octavian had used, but, instead, they came flying at me." She pointed. Elisa and I looked at the knives embedded in my kitchen wall, at each other, then finally at Tasmin. "One of them even cut me, but…" Her voice trailed off.

"But what, Tasmin?" Elisa asked in a soothing, calming voice.

Tasmin lifted her palm, but there was nothing there.

"I thought you said you cut yourself," I questioned, not quite understanding what she was getting at.

"I did! The blood's right there." She pointed to several huge droplets of blood drying on the Pergo hardwood floor.

Elisa and I stared at her for a few seconds before I spoke up. "So it appears that, in addition to being able to heal others, you can also heal yourself."

"Yeah, I kind of figured that out." Her voice held an annoyance with me that I hadn't heard before.

Elisa, picking up on the tension, asked, "So what did Octavian say about all of this?"

Tasmin shrugged, replying, "He didn't say much about the cut, except that it wasn't as bad as it should have been." I found the fact that he made that statement without further explanation intriguing. I'd have to talk to him about it later. "He did say that he thought I was telekinetic."

"Yes, so it seems," I acknowledged, walking over to the knives and pulling them out of the wall. "You definitely need to get a handle on this quickly before you kill someone."

I probably should have refrained from pushing her further, because before I knew it, the witches had unleased their anger on me, saying in unison, "Put a sock in it, Dafari!"

"You want me to deal with being able pick up on the feelings of other, something I only realized I could do when I got back into town; get a handle on controlling energy bolts coming from my hands, a power I just discovered less than twenty-four hours ago; completely absorb the fact that not only can I heal others, something else I just learned about less than twenty-four hours ago, but also myself, which I just learned not thirty minutes ago; and last, but certainly not least," she lambasted, using her hands for emphasis, "You want me to control moving things with my mind, a feat I just learned. Is that about right, Dafari?"

While nothing usually rattled me, looking at Elisa with her hands on her full hips and a look of scorn on her face, and Tasmin reflecting the same, gave me pause, lest I get blasted by an energy bolt in my own home. I chose my words carefully. "Yes, well, while I understand your clobbering Octavian was an accident, he is quite perturbed with you at the moment. As such, I have been tasked with being your companion for the day. That said I believe we should make our leave, sooner rather than later."

Without a word, Tasmin marched toward the stairs, I surmised to go upstairs and get dressed.

Elisa, on the other hand, stood in place looking at me, arms crossed over her full bosom that swelled each time she breathed in. The stern look on her face actually excited the male in me. Her fiery disposition was quite alluring.

"Cut her some slack, Dafari," she chastised. "I somewhat have a better understanding of this magick thing because I grew up here, but she didn't. You and Octavian need to back off a bit. I know there's a lot at stake but trying to bash us over the head with that fact constantly is not doing anybody any good. Besides, isn't patience supposed to be a virtue among your kind, the angel part anyway?"

"Yes, one I nor my brother possess," I retorted. "I suggest you follow Tasmin's lead, lest you be late for work."

Turning on her heel, Elisa began to walk away, but abruptly stopped. Then she wordlessly projected, "Go to blazes, Dafari, and kiss my tail!"

"Been there, and, again, I warn you to be careful what you wish for," I shot back. I obviously angered her even more, as she stomped off without a second look. That aroused me to no end.

A short few minutes later, Tasmin returned, dressed and ready to depart. She wore a pair of camouflage cargo pants that accentuated her slender curves, a black crop top, a black bubble jacket, and black high-top sneakers. Her long waist-length locs hung down, with most draped over her left shoulder. Elisa still had not come back downstairs. Although I wanted to say good-bye to her, I felt it best not to, not even telepathically, since she was clearly vexed with me at the moment.

Once we were in my car and on the road, Tasmin remained reticent for some time. Even for me, the silence was deafening, and no one loved silence more than I did. I knew that she was going through a lot with the discovery of her two new powers. The irony wasn't lost on me that they appeared to be a yin and yang of one another. Depending on how she used her telekinesis, it could kill, and her healing power could save lives, including her own.

"Your car has been taken care of," I said, breaking the ice.

"So quickly? How?" Tasmin queried, turning to look at me.

"I called in a favor. Also, your rental fees have been paid."

Letting out a deep breath, she replied, "Thank you, Dafari. Just let me know how much it costs, and I'll reimburse you."

"No need," I responded. "Consider it a very small token of my gratitude for saving my brother's life. In reality, no amount of money could repay what you've done. He truly would have met his demise had it not been for you."

"You're welcome, but I didn't even know I did it. It was a complete accident."

"Consider it a very fortunate accident. Take the win, Tasmin. Speaking of Octavian; I know he's annoying, antagonistic, and clearly knows how to push your buttons, but, at his essence, he has a good heart. At times, he has…difficulty expressing himself."

Tasmin had a look on her face. "Earlier, he mentioned that for beings such as yourselves, your language may be, for lack of a better word, stuck in the time period that was most traumatic. He said for him, it was 1855."

"What else did he tell you?" I inquired, raising an eyebrow.

"Not much else and I didn't want to pry."

I pulled up in front of my practice to check on the animals that were still bordering in the kennels. I also needed to refill their food and water dishes.

Turning to Tasmin, I said, "Shall we?" She followed me inside, walking with me to the back. I filled water and food dishes, Tasmin jumping in to help. "That was wise of you not to question him further. While it's not my story to tell, it was a very tragic time for my brother. What he endured I wouldn't wish on anyone. Like humans, we process our grief in different ways. All I will say is Octavian didn't handle it well. It took him a very long time, decades even, to get back to some semblance of life. Even now, I know certain circumstances will trigger him. I told you all of that to say my brother would not purposely hurt you as he knows the unbearable pain of being intentionally hurt."

"Thank you for sharing that, Dafari. I think I have a somewhat better understanding of Octavian now."

"Thank you for being so receptive." After I checked on the animals, I checked my office phone for any messages. There were none. "And thank you for your help. On to the bookstore?"

She smiled, something that had been rare in the past two days but was completely understandable. "On to the bookstore," she echoed.

We walked the short distance, noticing how calm and peaceful the street was. There was also a chill in the air. Trees gently swayed back and forth as if waving hello. It was still early, and most of the town's denizens had yet to venture out of their homes. With the shortening of the fall days, residents rose later and retired earlier.

Tasmin walked inside the bookstore and shivered. "I need to turn on the heat and the fireplaces," she remarked. "Dafari," she began, turning on the lights then taking off her jacket and placing it on the back of the chair behind the counter, "Would you care for something hot to drink?" She walked over to a wall with a thermostat and several switches. She turned on the heat and flipped the levers, the fireplaces roaring to life.

"That would be nice. What are you having?" I asked, walking over to a bookshelf, scanning the titles.

"Water with honey and lemon," she replied.

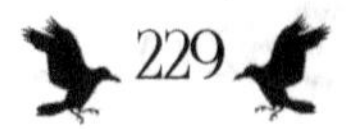

"Then I'll have the same. Lots of honey, please."

"You got it. Be back shortly."

As I continued to peruse the bookshelf, I reflected on how I would be heading to Elisa's café around this time. I was always her first customer for reasons all my own; I wanted her undivided attention first thing in the morning. It gave me the opportunity to spend some time alone with her, even if for just a few short minutes. I looked out the front window only to see a line forming outside the café. Elisa was usually there by now, but she wasn't. That was unlike her to be late. Since she was with Octavian, I wasn't particularly concerned. I knew they would arrive eventually.

Tasmin returned in short order with our hot beverages. "Here you go," she said, handing me a large mug.

I took a sip of the sweet concoction. "Perfect. Thank you. So Tasmin, what is your plan for today?"

"I would like to finish up this inventory, but we can't always get what we want," she said with a laugh. Her laugh was much like her aunt's, full of mirth. Standing in the bookstore and hearing her laugh made it feel as if Noreen's spirit was here with us.

"As your most estimable aunt would have said, 'You don't know how much you can accomplish if you don't try'. While the task may seem daunting, I feel that between the two of us, we can get it done. Where do we start?"

"Way to go, Dafari," she commented, laughing again. "Invoking Aunt Noreen to get me motivated was a cheap shot."

"My question is did it work?"

"Sure did. Let's do this."

Tasmin and I worked diligently throughout the morning cataloging the bookstore's inventory. I took a brief, yet unnoticeable, pause when Octavian telepathically connected with me, alerting me to a break-in at Elisa's home. Octavian detected my father's energy signal, thereby identifying him as the culprit of the break-in. I didn't want to alarm Tasmin until I knew more; therefore, I kept the information to myself. A short while later Octavian asked me about blue kyanite. When I questioned as to why he was asking, he quickly broke our connection, locking me out of his mind. I would definitely have to address the topic with him when we get home later.

"Wow, Elisa's going to have to hustle if she's going to get that line down," Tasmin remarked, peering out the window seeing the now-long line of patrons waiting for Elisa. "I wonder where she and Octavian are." Just as the words left her mouth, Elisa's SUV pulled up in front of the café.

Tasmin and I had planned to walk over to the café later for a short visit; however, we were so engrossed in the inventory, and our own conversation, that we lost track of time. Before we realized it, it was almost three-thirty, the inventory finally completed. We sat down, taking a well-deserved rest.

"You and Octavian are centuries old, you've lived through major world events, technological advancements, wars. What was one of your most memorable experiences?" Tasmin queried.

I had existed for three centuries, had witnessed empires rise and fall, institutions begin and end, societies being built from the ground up. I deliberated for only a short period of time before replying. "I would have to say being a scout for Harriet Tubman on the Underground Railroad," I began, making Tasmin's mouth fall open in incredulity. "Ms. Tubman was blessed and highly favored by the Powers That Be; as such Octavian and I were tasked with making sure she, and her many charges, arrived at their destinations safely. That, Tasmin, I feel is one of the greatest accomplishments of my life to date."

Tasmin, still looking amazed, answered, "I am in awe of you and Octavian. You guys worked in concert with one of the most iconic figures in history. Color me impressed."

I was about to respond when the door to the bookstore opened. In walked Mayor Lovett, still looking very much like a tanned vampire, as Octavian had described upon their first meeting. Tasmin and I stood. I could tell she felt uneasy, I suspect due to her empathic powers honing in on the mayor's smarmy nature.

"*Bonne après-midi*, Dafari," he began. "*Cher*," he continued, looking at Tasmin as if she were a freshly fried and powered sugared beignet. I wasn't an empath, but even I could pick up on Tasmin's feelings of disgust.

"Mayor Lovett," I replied coolly.

Tasmin walked behind the counter. Not caring for the way he was ogling her, I followed suit. "Good afternoon, Mayor. What can I do for you?" she questioned.

"*Non, non, mon tender*, I want to know what *I* can do for *you*." He placed his hands on the counter, leaning forward, causing Tasmin to move back a few steps. "Rumor has it that this fine establishment is up for sale. For a fair price, I'd be willing to take it off your hands," he said looking from Tasmin to me.

"First of all, Mayor, it's Tasmin," she calmly shot back. "Second, I haven't decided yet what I'm going to do with the bookstore. I might sell it. Then again, I just might keep it."

A look akin to dismay crossed the mayor's face. "Keep it? But why, *ch*...Tasmin? Won't you be returning to parts whence you came soon? Why not sell this place and leave with a nice chunk of change in those pretty little hands of yours?"

Putting her hands in the front pockets of her cargo pants, she replied, "Well, that's just it, Mayor; when I'm going home is kind of up in the air, and while I'm here I'm going to continue to enjoy this place. That said, Mayor, for foreseeable future, the bookstore is off the market."

I don't know what it was about Tasmin's words, but the mayor's color turned from tanned to three shades of red. "You are just as *délibérée* as your Aunt Noreen was."

It appeared as Tasmin was about to read the mayor the riot act, but the moment he spoke Noreen into existence, the most extraordinary thing happened. There had always been rumors that spirits inhabited the bookstore. Since I had never seen one, I put no stock in it...until today. While the fireplaces were already on, the low flames shot up, as if in an angry rage. And then there were the books; random books began flying off the shelves directly at the mayor, as if to say they didn't want him there. While Tasmin and I stood there in stunned silence, watching the mayor bob and weave to avoid getting hit was quite amusing.

Once the spirits finished having their fun with Mayor Lovett, the fireplaces dimmed and books stopped flying off the shelves, save for one book in particular. As the mayor was standing still in front of us, a book flew from behind Tasmin and me, hitting the mayor squarely in the face, leaving his thin nose bruised and battered. It then landed on the counter. The book was entitled *Becoming Free, Remaining Free: Manumission and Enslavement in New Orleans, 1846—1862*, which was ironic considering it was no secret that the mayor's family owned slaves in New Orleans.

"Well, it appears this *libarairie* is just as *obstinée.* Must be a family trait," he said, touching his nose, clearly flustered. "Perhaps it's best I make my leave before a I get hit by a chair or something," he laughed nervously.

"Perhaps that is best, Mayor Lovett," I replied, walking to the door, holding it open for him.

He was about to walk through the door when he turned to Tasmin, asking, "Tasmin, I would love to get you on the dance floor at the jubilee. Save me a *fais-do-do*?"

"Maybe," she replied, her façade of a smile replaced with a scowl once he was out the door. "Dafari, what was that?" she queried.

I told her about the rumors of spirits occupying the bookstore.

"Spirits?" she asked dubiously. "You have got to be kidding me."

"Tasmin, considering everything that's happened over the past few days, are you really *that* surprised?" I folded my arms in front of me.

She took a seat by one of the fireplaces. "Why haven't they revealed themselves before?"

"I'm guessing they thought you didn't need them until now. Also, they probably didn't want to scare you off. Their arrival was quite timely, wouldn't you say?" I took the seat across from her. "I thought that last book hitting the mayor was especially fitting."

"Actually, Dafari, I think that was me."

I looked at her inquisitively. "Explain."

"I had thought to myself that I wished I knew what would get rid of the mayor. That's when that book flew right at his face."

Despite myself, I smiled. "You're learning to control your telekinesis. It appears you also touched a nerve with the mayor. Well done, Tasmin, well done."

"Why thank you, Dafari," she giggled. "From what he was saying, I assume he was trying to buy this place from my aunt. I wonder why."

"I *know* why. This location is a magical epicenter. Very potent magick is inside, around, and under this structure. In the wrong hands, it could lead to catastrophic consequences for not just the Salix Pointe, but for the world as a whole. But we can discuss this further as a group. Elisa and Octavian need to know about this."

Tasmin stood. "You're right. Besides, it's getting late anyway." She turned off the heat and the fireplaces then turned off the lights. "Thanks for helping me out today. I don't know how long that inventory would have taken without your help. And thanks for backing me up with the mayor," she said, as she locked the door behind us.

"You are most welcome, but as far as the illustrious mayor is concerned, I think you handled him quite smashingly…literally." I looked across the street, noticing that the café was closed and Elisa's SUV was gone. I assumed she and my brother were on their way back home, which was timely, because we had much to discuss.

CHAPTER 18:
DAFARI

As I pulled up to the house, I observed Elisa's vehicle parked in front of one of the garage bays. After I parked my car into the garage, Tasmin and I headed inside. I was ready to wind down from what turned out to be a very enlightening day, but first, I needed to convene with my unexpected houseguests in order to have a much-needed conversation. I assembled the three of them in the kitchen with them sitting at the counter, Elisa on one end, Octavian on the other, and Tasmin in the middle. The tension in the air was palpable.

I immediately cut to the chase. "First of all, there have been some developments that we have to talk about, but, as this has been a very long day, they can wait until morning. I have more important issues to discuss. My life has been upended because of the invaders now residing in my abode," I said, as I saw their taken aback looks. "While I understand the need to keep both of you close," I continued, directly addressing Elisa and Tasmin, "I will not tolerate the continued disruptions to my home, and since it's abundantly apparent that this living arrangement may not change any time in the near future, I feel it's necessary to set some ground rules."

"Elisa, I'll start with you. Your training on how to guard your thoughts will start immediately, else I cannot be held responsible for my actions. Understood?" For a few seconds, she stared at me in astonishment then nodded in agreement. "And speaking of training, ladies, tomorrow you *will* start training like your lives depend on it, because they do. Any objections?" As expected, they shook their heads. "And lastly, Octavian and Tasmin. Brother, while I am used to your antagonistic, annoying, pretentious ways, Tasmin clearly is not. You are acting like a seven-year-old boy with a school-boy crush, but rather than telling her that you like her, you pull her hair or hit her instead." Yes, I called him out, but I felt tough love was necessary before the situation worsened. I then turned to Tasmin. "And now for you. My brother can be an insufferable dolt chauvinistically stuck in the Dark Ages. However, he did not intentionally mean to insult you, so please forgive him and no more teapots to the noggin. Both of you fix this, *now*," I rebuked sternly.

Turning to Tasmin, Octavian said, "Although I feel as if I've just been chastised by the headmaster of my primary school, Tasmin, I sincerely apologize."

"Apology accepted," Tasmin replied. "And again, I am so sorry."

Octavian took her hand. "And I, too, accept your apology." He bowed his head to kiss the back of her hand, but then stopped himself. "Promise not to hex me?"

Tasmin laughed, saying, "I promise. Not this time anyway."

He followed through, kissing the back of her hand. "Good, now that we've cleared the air, starting tomorrow, we can get down to real business."

"I agree," Tasmin replied, standing up. "If you all don't mind, I'm going to call it a night. I need to shower and practice moving things with my mind. Dafari, thanks again for today. Good night, guys." With that, Tasmin left the group.

I turned my attention back to Elisa. "If it's not too much trouble, I would like to speak with you later."

"It's no trouble at all. We do need to talk, but can I go take a shower first then meet you back here?"

Thinking about her taking a shower gave me pause, but I quickly brushed it from my mind. "That would be fine."

"Okay, see you in a bit," she said, strolling up the stairs.

"Brother, before you go, a word." I walked over to the bar, poured us two fingers of bourbon into snifters. Passing Octavian his glass, I continued. "We have a few things to discuss."

Octavian took a swig of his drink. "Agreed. You go first."

"Well, to start, after you stormed off this morning, Tasmin showed Elisa and I the cut on her palm, or should I say lack thereof. She showed us the blood on the floor, but there was no wound at all. She had completely healed."

"Yes, the cut was far less severe than I had expected considering the amount of blood loss. She is indeed a true healer, which should not be possible."

"Yet another mystery to add to our ever-growing list," I said finishing my drink, and refilling my glass. "And speaking of mysteries, what was with you mentally asking me about blue kyanite then shutting me out of your mind when I inquired why you were asking?"

Octavian began to pace in earnest, which he tended to do when he had something of major importance on his mind. He exhaled deeply before responding. "Brother, I found this at Elisa's home", he said, taking something out of his pocket, placing it on the bar.

I looked at the crystal in front of me. It was a shard of blue kyanite.

"Yes, blue kyanite. What's so unusual about that? It could be Elisa's."

"While that is plausible, it's highly doubtful."

I stared at Octavian, suspicion in my tone. "What are you not telling me, Octavian?"

Pacing even faster, he replied, "While I told you about your father's energy trail, I didn't tell you about the signs of a battle. Apparently, your father was wounded, as I found drops of his blood in Elisa's home. Also…"

"Continue," I demanded, anxiously awaiting his response.

"Like what occurred in Mother's flat, I could not read the energy of the room and there was only static. However, I smelled something familiar, something that I also smelled in Mother's flat; the distinct aroma of burnt cinnamon."

A light bulb went off in my head. "Blue kyanite. Burnt cinnamon. Octavian, are you thinking your parents were the ones who fought my father?"

"So it seems. As you and I both know, only another angel could injure him. Also, one of the Merry Widows had a necklace crafted from blue kyanite. My father's energy signature was all over it, plain as day."

"And your father's blue kyanite sword could definitely wound him severely. But that begs several questions, Brother; if Mother was indeed in Elisa's home, where has she been, and why would she fake her own disappearance? If she and your father are in Salix Pointe, why would they conceal that from you? And what is his connection to the Merry Widow? Their actions are extremely suspicious if you ask me."

Octavian turned to me, his eyes turning white. "Perhaps they arrived just in time to stop *your* father," he said in retaliation.

I remained calm, surprising myself. "That is a possibility. Still, if that were truly the case, why not contact you afterwards? Face it, little brother; your parent's actions must be questioned. Regardless, until we know more, I suggest we keep this information under wraps…for now. In the meantime, I suggest you try to reach out to your father and Mother to see if you get a response," I stated, walking back toward the kitchen. I heard Elisa's footfalls and was anxious to speak with her.

"Yes, Dafari, I will try to reach out," Octavian replied. He noticed Elisa standing by the counter, saying, "On another note, I thought you should know that the Merry Widows have been conspiring to couple you and Elisa for quite some time. They would appreciate it if you got your act together, dear

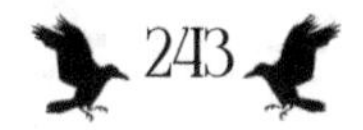

brother, sooner rather than later." Both Elisa and I just shook our heads. "Well, it's been quite a trying day, don't you think? I'm going to retire. Elisa, thank you for your immeasurable wisdom that far belies your years. I'm off to Bedfordshire! Pip pip!"

Elisa and I were now alone. "Forgive my brother. Obviously, subtlety is *not* his strong suit," I uttered, walking into the living room. I motioned for her to have a seat on the sectional.

Elisa let out a hearty giggle, sitting down next to me. "It's okay. The Merry Widows are also not known for their subtlety. They really did say they were hoping you and I would become an item."

"It's seems they have way too much time on their hands if they're worried about us becoming a pair."

She looked at me, a question in her big brown eyes. "Would that be so bad?"

"Us being a couple? Elisa, with all that's going on, I suggest we revisit that topic at another time. Besides, after what I have to tell you, you may no longer consider me an option."

"What—"

"Please, Elisa, there's so much I need to tell you, and I don't want to lose my nerve." She nodded. "First of all, I apologize for being so harsh with you earlier. I should not have been so…abrasive."

"Hey, I get it," Elisa chimed in. "You're not used to having all these people, with all our respective drama, in your space. Believe me, if I had any other place to go—"

"Elisa," I interrupted, "You are welcome here for as long as you want to stay. Please do not concern yourself with that. But in order for you to truly feel at home, you need to know some things about me. As you know, I'm three hundred years old, and that I am half angel, half demon. Also, you've already had the unfortunate displeasure of meeting my father, Azazel. My mother is an angel, and our relationship is…contentious at best, acrimonious at it's worse."

I took a deep breath before moving on. "My mother was aware that my father was a demon, and she knew of his demon nature, before they became involved and eventually married. However, from what I have gathered over the centuries, she felt that her love, fidelity, and commitment to him would instill the same values in him."

Elisa put a hand up. "I'm sorry, but when you say demon nature, what exactly do you mean?"

"My father is what is known as an incubus, an otherworldly being who provides…pleasure to women in their dreams, fulfilling all of their sexual desires."

Elisa's mouth dropped open in amazement. "When you say all of them—"

"I mean *all* of them."

"So why get together with your mother if he knew he wouldn't be faithful, even if it was only in other women's dreams?"

"That's a question you would have to ask Mother. However, I surmise that she felt she could change him. I found out she even went to a prophet to pray away his incubus nature to make him besotted to her and only her. It didn't work, and while he was good to her, and she never wanted for anything, he still could not shed being his true self. Whether it's because he couldn't, or just wouldn't, change no one really knows, but as a result, Mother left him, and took me with her."

Elisa put her hand on my shoulder, sympathy in her tone. "Did you get to see your father growing up?"

"Rarely," I said, "I thought it was because he didn't want to see me, but I later discovered that she purposely kept us apart in order to keep him from influencing me. He wanted to see me, but my mother wouldn't allow it because of who…because of what he was. While she physically kept me away from my father, *she* became more and more emotionally distant. I believe it was because I resembled my father so much."

"You do bear a striking resemblance to him, just younger with a darker complexion," Elisa confirmed. "But that never should have stopped her from loving you the way a mother should love a child. I'm so sorry."

"Yes, so am I. Anyway, several years after she left my father, she became involved with Michael, an archangel. They eventually married, and she became even more distant. Things only worsened when Octavian, her full-blooded angel who could do no wrong, was born. Then there was the epic battle between Father and Michael, who, by the way, happens to be my uncle."

"Wait, what?" a shocked Elisa asked.

"Michael and my father are brothers."

"Sounds like an episode of Jerry Springer to me."

"Yes, the entire incident played out like bad reality television, for sure. Apparently, my father couldn't get over my mother, and that only worsened when he found out about her and Michael. He felt betrayed. In the end, he and Michael fought; he lost and ended up chained to a mountain…that is, until he escaped. I was still a child when that happened, but old enough to know what was going on. By the time I turned eighteen, the tension at home was so unbearable, I left."

"You haven't spoken to your mother since?"

"I rarely speak to her. I thought it best to keep my distance."

I knew my story was a lot for Elisa to take in. We sat quietly for some time until she broke the silence. "I have to ask; you're half demon. Is your demon nature—"

"Yes, my demon side is incubus. It's not as strong as my father's because of my angel side, but it is still powerful nonetheless."

"How do you find these women? Do you just invade their dreams?" she questioned.

While the conversation had taken an uncomfortable turn, it was necessary if we were to co-exist, and possibly move further. "Women must call out to me; allow me entry, if you will. Consider it a form of supernatural consent."

She seemed apprehensive about asking her next question but continued. "You said you provide pleasure to women in their dreams. What about in the real world?"

"If you're asking if I've had carnal relations on the earthly plane, then yes, but that was for my own edification, and had nothing to do with my being an incubus. It has not occurred in some time. Seven years to be exact."

Elisa looked at me incredulously. "But you're a male, and a demon, at that."

"Color me an enigma."

"Have-have I called out to you?" she asked shyly.

"Yes, Elisa, you have."

"For how long?"

"You have been calling out to me for three years."

She stood up, clearly perturbed. "*Three years?* You're seriously telling me that we have been having…dream sex for the past three years? All this time I thought I was losing my mind, thought I was going crazy, and all the while you were playing mind games with me? Then why can't I remember?"

I hung my head in shame. "Because, I didn't want you to remember."

"Why not? Was it bad? If it was, I am mortified."

"No, not at all," I said reassuring her, taking her hand in mine. "I just didn't want you to feel any shame when we saw each other. Every encounter had always been quite…titillating. You are an extremely passionate woman, Elisa Hunte. I'm looking forward to one day experiencing that passion on this plane, when you're ready, that is."

As she sat back down, I saw her dark cheeks become rosy and felt the heat emanating from her body. "It really should have been my choice whether or not to remember."

"You're right, and I'm truly sorry. I won't make that mistake again."

"Since we've been…you know, have you…'pleasured' anyone else?" she asked, making air quotes with her fingers.

"Why, my dear Elisa, are you jealous?" I asked. She didn't respond. That spoke to the better part of my ego. I turned her face to look at me. "You have been the only one I've been pleasuring, and enjoyably so."

"Dafari," she said, looking me in the eyes and biting her bottom lip, "What if I want to remember?"

"If that is your request, so be it. But I must warn you, be sure this is what you want, because once it's done, I can't undo it."

"Her brown eyes stared into mine, determination in her gaze. "I want to remember."

"If that is the case, tomorrow I will teach you how to close off your thoughts," I answered, rising from my seat. "Tonight, I want you to be completely open and receptive to me. As you desire, so shall it be," I replied, leaning down, kissing her on the forehead. "Good night, Elisa. I'll be waiting for your call."

The next morning, everyone was already downstairs when I joined them. Elisa was behind the counter, preparing a bowl of cereal.

When she saw me, she spoke to me telepathically. "I remembered everything. I can't believe the things we did last night. I am so embarrassed by my behavior."

"You weren't the least bit embarrassed last night, my little temptress," I sent back. "In fact, you appeared rather empowered throughout rounds three, four...five. I was just playing off of your deepest desires," I noted. I reached into the refrigerator, taking out the orange juice. Standing directly behind her, I whispered something in her ear so low only she could hear, causing her to grip the counter hard, crossing her legs.

Tasmin and Octavian stared at us quizzically.

"Why do I feel like I need a cold shower?" Tasmin asked.

Octavian followed up, asking, "Would you two like to be alone?"

I smelled the arousal on her, thick and heady. What did I whisper? "You're the one who wanted to remember last night. I told you to be very careful what you wish for. You begged for it and you got it again...and again...and again. You've experienced my...tastes in the dream realm. Imagine how they are on the earth plane. Do you really think you're ready for that?"

CHAPTER 19:
TASMIN

The new day arrived before I knew it, but it was my own fault for staying up late trying to get a handle on my newly discovered power. In my head, if I could get through medical school, I could definitely master telekinesis. While learning this new power wasn't the easiest, I was getting better at controlling it.

As I prepared to get out of bed, I took a minute to take in my temporary residence. The bedroom was larger than any I had ever slept in. After seeing Elisa's room the day before, I recognized that the guest bedrooms were all similar. Mine differed in that the color scheme consisted of cream-colored walls. The bedding was in shades of blue, particularly Maya and Egyptian blue.

Dafari made such a big deal about Elisa and I starting training that I felt it was best to get an early start. Luckily, I was an early riser. So was my dad, which explained why my phone was buzzing before six o'clock.

"Good morning, Daddy," I answered cheerfully, glad to hear from him.

"Good morning, Tazzy. How's it going down there?"

"Things are…going," I replied hesitantly. I couldn't very well tell him what was really going on. Dad would have me back on a plane to New York before I could say boo. "I finally finished the inventory."

"That's great, sweetie. Really great." The tone in my dad's voice told me that something was up.

"What's going on? I know it's something because I can hear it in your voice."

He sighed. "You're right. I have news about the fire."

I was anxious to find out what that news was. I sat up, waiting to hear what he had to say.

"Kiddo, there's no easy way to say this, so I'll just give it to you straight. It definitely was arson. The problem is they couldn't identify the substance that was used, and there was no residue of any kind. They also couldn't locate any type of incendiary device. Not to mention the blast pattern was extremely unusual."

I swung my legs off the edge of the bed, standing up. I kind of tuned out after the word arson. "I don't understand. Why would anybody want to burn down my practice?"

"That's what the investigators are wondering. Since I know all of them, they are keeping me advised as a professional courtesy, especially since you're not here. I just can't be directly involved in the actual investigation. I do have to warn you; because the fire is unusual in nature, they are still looking into it. They may request some information, like your bank account numbers and cell phone records, to check for suspicious activity."

I shook my head. "Let me guess; they want to make sure I wasn't trying to cash in on the insurance money."

"You've paid attention to me when I've talked over the years." He laughed. "But, yes, among other things."

"They can check whatever they want. I have nothing to hide." I started looking for some workout clothes to put on since I knew the guys would be putting us through our paces today. At the rate I was going, soon I would need a whole new wardrobe if I was going to be sidelined in Salix Pointe for much longer.

"I know you don't, sweetheart. I don't want to get your hopes up, but I do have a lead of my own. I can't tell you much, but when I know more, you'll be the first to know. Well, second, after your mom." He chuckled. "She'll have my head if I don't keep her in the loop."

I laughed with him. "Don't I know it? Okay, Daddy, keep me posted."

"I will, Tazzy. I'm about to head into work. Love you and talk soon."

"Love you. Talk to you later." We hung up, but now I had more questions than ever.

I got myself together, first brushing my teeth. I had showered the night before, so opted to wash up instead, anticipating that I would need a long shower after today's training. I threw on a sports bra, workout tights, a sweatshirt, and cross trainers, unsure of the type of training we'd be doing today.

When I got downstairs, same as the day before, Octavian was the first one in the kitchen. I figured he was dressed for training, as he was wearing a black tee shirt with matching black joggers with the logo 'Manchester United', which meant he was a soccer fan. The shirt highlighted his broad chest and well-defined arms, while the joggers accentuated the muscles in his legs. Not that I was looking or anything.

"Good morrow, Tasmin," he greeted in that ever chipper British way of his.

"Morning, Octavian," I replied a bit distracted, the conversation with my dad still on my mind.

"Something troubling you, poppet? You appear to be a bit preoccupied."

I wasn't sure how I felt about Octavian calling me poppet, but considering what happened before, it had to be better than wench. I noticed he was preparing a cup of tea. I saw him drop in the green tea bag, adding honey and lemon to the cup. After he added the hot water from the teakettle, he stirred the mix, handing a cup to me.

"Thanks," I said, taking the cup after sitting at the counter, sipping the hot blend. "I just spoke to my dad. He was updating me on the status of the investigation regarding my practice burning down."

"Ah, yes, a shambolic affair, to be sure. And what did your paternal unit reveal?

"He said that it was arson, but no source was found. No chemicals, no bomb parts, nothing.

"I have a theory, but I would like to wait for Dafari before we discuss the matter further. Would you like one, Tasmin?" he asked while preparing a green smoothie for himself.

"No thanks," I replied, walking around the counter. Checking the cabinets, I found the ingredients to whip up some oatmeal. I grabbed a bowl from the shelf, filling it with some rolled oats, almond milk, diced peaches, honey, chopped walnuts, and cinnamon.

Once I put the bowl in the microwave, I turned my attention back to Octavian. "I'm fine with waiting for Dafari. My dad also said their investigation was on-going and they'd probably be looking into my actions to make sure I wasn't involved, and that he was working on a lead of his own. He'll contact me when he knows more."

Octavian sipped his smoothie. "Why would they be investigating you?"

"It's standard in cases like this. They want to make sure I'm not profiting from the building being demolished. I get it and I'm not concerned. What does concern me is why someone would purposely destroy what I worked so hard to build. It doesn't make sense." I took my oatmeal out of the microwave and returned to my seat at the counter.

Octavian joined me. "Perhaps it will make more sense once Dafari joins us. In the meanwhile, I've formulated an agenda for today's training. Dafari has a superb indoor gym, which means we can spend the entire day working on your martial arts and hand-to-hand combat skills, as well as your telekinesis." He sounded a bit too exuberant for my liking.

"Oh joy, oh bliss," I replied snidely.

"Tasmin, I know this is a lot to take on, but—"

"You don't have to say it, Octavian. I know Elisa and I need to train, and we need to learn to use and control our powers in order to become stronger witches."

He put up his hand, a slick grin on his face. "No, what I was going to say was that I know this is a lot to take on, but I promise that I will be here to help you every step of the way."

I admit it. I felt stupid for jumping to the wrong conclusion. "I'm sorry for assuming. It's just because you guys have been drumming into our heads how important all this is."

"Yes, and we've also seen where that's gotten us, now haven't we?" he said, letting out a hearty laugh. "As a professor, I've had to learn that the same approach doesn't work on every student. With you and Elisa, I've come to realize that a kinder, gentler approach works best."

"Thank you. I promise I will be your star pupil, Mr. Miyagi."

Octavian had an inquisitive look on his face. "Who?"

I couldn't help but laugh. "I really need to teach you some pop culture references."

"Good morning, you two," Elisa said, walking into the kitchen, her cheery disposition evident. "Beautiful day, isn't it?"

Octavian and I looked first at Elisa, then each other. "Good morning to you," I said. "Someone's in a good mood." She looked at me and smiled.

"Good morrow, Elisa," Octavian answered back.

She was already dressed in indigo colored leggings, a fuchsia colored tee shirt, and her combat boots, while carrying her favorite leather jacket in her hand, placing it on the back of a chair. The way she was dressed, I figured she was going to the café.

"I slept great last night," she said, taking a bowl out of the cabinet, and a box of cereal out the pantry.

"I'm glad someone did," I remarked. "I stayed up late practicing my telekinesis."

"Oh?" Octavian questioned. "And how goes it?"

There was a saltshaker on the counter. Thinking I wanted the shaker to move across the counter and stop in front of Octavian, I focused my mind, and was pleased with the result. From the gigawatt smile on Octavian's face, so was he.

"Good show, Tasmin! Just smashing!"

"Thanks, Octavian. I don't need a repeat of the knives and teakettle incidences."

"Well, you're off to a blinding start."

"High praise from the professor. It means a lot." I smiled despite myself.

Elisa leaned over, giving me a high five. "Way to go, girl."

"Thanks, Elisa. I figured if I have to embrace this witch thing, might as well jump in headfirst, literally."

"What did I just walk in on?" Dafari asked, appearing out of the shadows, his black pants and charcoal gray turtleneck adding to the effect.

"Tasmin has been doing an ace job of honing her telekinetic skills, Brother."

Dafari walked behind the counter. "Kudos, Tasmin," he replied to me, but looking at Elisa the entire time. It appeared those two were having a meeting of the minds, one that Octavian and I clearly weren't invited to. When he walked up behind her, and she suddenly grabbed the counter, I knew Dafari was probably whispering something he shouldn't have in mixed company, even if we couldn't hear him.

I saw how uncomfortable Elisa looked, so I quickly changed the subject. "Octavian, didn't you say that you wanted to talk to Dafari about what we discussed earlier."

"Ah, yes. Dafari, Tasmin advised me that the investigators have ruled the fire arson and could find no cause for it or the subsequent explosion that decimated her office. Yet, the adjacent structures were left intact. I have a theory; what if brimstone was used?"

Dafari leaned on the counter, a pensive look on his face. "A reasonable assumption, I suppose. Brimstone can be concentrated to only destroy the target. But if that is the case, only a demon can handle it, and we know it wasn't Father because he was attacking Elisa at the time."

"But he could have had one of his minions do it. Perhaps possess a human host and have him or her plant the brimstone before igniting it."

I cut in. "Guys, even if that is the case, it still begs the question as to why he would destroy my livelihood."

"Perchance to keep you in Salix Pointe, Tasmin. Without your profession to return home to, you could possibly remain in town indefinitely," Octavian postulated.

"Well, if your father was responsible, Dafari, he got his wish. Aside from my parents, I really have nothing to go home to. But what's his motivation?"

"That, Tasmin, has yet to be ascertained," Dafari replied. "The same holds for the reasons he trashed Elisa's home."

"Can't you just have some father-son conversation?" Elisa asked.

"If only it were that simple," Dafari countered. "He'll be found if, and only if, he wants to be found. For now, let's focus on those whose motives are abundantly clear, such as Mayor Lovett."

I filled in Elisa and Octavian, telling them how he offered to buy the bookstore outright, and how he became extremely distressed when I told him the bookstore was off the market indefinitely.

Dafari told them about the alleged ghosts inhabiting the bookstore, about the fireplaces lighting up, and the books flying off the shelves. "Tasmin even used her telekinesis to have a book smack the mayor square in the face. It was quite an amusing sight. But I can understand his interest in the bookstore, as it is the epicenter of magick for Salix Pointe."

"Excuse me," Elisa cut in, "Epicenter of magick?"

"Yes," Dafari continued. "Most of the magick in Salix Pointe is concentrated at the location that houses the bookstore. Anyone having access to it would have immeasurable power at their disposal."

"That explains a lot considering all the weird things that have happened there over the years," Elisa commented.

"All the more reason for you ladies to find your Book of Shadows." Octavian added.

"Book of what?" I asked.

"Book of Shadows, a tome where Ms. Chadwick and Mama Nall would have notated their spells, potent and elixir recipes, and the like," he carried on. "It would be in your best interest for you two to unearth the whereabouts of that book."

"I agree," Dafari added. "The book will act as your essential guide to using magick, which is why it's important that you both locate it sooner rather than later."

"Understood," I said.

Octavian stood up from his chair. "Well, good people, I think we're all caught up for the duration. Tasmin, shall we commence with your training?"

I stood to join him. "Yes, sensei," I said, giving him a martial arts bow, making Elisa snicker. "See you guys later."

We left Elisa and Dafari in the kitchen. With everything that was going on, I hadn't ventured much further than the kitchen and my bedroom. I soon discovered there was much more to Dafari's home than met the eye. I followed Octavian down a long corridor to other side of the house. We stopped when we reached the end of the hallway, standing in front of two glass double doors.

"Shall we?" Octavian said, opening the door for me.

"Thank you," I replied, walking into the gym.

To say that the large gym was amazing was an understatement. One wall was entirely adorned with hand-held weapons of all kinds, some of which I didn't even recognize. On the other side there was a climbing wall. I did always want to try one of those. One side of the room contained exercise equipment; weight machines, free weights, and cardio equipment. Although I couldn't fathom what an otherworldly being would need with all of that, hey, if he liked it, I loved it.

The space was large enough to do laps, which Octavian used to his full advantage. "Tasmin, you need to warm up. Give me ten laps, please."

I looked at him, wanting to say something smart, but thought better of it. I worked out on a regular basis but hadn't had the opportunity since arriving in Salix Pointe. Since it had only been a few days, I knew it really wouldn't be an issue. I just liked giving Octavian a hard time. I took off my sweatshirt, handing it to him. When I did, I took note of his reaction. He was watching me intently, lopsided grin on his face. I felt as if he was undressing me with his eyes, and when I say *felt* it, I meant it.

I started off at a slow pace just to get my muscles warmed up. It wasn't difficult to get back into the swing of things, and it actually helped me to clear my mind. I had so many thoughts swirling in my head. Running gave me the focus I needed to sort out everything. Top of my list was figuring out who was trying to ruin my life and kill Elisa and me. Right now, all roads pointed to Dafari's demon daddy, but if that was the case, why was he doing all of this? Then there was the mayor who was trying way too hard to buy the bookstore.

I was concentrating so hard that I initially hadn't heard Octavian calling out to me. I finally heard him yelling my name. "Tasmin!"

I stopped dead in my tracks. "Huh?"

"Did you realize you completed ten laps three laps ago?"

"No, I didn't. Sorry."

"Poppet, what has your thoughts so preoccupied?"

I walked around, slowing down my heart rate. Octavian followed. "What's not preoccupying my thoughts? Not too long ago, I was home in Brooklyn seeing patients. My life was great. Now, here I am, learning I'm a witch with major powers, my practice is gone, and someone is trying to kill me."

Octavian stopped me, turning me to face him, his hands on my shoulders. "Tasmin, I can't bring back your practice, although I wish I could, but I will tell you what I can do; I will protect you to the best of my ability, on that you have my word."

What he said had an effect on me. For some reason, I felt a sense of relief like I hadn't felt since arriving in Salix Pointe. "Thank you. I really appreciate that."

"You are most welcome. Now, I know something else that will make you feel better?"

"What's that?" I asked, crossing my arms in front of me.

He took a fighter's stance. "Come at me."

"Say what now?"

"You heard me, poppet," he taunted. "Try to hit me."

I put up my hands. "I don't think that's such a good idea."

"Why, are you scared?" he jeered, sending a jab in my direction which I quickly blocked.

"Not in your wildest dreams," I shot back.

"Tasmin, I don't think you want to know my wildest dreams." The look he was giving me told me that maybe he was right. "Come now, I need to know what I have to teach you."

"Okay," I said, squaring up in my own fighter's stance, guard up. "You asked for it."

I began to level a volley of punches and kicks at Octavian, much to his surprise. Little did he know

that I had several years of martial arts training when I was in medical school, and although I was a little rusty, much of it was coming back to me. We kept going back and forth, with one of us on the offensive, the other, the defensive. Octavian was right; I did feel better. I realized that much of what I was feeling was anger, mainly because Elisa and I had forces against us, and we didn't know who or why. I despised not having control of the situation, and I had built up a lot of aggression; this was great way to release it.

Octavian let me come at him hard but didn't let me get off easy. He was definitely like a sensei, correcting my form, giving me pointers where I needed them, and reminding me to keep my guard up at all times. I was actually enjoying our training session so much I hadn't realized that several hours had passed.

"Very nice. Why didn't you tell me you had previous martial arts instruction?"

"Because you didn't ask," I remarked as we were taking a quick break.

"Well you are quite skilled, I must say. I would like us to try something," he said walking over to a large mat. "I want you to try to flip me."

"You want me to try to flip *you*?" I asked, raising an eyebrow. I had flipped opponents in class before, but no one nearly as big as Octavian. Nonetheless, I was willing to give it a shot.

"Yes, you want to be able to grab your opponent by the arm and flip him or her over." He grabbed my arm, gently flipping me on to the mat. "Just like that," he said, helping me up.

"Okay, so I grab you by the arm and flip you like this?" I asked, firmly planting my feet and steading myself, flipping him squarely onto his back. By the look on his face, he hadn't expected me to get it right the first time. Then again, neither did I.

"Yes, well, precisely like that."

It felt a bit gratifying being able to take down someone so strong. "Not bad for such a small slip of a woman, huh?" I remarked, poking fun at him calling me that when we first met.

I reached out my hand to help him off the mat, but instead, he pulled me down, and I found myself on top of him. We stayed still for what seemed like a few long moments, our closeness enabling me to feel both of our heartbeats. My heart was beating fast, definitely faster than his. I felt one of his hands move to the small of my back, the fingers of the other moving slowly up and down my spine. I felt my heartrate decrease, as if it was trying to synch up with his. I tried to get a read on what Octavian was feeling, but, for some reason, I couldn't pick up on anything, as if something was blocking me.

"Tasmin," he said, his black eyes staring into mine.

"Yes, Octavian?"

"Always keep your guard up. Doing so may one day save your life."

"Duly noted," I replied.

I knew I should have gotten up, but, much as I tried, I couldn't. It was as if Octavian has some sort of hold on me, a tether that couldn't be cut.

I was finally pulled out my trance when I heard someone clearing their throat. When I looked up, I saw Dafari and Elisa standing by the gym's entrance.

"If you prefer to be alone, we can come back later," Dafari said in that dry tone of his.

I quickly jumped off Octavian, grabbing my sweatshirt. I got out of there as fast as I could, carrying my sweatshirt, along with my embarrassment, with me.

CHAPTER 20:

ELISA

No. Dafari wanted to know if I thought I could handle him live and in living color. The answer was no. I was barely able to wrap my mind around the fact that he and I had made the earth move in my dreams the night before. Now he had me gripping the edges of the counters and sinks because I knew what it was to feel him at his full prowess.

I felt the way his energy attached to mine. It was as if I could feel him touching me, kissing me…I felt the hairs on my neck stand. Then felt goosebumps cover my skin as heat ran up my spine and chills ran down it. I was embarrassed to be behaving as such, especially in front of Tasmin and Octavian. I was more than happy when they left us to go do some training.

I whirled around to face Dafari. "I think it's best you move back lest I be the one not responsible for her actions."

I'd intended for that to come out angrily, but judging by the smirk adorning Dafari's features, I'd say I missed the mark. Still, he took his orange juice and backed away. As the day progressed, Dafari shadowed me. While I was relieved to know that his father wouldn't attack me while I was with him, it was still hard to focus when an incubus had his hooks in me.

I got to the shop in plenty enough time to put up a **HELP WANTED** sign and to put up a note to let everyone know the café would be closed for the day. I knew a lot of the townsfolk would be annoyed, and some even upset, by the news, but I had to carve out some time to focus solely on learning the tricks of the trade of witchcraft.

"I want to go by your house," Dafari said as we left my café and headed to his car.

He'd refused to let me drive myself for some reason. He opened the passenger side door for me, and I slid in.

"Why?" I asked once he'd gotten in.

"I'd like to assess the damage and see what I can pick up—"

"Why don't you believe your father had anything to do with Ms. Noreen's death?" I asked out the blue.

It was something I'd been meaning to ask him since after he'd revealed that demon was his father. I noticed, while listening to the conversation between him and Octavian, that he was more than skeptical about his father being the perpetrator.

"It's not his style," he said then gave a one-armed shrug as he pulled into the minimal traffic. "My father would have wanted the world to know he'd been there. He'd have left his mark."

"What do you mean?"

"If my father had murdered Noreen, she'd have been strung up on an upside-down crucifix or something else just as egregious. He wouldn't have had the decency to stage the scene to look as if she'd died of natural causes."

I was appalled as could be seen by the open-mouthed shock on my face. "Your father's a psychopath."

Dafari glanced at me. "My father's a Fallen. They live up to every stereotype they've been given."

"And you?"

"What about me?" he asked.

"As the son of a Fallen, are you—"

"Am I what? A psychopath?"

I nodded timidly, not wanting to offend the man.

He chuckled without mirth. "I would be offended, but your question has merit," he said then stopped talking. He rubbed a hand over his chiseled jaw as if in thought. He was quiet so long, I assumed he wasn't going to answer. "I'll be completely honest with you, Elisa… I'm capable of anything if pushed. If my brother, you, and even Tasmin, or anyone we love or care about are threatened, I can't say what I won't do. With that being said, I'm also the son of a high-arch. I do have filters." He laughed lightly after saying that as if it was all comical to him.

I didn't know how to respond to that. How could I respond to that? I didn't know if I should be shocked or scared.

"Both," he said then cut his eyes at me.

"Excuse me?" I said.

"Be shocked and be scared. But while you're doing that, guard your damn thoughts," he snapped.

I rolled my eyes.

He said, "Remember our lessons from last night. It's easier than you think. Even when you're around those you love and trust, it's still important to guard your mind. You're not the only telepath in this town. Not only is guarding your thoughts important because you don't want pertinent information to get out, but your mental well-being is of utmost importance, especially when my father is around. If you leave your mind wide open, he will infiltrate, without permission, and he will take full advantage of it, good or bad. Right or wrong."

I was all set to rage against him until he said that last part. It brought me back to the reality that I needed to take this more seriously than I already was.

I took a deep breath then remembered the lessons he gave me in my dreams the night before.

As he drove, I calmed my mind and thought of happier times with my parents. I saw my dad's smiling face. Mama used to always tell him he was as black as night, tall and strong as a mighty Sequoyah, and as handsome as the devil himself. I always found it odd that she would compare him to the devil.

Mama always reminded me that the Good Book said Lucifer was the finest angel in the land. Then she would laugh and share a knowing look with my father who always had a charming smile for her. I inwardly smiled at the memory. I felt myself get emotional when an image of my Amazonian grandmother, Mama Nall, popped up. She was a thick, tall woman with rich ebony skin. Her vibrant brown eyes always held a twinkle.

"Perfect," I heard Dafari say.

I jumped back to the present and looked at him as he pulled in and parked in my driveway.

"What?"

"For about five minutes, I couldn't read your mind," he said.

"You tried to?"

"I always do… It's how I knew you wanted me for seven years now," he said, then chuckled and got out the car.

At this point, there was no need for me to be embarrassed about anything when it came to him. I got out the car and looked up at my house. Someone had boarded up the windows and put a thick piece of wood up where the door used to be.

"I called Carpenter John last evening and asked him and his son to come over and do this," Dafari said.

Carpenter John was another citizen of Salix Pointe whose family could be traced back to the beginning years. He'd built most of the homes in the area just like his forefathers before him had and he also helped me remodel the home I was standing in front of.

"Remind me to thank him and his son," I said.

I watched as Dafari walked up to the makeshift door and gave a slow wave of his hand. The door moved as if someone behind it moved it to the side. I glanced down at my hands and wondered if I could do that.

"More or less," Dafari said then held his hand out for me.

I felt a sense of dread as he ushered me inside. The damage was more than I could have imagined. Sure, Octavian had told me it was inhabitable, but by all the great Orishas, this looked beyond repair.

"My God," I whispered.

I was about to walk ahead but almost tripped over the earth, the literal ground, protruding through the floors. Dafari caught my arm and pulled me closer to him. "Watch your step," he said against my ear.

I rolled my neck to stave off the immediate, visceral reaction my body had to that simple act. I cleared my throat, set to turn so I could thank him when he shoved me. Clear across the room, he shoved me, and it was so hard that when I landed, I felt as if I'd broken something.

I groaned, disoriented a bit. My vision blurred. I grabbed a hold of a board sticking from my dilapidated wall to pull myself up, only to be knocked back on my ass by a golden ball of energy from Dafari's hand.

I screamed then yelled, "What the fu—"

My words were stopped short by a force that picked me up and tossed me back to the entrance of the house. That knocked the wind out of me. So much so that I coughed erratically as I turned over and looked up at Dafari. He stood over me, tall and proud with glowing red eyes. I didn't know what was going on. I was confused and scared. Why was he attacking me? Was he an enemy and not the friend he pretended to be? Had I gotten it all wrong?

"No," he said as he knelt in front of me. "But your reality now dictates that you should always be ready for whatever, whenever. I attacked you as any other otherworldly entity would if they wanted to hurt you or kill you. This isn't a game, Elisa. Get up. Fight." He stood then cockily beckoned me.

I was far too disoriented to get a grasp on what was happening.

"Get up, Elisa. By now, any other demon would have killed you. Get up and use your magic," he demanded just before a burst of wind from his hand lifted me from the debris and tossed me behind where he stood.

In the future, I'd never be able to explain the rabid rage that coiled in my gut and took a hold of me. Like fire had been injected into my veins, madness overtook me. My fingertips burned like I'd stuck them on an open flame. Through the pain and delirium, I jumped to my feet. Before his red eyes could blink, I jutted my hands forward and witnessed my own magic. Fireballs, the size of small planets chased Dafari.

He deflected them with ease as he backed away from my rage. He smirked then chuckled. "Is that all you got?" he taunted.

A growl erupted from somewhere in my gut as I launched at him. Magic be damned, if I got my hands on him, I'd beat his ass like we were in a good ole street fight. How dare he attack me in the guise of training! I'd show him. I was on him so fast, it was lost on me that my floor was still upturned and earth, as were dense tree roots that protruded from the ground like thick gnarled fingers and veins.

We fought like mortal enemies, hard and fast. He deflected most of my offensive fighting and sent me on the defense more than I would have liked, but I gave him all I had and then some. I swung for his face. He grabbed my wrist and slammed my back against a wall. He threw a big, solid fist at my face. I yelped, moved my head in time, then kneed him in the groin.

When he doubled over in pain, I caught him by his hair and slammed my elbow down on the back of his neck. He tried to lean in with his shoulders to lift me from the floor, but I still had a hold of his hair. I gripped it tighter then yanked him backwards. He fell on the floor so hard, it almost felt as if the earth shook. I bent and picked up some soil then tossed it at his face, his eyes in particular.

He was up in a flash. Eyes flashing between golden and red as he angrily swiped at the dirt on his face. It was my turn to taunt. "Is that all you got?" I snapped, fist balled in a fighter's stance.

He flew at me, well he tried. The earth and roots of the trees attacked him. The roots sprouted up and around his legs, crawling up and growing like weeds.

The dirt from the floor shot up like spears and caged him inside while the roots from the trees coiled around his wrists. The dirt had caged him in while the roots held him captive.

I gasped and slapped a hand over my mouth when he strained against the roots and yelled out in annoyance and anger. I didn't know what was happening. Had no idea how to stop it. The coiling roots got so tight around his wrists that blood started to trickle down.

"Oh my Loa! Stop," I screamed, running over to reach through the dirt bars to grab at the roots.

In an instant, the roots scaled down, while the dirt bars sunk back into the ground. Once free, Dafari dropped down to one knee with one hand balled on the ground. His back was rising and falling slowly as if he was struggling to breathe.

"What was that?" I asked, breathing just as erratically.

He cut his eyes up at me and through a mouth full of jagged fangs, he snarled, "You're an elemental… I wasn't expecting that."

"I am what?"

He stood then took a deep breath. "You can control the elements. I saw the fireballs earlier, but just assumed it was energy blasts again, but the roots attacking me and the dirt caging me in after you'd touched it proves otherwise."

He made a step toward me and I moved back, ready to defend myself again if need be. Dafari reached for me and I pulled away. Even with the shock of that revelation that I was an elemental, I was upset with him.

"You attacked me," I said.

"Yes, but for good reason."

"There was no good reason to outright attack me, Dafari. We could have gone about this so many other ways," I snapped.

"We could have, but that was what you expected. When you're on the defense, you won't get a warning. Get over it," he shot back.

"Get over it?" I asked incredulously.

"Yes. Get over it. I gave you a crash course in defending yourself first because people, other witches, have been murdered, Elisa. Murdered. That includes your grandmother and your parents. So, yes, be mad. Be upset, but I'm not going to stand by and hold your hand while danger is lurking and ready to pounce," he said, speaking emphatically as he used his hands to get his point across.

I was still mad as hell, still wanted to sock him in his glowing eyes, but I knew he was right. Being reminded that three of my elders had indeed been murdered made my anger at him seem a bit stupid. Afterall, he had said he would be training me. His first lesson had been in my dreams the night before when he gave me succinct lessons on how to guard my thoughts. Once I got it down, he rewarded me with erotic pleasures no earthly man would even think of. And here I was today, mad enough to gut punch him.

I turned away and stormed from my house. I huffed down the steps to his car then slammed the door after I got in. He followed me a few minutes later. Only he stopped on the porch, looked down and then stooped to touch a red drop on the porch. I watched as he rubbed his thumb and index finger together then nodded like he was answering a question only he could hear.

Once he was in the car, we left. He tried to make conversation with me, but I was over it, too mad to even nod when he asked me a question. By the time we got back to his house, I had simmered down some, but not enough to talk to him. My body ached and I'd started to feel all the bumps and bruises. I couldn't wait to get in the house to shower and relieve some of the discomfort.

As soon as he parked, I got out the car and headed inside. We didn't see Tasmin and Octavian. I would have assumed they'd gone until Dafari told me he could feel his brother in the house. He led me to the gym because I wanted to check on Tasmin. I hoped Octavian hadn't dragged her through battle and called it "training." To my surprise, however, we walked in to find Tasmin laying on top of Octavian in what could only be considered an intimate embrace.

I was embarrassed for her when Dafari cleared his throat and made a suggestive comment. Tasmin looked as if she would have rather been caught stealing than what we'd walked in on. She flew out of that gym like she had been caught by her parents. I shook my head at Dafari's antics and then turned to head upstairs myself.

CHAPTER 21:
ELISA

Over the next couple of days, Tasmin and I were put through our paces. Three times in one week, we were awakened from our sleep, scared within inches of our lives. Frightened to the point that we fought like our lives actually depended on it. I didn't give two hoots what anyone said, seeing a full-blooded archangel in true form was frightening. Octavian may have been a professor and one of the good guys, but I never wanted to see him in his full form come after me again. When they weren't pressuring us to train harder, they whispered and convened in secrecy, locked away in Dafari's home office or meeting at his practice.

On top of all that, Tasmin and I still had to work the café and bookstore. My help wanted sign had brought in all kinds of people. Out of seventy-five applications, I called ten people back to interview them. I ended up hiring two high-school girls and one college student. The college student kept burning the coffee and pastries. I had to let her go. One of the high school students kept getting so nervous she broke two sets of bowls, four mugs, six glasses and five plates. I had to let her go before I ended up having to order a whole new inventory of dishes. The last high school student was great with customer service but refused to learn how to run the register or bake the pastries. In the end, I was back at square one.

By the week of Halloween, all anyone in the town could talk about was the jubilee at the mayor's manor. Since I'd never been to a jubilee, I didn't know what all the hype was about. However, the town was abuzz like never before. Anytime someone came in the café, they asked me if I knew for certain that Dr. Battle and his brother would be there. The women, and some men, were as giddy about them being there as they were about the actual Halloween party.

I did notice that Tasmin and Octavian had been getting closer even though things were a bit awkward after Dafari and I had caught them in that compromising position. She wasn't looking for ways to string him up anymore. Every morning, they were the first ones up and would be downstairs sharing libations over breakfast. I often wondered if she noticed the ways in which he would gaze upon her. He looked at Tasmin as if she were the Second Coming.

The Merry Widows hadn't been back to the café, and I'd started to worry that Octavian had scared them off. I made a note to ask Tasmin if she wanted to go with me to check on them later. Speaking of Tasmin, she and I had gotten closer. She'd become the sister I never had. If we weren't at our wits end with the training, we were thinking of ways to find, what Octavian had called, our Book of Shadows.

"It's got to be here," Tasmin said as she browsed the shelf of magic books.

I was on the other side of the aisle doing the same. We were in the bookstore. I'd come over after closing the café for the day. We'd agreed to meet there after we'd searched Ms. Noreen's home and came up empty. After searching the same row for the second time, I shook my head.

I stood up. "This is useless," I said on a heavy sigh. "Maybe we're looking in the wrong place. Maybe this is too obvious."

Tasmin climbed down the ladder on her side then stood next to me with her hands on her hips. "You may be right, but where else is there to look?"

"We haven't searched my grandmother's house. Could be there," I said.

Tasmin looked skeptical. "I don't know," she said shaking her head slowly. "Do you think they would put it there? I mean since it wasn't at Aunt Noreen's? We turned that place upside down."

I shrugged. "It couldn't hurt to look."

It was her turn to sigh. "True… well…want to head over that way?"

I took a gander at all the mess we'd made. "I suppose we should clean the place up first. I can't believe all the business you've been getting. It's like Ms. Noreen is still alive and running this place."

Tasmin laughed lightly. "I can't believe I'm about to say this, but I'm actually enjoying this."

"Enjoying what?" I asked, picking up books.

"Running the bookstore."

I quirked a brow, a wide smile adorning my face. "Really?"

She nodded.

"Does that mean… you won't sell and that you plan to stay?" I asked, hopeful.

Tasmin glanced around then gave a one shoulder shrug. "Perhaps…"

I squealed, dropped the books I was holding then rushed to hug her.

While she hugged me back and laughed at my shenanigans, she said, "Goodness, Elisa. Calm down. I said perhaps."

I pulled away and looked at her. "That's much better than a no and far better than what you'd intended to do when you first got here."

I was about to joke and tell her that I was going to put a spell on her to make her stay when just beside the basement door, I saw a figure. No…a person? I gasped so hard my chest felt as if it was about to cave in. It was the same woman I'd seen looking at me from the bookstore window a few weeks ago.

"What?" Tasmin asked, alarmed.

I pointed toward the basement. "Look!"

Tasmin whipped around. "What? I don't see anything." Alarm still in her voice, she rushed behind me as I raced toward the basement door. "Elisa, slow down! What on earth is the matter with you?"

"She's right there," I said then stopped cold in my tracks.

The basement door opened, and the woman disappeared into the darkness.

"Okay, now that I saw," Tasmin said stopping beside me.

"You saw her?" I asked, turning to look at Tasmin.

She looked befuddled. "Ah. No. I saw the basement door open though."

I shook my head, knowing darn well I'd just seen a younger looking Ms. Noreen disappear into the basement. I timidly walked over to the door then flipped the switch to the right of it. A flight of about eighteen stairs greeted us.

"You been down there since you've been running the store?" I asked Tasmin.

She shook her head. "No. Not sure if I want to go down there now, especially since you're seeing…what is it that you saw?" she asked with a curious frown as she looked up at me.

"So you really didn't see her?" I asked.

"See her?"

"Yes, the-the-the woman in the plum dress. It looked like a dress from the 19th century, but that's beside the point. She was standing right there! I saw her!"

"Elisa, are you telling me you see…ghosts?"

I struggled to answer. I didn't know what it was I'd seen. I suppose it was possible it was a ghost…

"I suppose I am. I mean, I guess?" I shook my head. "Anyway, let's see what's down there."

We eased down the stairs. We were apprehensive being that I'd just told Tasmin I saw a ghost disappear down there. Basements and attics had always given me goosebumps. This time was no different. When we got to the bottom, I expected to find creepy old boxes, spiderwebs, a stench of staleness, rats, roaches, bats, and only the Ancestors knew what else.

Instead, we found a clean basement with built-in bookshelves for walls and concrete flooring. The shelves were filled with books that didn't appear to be inventory, as inventory was kept in the storage room upstairs. There were seven wooden chairs on the left side of the room, an old cook stove in the middle of the room, and on one of the shelves on the right side of the room were candles of all colors, crystals, sage and rose bundles, palo santo sticks, stones, things for runes, different decks of tarot cards, and many other things that I was too wired to put a name to at the moment. On the right side of the room sat seven hand-carved round tables with names etched in them. On top of each table sat various crystal balls.

"Amabelle, Noreen, Cara, Mary, Martha, Duma-Nolan and Hondo," Tasmin read in a soft voice.

"Amabelle was Mama Nall's first name," I said. "Duma…was my father," I continued then slapped a hand over my mouth to stifle the sob I almost let out.

I didn't even know why I got so emotional. I felt a sense of overwhelming grief. It just hit me hard that my grandmother and her son, my father, and Noreen were gone, snatched away from us.

Tasmin walked over and rubbed a comforting hand up and down my back. "I know. I feel it, too," she said, voice shaky. Then she asked, "Who is Hondo?"

"Hondo was Martha's husband," I replied. "He was a tree cutter who died in a work accident seven years ago. He was killed instantly."

I took her hand and gave it a gentle squeeze. As soon as our hands linked, our bracelets buzzed then glowed golden, the crystal balls shone, several candles flickered on, and a book on the left wall of the bookshelf shot out and flew over our heads. Tasmin and I yelped and ducked and then watched the book land on the table with Noreen's name. Then, just like that, all the commotion stopped.

Tasmin and I looked at one another then eased over to the table. In a beautiful script read: ***Book of Magic Enchantment: To attain knowledge, go seek. To attain wisdom, go listen. Get knowledge. Get wisdom. But of all things, get understanding.*** There were also several Adinkra symbols, drawings, and etchings on the cover. She and I stared at it like it was a rare artifact. Technically, to us, it was.

"We found it," I said just as Tasmin and I reached out to touch the book.

Energy sizzled through my fingertips and crawled up my arm. Judging by the way Tasmin gave a slight shiver, I knew she felt it, too.

"Do we move it? Take it with us?" Tasmin asked.

"I don't know…"

"Octavian and Dafari will be happy to know we've found it," she said.

I nodded. "I say we leave it here until we have time to look over it thoroughly. That way we can take our time looking at it, for now anyway."

We stood in companionable silence for a moment, not sure of exactly what to do now that we'd actually found the book. It was safe to say I was nervous. I wasn't sure what Tasmin was feeling, but anxiety accompanied the nervousness I felt.

"Should we open it?" I asked.

"That's better than just staring at it I suppose," she said.

1 Your Becoming: Welcome

For the witches who came before us, and for those who will continue after us, use the pages as a guide to your journey of becoming. Your becoming will send you many trials and tribulations. There will be some who will welcome you with open arms, and then there will be those who will shun you and wish you harm. Be ready for anything, our future coven members. Protect many, but trust few. Be responsible with your magic at all times. Never take it for granted. Never take it lightly. Protect your magic at all costs as it can be stolen. A witch who loses her magic will suffer a terrible fate, one that not even the most evil of humans deserve.

Your magic decreases when you use it for gain or profit. Your magic increases when used for good. Many will tell you that black magic is bad magic. By itself, black magic isn't a bad thing, but with the wrong intentions, it can inflict terrible harm. Sometimes, to protect those you love and the innocent, you must tap into a darker kind of magic because it will be the only kind of magic the evil you'll be up against will respect. While those times are rare, you will be faced with hurdles that will require you to use such magic. Not everything that's good is good and not everything that's evil is evil.

Those words may confuse you at first, but as time goes on, you will understand. Find your coven as soon as possible. There should be SEVEN of the coven at all times. When there isn't SEVEN, the ranks can be easily manipulated.

Repeat these words three times before turning the page: I am becoming who I am destined to be. No harm shall come to me. By all the Ancestors who came before me, I am becoming who I am destined to be. I will honor this coven, and even when there will be things that will test me, I will become who I am destined to be. The number 7 is sacred to me and will always balance the scales to favor me. By all the Ancestors who came before me, I am becoming who I am destined to be.

As soon as Tasmin and I finished saying those words, the crystal balls shone brightly while seven different crystals on the wall glowed and floated just above the shelves. An electrifying charge surged forward and hit both Tasmin and me square in the chest. Blackness overcame me.

I woke up hours later. It took me a minute to get my bearings about me. Tasmin sat up beside me.

"What was that?" she asked.

"I have no idea, but I think that's enough for today," I said.

"You ain't lying. What time is it?"

I checked my watch then my eyes widened. We'd been down in the basement for four hours.

"Four hours?" Tasmin yelled after I told her the time.

We stood. "Let's close the book, lock the basement and get out of here," I said.

We got to Dafari's place just in time for dinner.

Dafari greeted us at the door in a blood-red apron while drying his hand on a towel. "You could have let me know you were still with them," he said as he looked into the yard behind us.

We turned, startled by the fact Octavian was behind us.

"Where else would I have been, dear brother?" he asked as he jogged up the steps onto the porch behind us. "These two were busy searching for their book. Dare I say, they found it being that they were in the bookstore's basement for hours."

"You were shadowing us?" Tasmin asked.

A smiling Octavian nodded.

"We never even saw you," I said.

"That was the point, little sissy," he said to me, then dipped his head and as bold as day, cupped Tasmin's chin and laid a kiss on her that left her reeling.

Then he walked on in the house as if that had been the most normal thing to do. Tasmin laid a hand over her heart as if she were in a daze.

"Err…is there something you need to tell me?" I asked her while she looked up at me with dazed eyes.

"If so, tell her inside," Dafari said dryly. "Wash up and dinner will be served within the hour."

For the rest of the week, Tasmin and I sat with the Book of Magic Enchantment whenever we could, which wasn't much considering how busy we were with the café and bookstore. Not to mention, I had to have my dress refitted for the jubilee. My breasts kept spilling out of the original design. Training still continued while the town was in a frenzy. By the time Saturday rolled around, it was in a complete uproar.

"Ladies," we heard Octavian call from downstairs. "Time is passing us by. If we want to get answers this evening, we must get going."

"Coming," Tasmin and I yelled in unison.

"You are really trying to give the men in Salix Pointe heart attacks," I said to Tasmin.

She was dressed sexily in a black sleeveless halter train jersey dress. The bottom half had a sweeping brush train and a slit so high up her thigh I feared if she moved the wrong way, she would definitely give the old geezers something to smile about on their way to glory. Her sleek brown skinned thighs were sure to call attention to the way the darn near backless dress fit her curvy slender frame. I said darn near backless because there was at least a thin strap adorning her waist to keep the haltered neckline dress in place. The tall heels she had on accentuated every curve she owned.

I said, "Sooo, I've been meaning to ask since the other day, what's going on with you and the professor? That kiss he laid on you was…wow!"

Tasmin blushed so hard, her eyes even twinkled. "I know you're not going to believe me, but I don't know what that kiss was about. It was out of blue—"

"And apparently it knocked your socks off. You laid a hand on your chest like he'd given you heart palpitations. He likened to gave you fits." I laughed.

"I won't even pretend that the kiss wasn't…whew," she said then blew off steam like just thinking about it got her hot and bothered. "But I don't know what that man's game is. However, I intend to ask him what his intentions are."

She had a natural look for her makeup with smoky eyes and a plum color made her lips pop. Sleek diamond chandelier earrings dangled from her lobes with a tennis bracelet on her right wrist to match. Her long locs had been swept up on one side while the other side curtained her beautiful face. She looked, for a lack of better words, damn good.

"Thank you, Elisa," she said with a smile. "And you're not half stepping either. Your breasts look amazing in that dress. Whoever adjusted the top half for you did a great job!"

I laughed then turned to look in the mirror. She wasn't lying. I was a lot more comfortable in the dress I'd picked out since taking it to Sharon's to be altered to hold my breasts better. I had a nice hefty pair and if not careful, I would have had a wardrobe malfunction that would have embarrassed me to the high heavens.

I'd chosen to go with a black ball gown with a dangerous low V-neck cut at the top and a court train tulle at the bottom. It flared out over my hips while the top was tapered to my waist. On my feet were purple platform heels that clasped around my ankles and made me strut with a regality I hadn't known I possessed.

For my hair, I'd done something I hadn't ever done. I pressed it and it hung down just past my shoulders and curtained my face. I went with simple pearl earrings, a natural makeup look like Tasmin, and berry colored lips. Neither of us removed our other bracelets. We didn't think it would be wise.

Tasmin and I looked out the window when the wind howled. "Something's in the air," she said.

I agreed. The night was cool and the winds blew the leaves on the trees softly. There was a full blood moon shining in the sky that caused Tasmin and I to wonder what was in store for us.

Without further ado, after some minor last-minute primping, Tasmin and I left my room to head downstairs.

CHAPTER 22: TASMIN

Elisa and I started to head downstairs. Before we did, we took a selfie, which I sent to my parents. I had mentioned the jubilee to them, and they had asked me to send them a picture. Elisa grabbed her clutch bag, which matched her purple platform shoes. She dropped her cellphone, lipstick, and compact inside. I did the same with my black clutch bag.

When we got to the bottom of the stairs, Octavian and Dafari were there, waiting for us. I must admit, Octavian looked very handsome in a black double-breasted tuxedo jacket and black tailored dress pants that highlighted his muscular thighs. The white tuxedo shirt with black tuxedo studs for buttons, plum bow tie, and matching plum pocket square complimented his look nicely. With his smooth burnt honey-colored skin, freshly-cut tapered mane, and undeniably good looks, he looked like he had jumped right off of the pages of GQ magazine.

Dafari, on the other hand, went against the classic black tux, instead opting for a ruby colored, single-breasted three-piece suit. The custom single-button jacket with peak lapels, fancy vest, and flat front pants fit his well-built frame to perfection. His white high collar dress shirt and ruby bow tie completed the ensemble. His outfit, along with his dark skin and black wavy hair that hung loose around his shoulders, reminded me of a high-born Black man from another time period that I had only seen in pictures. I could tell by the look on Elisa's face that she was quite taken with his appearance. Tonight, Dafari would be her arm candy.

When I stood in front of him, Octavian did that lopsided grin thing, undressing me with his eyes. He took my hand, spinning me around, getting a full view of my dress. "Tasmin," he said, a look of what I can only equate to lust in his eyes, "You look absolutely ravishing. I fear I may have to fend off some suitors vying for you attention."

Much as I tried to fight it, Octavian made me blush. "How chivalrous of you. I'm sure you'll keep them in line. And I must say you clean up nicely yourself."

"Thank you, M'lady," he said, presenting his arm for me to take.

I didn't know what to make of the look on Dafari's face. He seemed to be unnaturally fixated on the top half of Elisa's dress. "I suggest you stick close to me tonight; *very* close." He held out his arm to Elisa. We looked at each other, shaking our heads.

"The mayor is a pretentious, pompous sod," Dafari remarked, as we all climbed into his Mercedes Benz.

"Which is why we're taking your car, correct?" I asked.

"Precisely," he replied. "Two things he and that loathsome wife of his respect are power and prestige. As a long-standing, well-to-do resident of Salix Pointe, I have both. As you all are with me, that privilege auspiciously extends to you."

"The fact that you and Octavian are going to the jubilee is enough to get us in the door," Elisa remarked. "I would bet that the only reason half the town is going is to see you two show up."

"I do believe you're exaggerating, Elisa," Dafari countered.

She crossed her arms in front of her. "You didn't see how many of my customers were inquiring if you and Octavian were going to the jubilee."

If I didn't know any better, I would have thought that Elisa was jealous. Then again, the way she and Dafari were interacting lately, one would have also thought they were lovers. My feeling was they were hiding something.

Octavian must have picked up on the tension. "Yes, well I'm a relative newcomer to town, and a foreigner to boot, so it would seem reasonable that there would be some curiosity. As far as my brother is concerned, the townsfolk are probably shocked that Salix Pointe's resident recluse is actually gracing them with his presence," he said, chuckling.

"You laugh, dear brother, but the way Ilene Suzanne was ogling you at my office, I'm sure she'll be quite pleased you're gracing her with *your* presence. By the way, you cannot call that woman an octoroon again. In this day and age, it's considered offensive."

"Her very existence offends me. However, as we are on a reconnaissance mission, I will refrain from calling her the octoroon that she is."

"Okay, guys," I chimed in, "Can we go over the plan for tonight?"

"Most assuredly, Tasmin," Octavian replied. "Dafari and I have decided that he and Elisa will fraternize with the guests since they know most, if not all, of Salix Pointe's residentiary, while you and I will investigate the mayoral manor."

Elisa turned around from the front seat to look at us, a mirthful grin on her face. "So what you're saying is Dafari and I will hobnob while you and Tasmin will go snooping."

"Basically," I acknowledged.

"Of course, we all need to keep our wits about us. However, to our advantage, Elisa can read thoughts, and I'm sure most of the guests will not be guarding theirs. The ultimate goal is to see if we can discern if any of the residents may be involved in the murders and the attempts on your lives," Dafari added.

Just as he finished that sentence, he made a left turn into a driveway, driving toward a palatial-looking structure, which I assumed was the mayor's manor. He drove around, parking his car at the back of the property. Cars of all makes and models filled the large parking area. As we exited the vehicle, I took note of the décor which could only be described as macabre. Jack-o'-lanterns with grotesquely carved features were lit along the periphery of the lot, as well as the pathway leading up to the manor. I noticed fake bloody hands poking out from beneath the extensive well-manicured lawns on either side of the parking structure; at least I hoped they were fake. Full-sized zombie mannequins in various states of decay, along with several coffin-shaped holes, were strategically placed all over the still-green grass. Adding to the gruesome sight was what appeared to be an enormous hedge maze sitting on the other side of the lot, eerie colored light patterns emanating from it. Sounds coming from the large outdoor speakers completed the creep factor.

When we finally reached the manor itself, I took in the all-brick and mortar structure that reminded me of a medieval castle. On either side of the ornate glass double doors sat life-sized moving figures; one the embodiment of Bloody Mary, the other a huge gargoyle.

"Where did they shop for their décor, Horrors R Us?" Octavian asked, making us all laugh.

Two men dressed as ghostly butlers open the doors for us, Elisa and Dafari leading the way. As we walked through the door, the room became eerily silent. Murmurs of "That's Dr. Battle" and "That's his brother" could be heard throughout the large receiving hall.

Then I heard someone say, "As fine as Dr. Battle is, why is he with Fatso?"

Another could be heard saying, "His brother's easy on the eyes, too. And yet, he chose such a common woman."

I knew that was clearly a jab at me, but I wasn't phased in the least bit. Call me common all they wanted, but I had more class in my pinky than those trolls had in their entire bodies. It was Elisa I was worried about. In the days leading up to the jubilee, I knew she was apprehensive about wearing such a revealing, sexy dress. I told her that I didn't see a problem with it because I knew she would rock it. Clearly, she did as evidenced by Dafari's reaction.

Standing in front of me, she kept her head held high. If the comment had gotten to her, she didn't show it.

Call me petty, but I couldn't let the callousness of those few individuals go. I had more or less learned to control my telekinetic powers, a mere thought no longer causing catastrophic consequences. Controlling my thoughts, I wished that those who had berated and demeaned us would either spill a drink on themselves or someone would spill it on them; that's exactly what happened. Gasps and curses could be heard as they tried to clean themselves off from the dousing. Elisa reached her hand back palm side up for me to slap.

"Okay, ladies, if we're finished congratulating ourselves, let's get down to business," Dafari said, chastising us. Then I heard him chuckle low in his throat.

Looking around the great hall, the first thing I noticed was the numerous servers; the women dressed as vampires, the male as grim reapers. As for the manor itself, the floor tiles were alternating gold and white in color. Elaborate chandeliers hung from the ceiling, faux spider webs hanging from them. Realistic looking spiders dangled from the spider webs. On either side of the room, off to the side were tables with tablecloths, napkins, and plates in purple and black, with finger foods sitting on gold trays.

Next to the tables were bartenders mixing drinks at the open bar stations. Oversized smoking cauldrons containing some sort of punch were placed throughout the hall.

A slim Black man with effeminate features and dressed as a town crier rang a bell, stopping all activity. "Hear ye, hear ye, announcing Salix Pointe's most esteemed mayor, the honorable Ephraim Lovett and the first lady, the honorable Ilene Suzanne Lovett."

"Who's that?" I asked.

"Lavell Turner, the mayor's sidekick," Elisa responded. "Rumor has it he's more than that."

The man then directed our attention to the top of a dual staircase. Trumpeters played as the Lovetts appeared at the top of the stairs. In an over-the-top display, they paraded down hand-in-hand as if they were British royalty. Ilene Suzanne even performed a fake wave as if she had just been crowned Ms. America.

Even worse than their excessive presentation were their costumes. The mayor was dressed in an eighteenth-century gold and purple tailcoat with matching pants and a white lace ruffled shirt. A white colonial wig sat on top of his head.

"He looks like Beethoven, and not in a good way," Octavian remarked. "Clearly, he thinks he's a dapper geezer. Not even I would wear that atrocity."

His wife was just as overblown. Her long sleeve purple tulle ballroom gown had rhinestone embellishments with a ruffled flared skirt. The dress train clasped to the sleeves. Her purple Marie Antoinette wig brought even more to the hideous outfit. The abundant amount of purple eyeshadow, burgundy rouge, and purple lipstick made her look every bit the clown I thought she was.

To add insult to injury, all the guests were lined up in a procession to greet the Lovetts, with Lavell keeping the flow moving.

"This is beyond ridiculous," Dafari quipped. "If we didn't have a purpose for being here, I would leave right now."

"Agreed, Brother, but we need to stay on mission," Octavian noted as we got closer the mayor and his wife. "Once we finish this errant burden, we can get on with what we set out to accomplish."

"This place is huge," I said. "I hope we can find something useful."

"So do I. At least it would make this whole affair more palatable," Elisa noted in agreement.

We had finally reached the Lovetts, with them greeting Dafari and Elisa first. "Well don't you look handsome?" Ilene Suzanne remarked to Dafari, stepping closer to him.

"And Elisa, you look just divine. You need to come to our gatherings more often," said the mayor, looking squarely at her chest. The man was beyond smarmy.

Dafari spoke for both of them, standing in front of Elisa. "If invited, *we* may attend. You both know I'm not one for large gatherings. Mayor, Ilene Suzanne." He gave them both a quick nod, quickly whisking Elisa to the side.

Then it was my and Octavian's turn. The mayor looked me up and down, making me want to bathe in a vat of disinfectant. "Tasmin, you are a vision. I hope you decide to grace our little town with your presence a bit longer. You might like what we have to offer."

He made the bile rise in my throat. "Like I told you before, Mayor Lovett, my plans are still up in the air. Only time will tell."

"Indeed, Tasmin, indeed. Still, save that *fais-do-do* for me, will you?"

I simply nodded.

"Well I do hope *you* plan to stay in town for a while, Professor Jerrod," Ilene Suzanne said, touching his chest while looking at me.

"I plan to stay for as long as Tasmin wants me around," he retorted, removing her hand from his chest. “On that note, we’ll let you get back to greeting your other guests.”

“If you don’t mind, Professor Jerrod, I would like to speak with you for a moment,” Ilene Suzanne implored.

Octavian turned to me, saying, “Poppet, can you indulge me for a moment? I’ll return forthwith.”

Without a word, I walked back over to Elisa and Dafari.

“Where’s Octavian going?” Elisa asked.

“No idea. All I know is Ilene Suzanne requested his presence,” I replied, annoyed.

Dafari chuckled. “I wouldn’t worry, Tasmin. Trust me when I say Ilene Suzanne will regret trying to pull Octavian away from you.”

No sooner had he said that did we see Octavian walking back in our direction; however, there was no sign of Ilene Suzanne. I looked at Octavian, who didn’t say a word. I took it upon myself to walk over to where I saw Ilene Suzanne walk with Octavian, only to find her cowering in a corner, looking even paler than she usually looked, as if she had the life scared out of her. Not wanting to draw attention to our little group, I left her there.

Walking back to Octavian, I asked, “What did you do?”

In lieu of a response, he gave me the evilest grin reminiscent of the Grinch Who Stole Christmas. "Don't ask," was all he would say, presenting his arm for me to take. I left it alone.

For a while, we stood together talking and acting like we were enjoying the party when, in fact, we were surveying the crowd and our surroundings. Elisa wasn't picking up any thoughts from people who wanted to hurt us. Sure, some of them were hateful because they wanted to get at Octavian, Dafari, or both, but nothing to indicate they wanted us dead.

I was picking up some weird vibes. There was a lot of sexual energy all around us, and the longer we were there, the more it was increasing, but I wasn't sure why.

Just as we were about to figure out our next move, a short stubby man with a deep brown complexion and a comb-over walked up to us, his grim reaper costume and the empty tray in his hand telling us he was a server.

"Hey, Elsie and Dayfari," the little man said, completely butchering Elisa and Dafari's names. I found it funny that he actually called Dafari by his first name. Up until recently, even Elisa addressed him as Dr. Battle.

Dafari shook his head. "Good evening, Rufus," he replied, not even attempting to correct the man.

"Hi, Rufus," Elisa said. "Have you met Ms. Noreen's niece, Tasmin, and Dafari's brother, Octavian?"

"No, but it's nice to meet you, Tasmania and Octovian," he said, extending his hand to both of us. He shook mine so vigorously it felt like he was going to shake it out of the socket.

"Nice to meet you, too, Rufus. And it's Tasmin."

"That's what I said, Tasmania."

I let the error go.

"Elsie, I saw the help wanted sign you put up. You know you could have asked old Rufus for help," he said energetically, referring to himself in the third person.

"I know, Rufus, but I didn't want to bother you," she said. I could tell she was trying to let him down gently.

"No bother at all. Oh, would y'all like a drink? Lemme get y'all a drink. I'll be right back." Before we could protest, he was gone.

Octavian and I looked at Elisa. "Rufus is eccentric but harmless. He's lived here for decades. Can't get a name right to save his life, but he means well."

He quickly returned with a bottle of Dom Pérignon Rose Gold champagne. The mayor had extremely expensive tastes. Placing the tray, which now contained four champagne flutes, on a table, Rufus uncorked the bottle, poured some in the glasses, and handed one to each of us. "Oooh, wee! Elsie and Tasmania, I must say, you ladies are lookin' like a whole snack. Makes somebody wanna put cha on a plate and sop ya up with a biscuit, I tell ya!"

Dafari gave Rufus a side eye so serious I thought he would incinerate the poor man.

Octavian, on the other hand, was amused. Giving a low chuckle, he took a sip of his drink then muttered under his breath, "Old fool."

Then Rufus did something unexpected. He motioned for us to all come closer, as if he had some big secret to share. Looking around to make sure no one else was within earshot, he stated, "Don't tell nobody, but I wouldn't drink that witches brew." He looked in the direction of one of the smoking cauldrons. "After they drank that, people started wilin' out. There's a lot of freak-a-leakin' goin' on upstairs." He then handed Octavian his tray, saying, "I ain't gotta go home, but I'ma gettin' da heck up on outta heah. Elsie, I'ma see ya next week fa that interview. Bye y'all!" He was gone in a flash.

"What a strange little man," Octavian remarked.

"A strange little man who just gave us several leads," I countered.

"I concur," Octavian said.

Taking a sip of her champagne, Elisa replied, "I guess this is the part where we split up. But before we do, it would be a shame to waste such an expensive bottle of champagne."

"Elisa is right. If the mayor is going to flaunt his avarice, I, for one, am going to enjoy it," Dafari voiced in agreement. We finished the bottle of Dom Pérignon in short order.

"On the subject of drinks," I started, "Rufus mentioned the guests' behavior after drinking whatever's in those cauldrons. As he called it, a lot of freak-a-leakin'. I wonder if it's spiked."

Dafari rubbed his chin. "That's a good question, Tasmin. Perhaps we should get a sample to analyze. Elisa and I can work on procuring one."

"Good deal. Since Rufus gave us those clues, Octavian and I should start upstairs. I feel like we're the Scooby gang, splitting up to look for clues," I said, laughing. Elisa, and even Dafari, agreed.

"Oh, do you mean Scooby-Doo, the animated show on the tele with the dog who can barely talk?" Octavian asked. We all looked at him in amazement. "What?" he continued. "Tasmin kept ribbing me about not knowing any pop culture. I rather feel a kinship with that bloke Fred. His ascot is just snazzy, innit? A real thinker, that one."

We shook our heads. "Yeahhhh, come on, Fred." I said taking Octavian by the hand, leading him up the stairs to the second floor.

When we got upstairs, we took note of the floor-to-ceiling stone pillars, couches, and love seats immediately to the left and right of us. Many of the seating areas were filled with party goers, making amorous overtures toward one another. Once we passed those, we observed doors on either side of the long hallway. The muffled sounds coming from behind them gave us pause. Opening one of the doors slowly, we quickly realized the sounds were moans and screams of passion. In what appeared to be a large stateroom were several people. It was hard to tell exactly how many because bodies and limbs were all over the place.

"Just like Rufus said, a lot of freak-a-leakin'," I whispered, awestricken by what I was seeing directly in front of me. "And it's like they don't even see us. Something is definitely up with that brew."

Octavian looked on in disbelief. "This reminds me of the Ancient Roman orgies I learned about in my studies. This place is a den of iniquity."

I closed the door, moving on to the next one. What I saw made me want to vomit in my mouth. On the oversized four poster bed, I saw the mayor, Ilene Suzanne, and Lavell engaged in what looked like a human sandwich, animalistic noises coming from all three of them. I quickly closed the door.

Octavian looked mortified. “Have they no decorum?” he asked, clearly astounded by the sight. “Please remind me to throw dirt in my eyes once we get to hallowed ground, as I cannot unsee this.”

“Only if you remind me to drink a gallon of Holy water,” I pleaded.

Octavian nodded. “You have my word.”

“Since the mayor is otherwise occupied, we should see if we can get into his office. No telling what we can find in there.”

“Excellent idea, Tasmin. Best to head there while the opportunity is presenting itself.”

We went back downstairs; saw Dafari and Elisa keeping an eye on the other guests.

“Back so soon?” Elisa asked. “What happened?”

“Words cannot describe the debauchery we beheld,” said Octavian, clearly disgusted.

Dafari gave a slight smile. “No description necessary.”

“Where’s the mayor’s office?” I asked both Elisa and Dafari. “I want to check it out since he’s…busy.”

Elisa laughed. “I don’t even want to know.” She pointed. “It should be down that hall, make a left, and the last room at the end of the hall on your right. I remember that because we visited the mayor’s office when I was a child, way before Mayor Lovett arrived in Salix Pointe."

"Okay, guys. We'll be back. If you see the mayor, Ilene Suzanne, or Lavell, let us know so we can get out of there."

"Will do, and be careful," Dafari replied.

CHAPTER 23:
DAFARI

Octavian and Tasmin were off sleuthing, looking for whatever evidence they could dig up on the ever-depraved Mayor Lovett. I may have been a half-demon, but at least I had morals, unlike Salix Pointe's oily mayor. On occasion, Noreen and I would talk about the mayor and his shenanigans. She shared with me that she believed he stole the election by some nefarious means, although she could never prove it. It would not have surprised me. Hopefully, Octavian and Tasmin would find something worthwhile.

I turned my attention back to Elisa. An Argentine tango, a form of the tango danced by African immigrants and Europeans in nineteenth century Buenos Aires, was playing, and while I knew we needed to stay on task, I also knew Elisa and I needed to blend in. As I brought her onto the dance floor, I appreciated the complexity, fluidity, and improvisational nature of this variation of the tango, the sensual elements of the dance speaking to me. While I was aware that Elisa was light on her feet, she impressed me with her ability to match me step-for-step, move-for-move. Then again, perhaps I shouldn't have been surprised, knowing what a sensual being she was in general. The dress she chose for tonight's occasion spoke to that.

The way Elisa's dress hugged every delicious, full-figured curve caused a visceral reaction in me so strong I almost couldn't control it. Right then and there, I wanted to physically couple with her in ways only married people should. I touched the lowest part of her back, causing her breath to hitch.

"Dafari, what did you do to me?" she asked, confused by what she was feeling.

"Only giving you a small sample of the emotions going through me at the moment. Don't think I'm unaware as to why you're wearing a dress so...seductive, Elisa."

"Dafari, I wasn't..."

I put my finger to her lips to quiet her. "All I will say, my alluring little enchantress, is if you call me to your bed when we get home, be prepared for a very...long...night. You already know I'm more than capable." She swallowed hard in her throat, the look in my eyes telling her they held no lie. Her reaction made me think back to the night after I gave her a crash course in training...

After my attack on Elisa, she still refused to speak to me, even on the ride home. While her anger was in some small way justified, she needed to get it through that stubborn head of hers that we were at a crucial point where the enemy could strike anytime and anywhere. No one was going to walk up to her directly and say, 'Hello, Elisa Hunte, I'm going to attack you now'. We were way past baby steps and easing into her new reality was not an option.

When we arrived back home, the only time she even remotely acknowledged my presence was when she was looking for Tasmin. We found Tasmin and Octavian in the gym in a very compromising position. Maybe my baby brother was further along than I thought in his pursuit of the good doctor.

I was resigned to Elisa being angry with me, at least for the remainder of the day. She'd get over it. After taking my shower, I was set to relax alone for the rest of the evening. I had gotten no further than putting on my boxers when I heard Elisa's thoughts. Whether she had accidentally forgotten to guard her thoughts, or purposely wanted me to hear them, I couldn't be sure, but they came through, loud and clear.

"I can't believe him! Look at all these bruises! I swear if Dafari Battle was in front of me right now, I'd slap the mess out of him."

So you wished it, Elisa, so it shall be. I materialized in her room, stood directly in front of her, and looked at her clad in nothing but a towel. "Prove it." I thought she was more bravado than anything else until she pulled her arm back and slapped me with the full force of her might. My eyes became as small as slits, as I held back my anger for her sake." If you know what's good for you, you won't let that happen again."

Elisa had a sneer on her face, no fear in her eyes. Just when I thought she couldn't hit me any harder, she did, causing my neck to snap back. I looked at her with red eyes, her brown ones looking back at me.

"What?" she asked, hands on her full hips.

"Did you get all your frustration out?"

She ignored me, instead giving me her back, walking away.

I hated being rebuffed. Grabbing her by the arm, I attempted to turn her around. None too pleased, she balled up her fist, swinging on me. This time I was ready for her, blocking her hits and grabbing her arm. Pulling her close to me, I kissed her passionately. She didn't resist, but instead kissed me back with a ferocity that matched her fighting skills. Backing her up to the bed, I ripped her towel from her body, kissing all her bruises, seen and unseen. Then I gave her what she wanted with a passion she had never experienced before with any man on the earth plane. She felt all seven...years...of pent-up...frustration in each thrust of my pelvis, and I felt hers as she matched me thrust for thrust, digging her nails into my back. I knew she was mine when, as her body released, she called out my name. I already had her mind and her soul. Now I had her body, as well.

As the music stopped and our dance ended, I leaned down, giving Elisa a long, lingering kiss, for all to see. It caught the attention of more than a few of the guests. While I had admonished Tasmin and Elisa earlier after Tasmin retaliated against those who had disrespected them, I found myself having my own moment of antipathy. Neither one of them deserved to be demeaned. As long as Elisa was with me, I would not allow it.

"What was that for?" Elisa asked, a flummoxed look on her face.

I smiled down at her, replying, "Do I need a reason?"

"Sometimes you really surprise me, Dafari."

"Good. Would you like another drink?"

"Yes. Please," she replied.

Nodding to her, I then walked over to one of the open bar stations, requesting two glasses of champagne. When I turned around, I saw Elisa talking to someone. Adour-Nuru Citlali Daystar, an attorney and one of Salix Pointe's life-long residents. A Black Taino Cherokee mix, from what I gathered, his family migrated from Oklahoma after they refused to be made to walk the Trail of Tears. Like the Chadwick and Hunte families, the Daystar family was one of the founding clans of Salix Pointe, and, as such, had considerable standing in the community and was well-respected.

"Attorney Daystar, nice to see you," I said, handing Elisa her champagne.

"You as well, Dr. Battle. I was just complimenting Ms. Hunte on how beautiful she looks this evening; no disrespect to you."

"None taken, and she does look quite beautiful. I'm surprised to see you here. Social gatherings usually are not your forte."

"No, they're not. However, it is customary for a member of my family to make an appearance at all major social affairs. Unfortunately, for the jubilee, I drew the short straw," he said with a chuckle. "If I may be so bold, I could say the same of you. This is the first time since you've arrived in Salix Pointe that I've seen you at the jubilee. But I can understand since you have such a lovely companion to escort you."

I never had a reason to take issue with Attorney Daystar in the past, but if he kept looking at Elisa as if I wasn't standing here, that could easily change.

Elisa chimed in. "I wasn't going to attend either, but Dafari convinced me. He can be very…persuasive."

"I noticed that public display of affection earlier. Are you two a couple?" Daystar asked.

I put my arm around her waist, pulling her closer to me. "Yes, we are."

Although she didn't show it on her face, the thought Elisa sent to me showed how much she was bewildered by my sudden declaration. "We are? Would have been nice if you told me."

"I thought my kissing you in public for the world to see told you that," I sent back to her.

Attorney Daystar smiled in a way that gave me pause. "Kudos to you both. You're a lucky man."

"Yes, I am, without a doubt."

As I was standing there, I was almost blown over by the booming voice of my father in my head. "Well now, did I hear correctly? You and the café owner? My, how being thrown together can change things in such a short time. Was that coincidence? I think not."

"Where are you and why are you here?" I asked.

"Very good questions, indeed, my progeny. In response to your first question, I'm in the hedge maze at the back of the manor. As to your second, if you really want answers, you know where to find me. Come alone and don't keep me waiting too long."

My father had put me in quite the quandary. He would not have revealed himself to me unless he had a very good reason. However, I didn't want to leave Elisa alone. Octavian and Tasmin had yet to return, but my gut was telling me that if my father truly had information he wanted to share, I needed to leave now. I did something that I hoped I wouldn't regret later on.

"Excuse us for a second, will you?" I said to Daystar, taking Elisa by her hand, moving far enough away so he couldn't hear us.

"I need to take care of something urgently, and I need you to not ask any questions." I said to Elisa.

"What's going on, Dafari?" she queried, a look of incertitude on her face.

"Elisa, I said not to ask any questions. I just need you to trust me on this."

She now looked worried. "Can you at least tell me where you're going?"

I put my hands on her shoulders. "It's best you not know, Elisa. Look, if I need you, I will call out to you. In the meantime, I need you to stay here where it's safe and wait for Tasmin and Octavian to return. Can you do that for me?"

"Do I have a choice?" she asked rhetorically, crossing her arms in front of her chest.

"You already know the answer to that. Now come," I said walking over to Daystar. "Attorney Daystar, while I am reluctant to ask, until my brother returns, I need you to keep an eye on Elisa. Don't let her out of your sight, not even for a moment."

"You have my word, Dr. Battle. I will not let her out of my sight," he said, all the while looking directly at Elisa.

"Yes," I simply said. I kissed Elisa one last time before walking out the door.

When I arrived at the hedge maze, my father was indeed there, in all his glory. Dressed in an expensive three-piece midnight blue tuxedo with contrasting black lapels and buttons on the jacket and vest, and matching custom-tailored pants, Father commanded authority. Knowing him, the white dress shirt, silk black tie, and leather shoes were of the highest quality. Like me, he tended to wear his wavy hair cascading over his shoulders. Save for the difference in our skin tones and the gray streaks in his hair, I was my father's spitting image.

"So, you decided to show up," he said.

I kept a healthy distance from him. "You said you had answers. Why would I *not* show up?"

"Is that the only reason you're here? I mean, you don't call, you don't write."

I was becoming impatient. "Enough, Father. You're the one who escaped and came to Salix Pointe but hid your presence from me. The only reason I knew was because Octavian told me."

"Of course, that Dudley Do-Right brother of yours would have told you," he spat. "I see he's no worse for wear after the gutting I gave him. More's the pity. It was fortunate you had a healer on hand."

"Fortunate, indeed," I growled. "Can we get to the point of this tête-à-tête? I need to get back."

"Back to Elisa, I presume. Ah, my wayward son. Teetering the thin line between good and... not so good. Still trying to live up to what your mother wanted you to be," he taunted.

I moved a bit closer to him, "I'm living up to whom I want to be. Mine is the only opinion that matters."

"You keep telling yourself that lie, Dafari. You may be able to fool all those, well, fools, but I see you, Son. You cared about what your, shall I say, surrogate mother, Noreen Chadwick thought."

"Keep her name out of your mouth," I hissed.

He grinned. "I meant no disrespect to the irreproachable Ms. Chadwick. Truth be told, she treated you far better than your own mother. If it eases your tortured soul, she regarded you as the son she never had," he said mockingly.

My eyes turned red. "Is that why you killed her? Jealousy?"

"Think, Son, what reason would I have to kill her?" he asked, chuckling. "I may not be father of the year, but why would I get rid of the one person who saw nothing but good in my only son?"

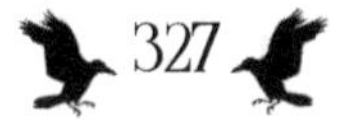

My eyes returned to normal. “If not you, then who?”

“We’ll get to that in due course. Meanwhile, back to you and your incessant need to please those you care about. You care what that angel whelp of a brother thinks. You even care what the erstwhile doctor thinks of you. Good job befriending her, by the way. You might be able to glide in there since your brother hasn’t seemed to make much headway with her.”

“That’s more your style, Father, not mine.”

“More my brother’s style, actually. Or should I say your uncle? Step-father? Ah, no matter. Most of all, you care what the thick and tasty baker thinks about you. I couldn’t fathom why you would settle in this vapid little town and as a pet doctor no less,” he said, looking at the well-manicured nails on his left hand. He paused then looked at me. “But, upon further reflection, I realized it’s because of the delectable tart maker. Now that’s one human who might even give me a reason to stay in town. It may have only been in her dreams, but don't forget, I've seen Elisa naked. I should have sampled her flesh, and other parts of her, when I had the chance. I smelled her fear...and her arousal. It was an intoxicating mixture. It would have been so easy for me to slide between those thick, luscious thighs of hers, and give her exactly what she feared, and yet, desired."

"You will never go near her nor lay another hand on her again," I sneered.

"Or else what?" he said, stepping closer to me, eye to eye.

"I will end you," I replied, no fear in my tone.

"Ah, Son, even on your best day, you could never get the better of me. Our last battle proved that. Neither you nor your weak brother has the skill to conquer me." I knew my eyes had again turned red. I felt myself bulking up. "Then again, maybe a woman can bring out strengths even you weren't aware of. One last question; tell me, Dafari," he said, whispering in my ear, "Now that you've actually been with her on this plane, does she taste as sweet as she looks? You know what they say, the blacker the berry..."

That was it. I was done with his taunting. I punched him hard, my balled-up fist connecting squarely with his jaw. He fell to the ground, stunned. I didn't give him a chance to recover. I grabbed him by his lapel with one hand, the other continuing to connect with his jaw, over and over and over. And yet, all he did was laugh, a laugh so maniacal it chilled even me to the bone. Why was he so calm? Why was he not fighting me? My father was a sadistic individual, so why was he taking a masochistic beating from his own son? What was he up to?

"Fight me," I yelled.

He would not. He let me continue to pummel him until I tired of the beating. I stood over him, looking in disbelief.

"Feel better now?" he asked, through a bloodied and battered mouth.

"Why would you not fight me, Father? You baited me; why not finish what you started?"

"Because one thing I always sought to teach you was to choose your battles wisely. You're fighting the wrong person. Think, my son, think. You know me. You yourself said Noreen Chadwick's mode of death was not my style, neither was the death of your little tartlette's grandmother, nor her parents, for that matter."

"If not you, then who?"

He laughed deep in his chest. "Now what fun would that be for me to just tell you? I will give you a hint, though; the obvious choice is not always the correct choice. What's good is not always good, and what's evil is not always evil. You'd do well to remember that, fruit of my loins."

I was still holding him by his lapel. "What does that even mean?"

"Figure it out," he replied, goading me.

"Well you did try to kill Elisa and Tasmin," I retorted.

"Did I? You see, my son, I didn't actually harm the witches, just scared them. And even though I relished in their sweet, luscious, delectable fear," he said, accentuating every word, "My actions served a greater purpose; the evolution of their powers. You're welcome, by the way. Keep this anger. It will serve you well shortly."

With his parting words, he disappeared, leaving me standing there alone, more perplexed than ever.

"Octavian, to me, now!"

CHAPTER 24:

TASMIN

Octavian and I followed Elisa's directions and located the mayor's office quickly. You couldn't miss it because of the extravagant name plate on the door that read '*The Most Honorable Mayor Ephraim Lovett*'.

I pointed to the name plate. "That's just extra."

"He is rather egocentric, but this lavish jubilee speaks to that," Octavian said.

I noticed the door to the left of the mayor's office with a **SECURITY** name plate on it. Something told me to check it out first. I tried the door, but it was locked. I had learned to move many things with my telekinesis, but I had never tried unlocking a door. There was no time like the present. I thought about the lock turning to the open position and smiled when I heard the locking mechanism move. I tried the doorknob, and the door opened.

"Why you little criminal," Octavian said, smiling from ear to ear.

"When you're a kid and you forget your house keys at home as much as I did, you learn a few things. My parents and I would all leave at the same time, and they would always lock up, so having my keys wasn't the first thing on my mind. They would get so annoyed with me because I would have to call one of them to come home from work to let me in. I eventually figured out a way to get into the house without them knowing. They were none the wiser."

"My, you are a sneaky little minx. I learn something new about you every day."

"Funny, I can't say the same about you," I retorted, staring up at him.

He smiled before saying, "In due time, poppet, in due time."

Once inside the security room, we observed the numerous monitors on the wall, each labeled according to the room where a camera was placed. I studied the screens, realizing that most of the property was being surveilled and recorded, including all of the upstairs bedrooms. I even recognized the one that Octavian compared to an Ancient Roman orgy. The only room that wasn't being monitored was the one where the mayor, Ilene Suzanne, and Lavell were holed up. So the mayor was recording his guests. One could only wonder why.

"Well this is a sticky wicket. It appears the illustrious mayor is a voyeur," Octavian said.

"Straight up freak is more like it," I countered. "Let's go to his office. We may not have much time left."

After we left the room, I made sure to lock it back then I opened the mayor's door. I turned on a standing stained-glass office lamp then Octavian closed the door behind us. The office was a large space with an oversized antique mahogany office desk and high-back leather executive office chair in front of us, a mahogany wall-to-wall bookshelf to our left, two fancy arm chairs in front of the desk, and a couch against the wall near the office door. A huge portrait of the mayor and his wife, dressed like they were relics from the antebellum south, hung above the couch.

"Octavian, please watch the door while I check things out. I know Elisa and Dafari will let us know if they see the mayor ahead of time, but we don't want anyone else catching us either."

"Sure thing, Tasmin. Just make haste."

I figured the best place to start was the mayor's desk. Of course, it was locked. Like I let that stop me. Checking the largest drawer allowed me to hit pay dirt. I found a book with an upside-down pentagram on it. It seemed the mayor had his own Book of Shadows. I took it out the draw, placing it on the desk. When I opened it, the first thing I saw was a mind control spell. The next page contained a drink recipe used to decrease one's inhibitions, more so than alcohol. Most likely the recipe for the witches' brew.

Thank you for the warning, Rufus, I thought.

Taking out my cell phone, I snapped pictures of both spells. The next spell was particularly interesting. It was a spell to trap a disembodied spirit. Clipped to the page were slave papers for a man named Afolabi, as well as a piece of paper with the same spell written out with two names; Afolabi and Disempsi. Disemspi was Ilene Suzanne's cat. Some poor soul was trapped inside that mangy creature's body. Maybe Elisa and I could figure out some way to free him. Like the other two spells, I photographed everything. The mayor being in possession of his own book of spells confirmed why he was so bent on buying the bookstore.

I put the Book of Shadows back where I found it, moving on to the middle drawer. In it, I found a ledger with names, dates, dollar amounts, and some notes next to each entry. I actually recognized some of the names in the ledger. It looked as if the mayor was blackmailing some of the townspeople, which was probably how he got elected in the first place.

"Tasmin, I don't mean to alarm you, but the mayor and Lavell are coming this way. The mayor said something about a silent alarm being tripped."

Darn, I should have known this was too easy. "What do you mean they're coming?" I asked, hurriedly putting away the ledger and locking the desk. "Why didn't Dafari and Elisa warn us? I don't hear anything. How is it that you can— " I was rambling.

"We can ask Dafari and Elisa about that later," he interrupted. "As for me being able to hear them, as an archangel, I have superior hearing. Unfortunately, they're close enough now that we're effectively trapped. Tasmin, do you trust me?"

"Yes, I do trust you, but what does that have to do with—"

"No time to explain," he said, cutting me off.

He took off his jacket, tie, and shirt, tossing them on the couch, causing me to raise an eyebrow. I couldn't help but notice his muscular chest and abs. When we trained, he always had on a tee shirt, so I never got to see the full effect of his muscular physique. If the situation wasn't so dire, I might have enjoyed the view more. He then knocked everything off the mayor's deck.

"Octavian! What the heck?" I whispered.

"They'll be here in a few minutes. They're going to the security office first to assess the threat. Just play along."

He sat on the desk, reaching out his hand to me. When I gave him my hand, he pulled me close, and before I knew it, we were on the desk, me on top of him. The way I imagined it in my head, we probably looked like the book cover of some cheesy romance novel.

"This is starting to become a habit," I said, thinking back to our first sparing session.

He chuckled. "I rather like having you this close."

"You've made that abundantly clear, Octavian." I looked in his eyes, eyes so dark it was like peering into two black pools. "So what's the plan?"

"Now I kiss you, if you allow me to."

"Now you want to ask permission? You didn't the last time you kissed me. I should have hexed you then," I teased.

"Now what fun would that be?" he said, a twinkle in his black eyes. "May I kiss you, Tasmin?"

I didn't answer, but instead kissed him, catching him completely off guard. As our lips locked, it was as if he had completely let his guard down, his emotional flood gates opening all at once. Like the teapot that smacked him in the face, his unadulterated feelings smacked me upside the head. The more I deepened our kiss, the more I could feel his lust, desire, and passion, for sure, but I felt something else…genuine affection. Now it was my turn to be caught off guard.

I finally heard the mayor and Lavell coming toward us, opening the door to the security office. Octavian broke our kiss long enough to say, "The mayor is watching. He's wondering how we got in here, but he's amused that we went to all this trouble just to be alone. He thinks we drank the witches' brew."

"So we need to make this look good," I replied, kissing him again.

I felt Octavian's hands on my back, his fingers gently running up and down my spine then moving lower. His hands slid beneath the back of my dress, hands grasping my hips, pulling me closer to him. When he did, that part of him that made him male rose to the occasion. He groaned low in his throat, his grip on me tightening. As Octavian moved his hips in an upward motion, his maleness stroked, through my lace boy shorts, that one part of my anatomy that was only meant for pleasure. I couldn't help but let out a moan, never having experienced anything like that before. That seemed to arouse him even more, his movements becoming more vigorous. The way the skirt of my dress was covering us, and the way I was straddling him, it was easy to portray the illusion of engaging in the ultimate carnal act.

Octavian played it up for all it was worth. He continued his upward thrust, hitting his mark every…single…time until my body betrayed itself, my lady parts doing somersaults of satisfaction. Octavian kissed me passionately, holding me in his arms until my body relaxed.

I heard the door to the security office close, the mayor talking to Lavell in a loud voice. "My, my, my. Who knew Tasmin had so much fire in her? I'd gladly trade places with Octavian for one night with her. I would love to see what her salad tastes like after she's had a long run. I'm going to enjoy watching that video later. Come on, Lavell. I don't know about you, but I'm ready for round two," he remarked, laughing as the two men walked away.

The mayor was such a vile, poor excuse for a human being. I immediately felt sick to my stomach hearing the disgusting things he said. I looked at Octavian and for a quick second, I thought his eyes flashed red, but then chalked it up to my imagination.

I sat up, still straddling Octavian. "We need to get going," I said climbing off of him.

"You're right," he concurred. Rising from the desk, he put his clothes back on.

I smoothed out my dress then worked on fixing my locs. As I moved most of my locs to hang over my left shoulder, I felt Octavian come up behind me.

Wrapping his arms around me, he placed light kisses down the right side of my neck. "You're not playing fair," I giggled.

"I beg to differ. All's fair in love and war, poppet," he stated.

I turned around, pulled him down by the front of shirt, kissing him once more. When I looked down, I saw the outline in his pants showing that he was still at full attention. "You might want to take care of that."

"What do you have in mind?" he asked, pulling me into an embrace.

"Not what you're thinking," I said, playfully pushing him away. "Think of something that's a turn off, like Ilene Suzanne."

"Nicely done, Tasmin. That did the trick."

"Anytime, Octavian." I laughed, winking at him. "Well, we didn't find anything useful to implicate the mayor in the deaths, or whether or not he's the one targeting Elisa and me; however, the information we *did* find is very helpful. Mind control; drugging people, albeit by magical means; blackmail; spirit trapping. This guy is a piece of work."

Octavian turned up his nose in disgust. "Yes, Mayor Lovett is a filthy mongrel."

I started for the door. "We should get back to the others."

"Tasmin, wait," Octavian said, stopping me by taking my hand. "When tonight is over, we need to talk."

I looked up at him. "I agree, we do, and we will; after this night is over."

"Just one more thing," Octavian said, waving his hand. Suddenly all the lights went out, leaving us in complete darkness, and I heard popping sounds coming from the security room.

"What was that?"

"I sent an electromagnetic pulse throughout the manor. It will disrupt all things electrical and will erase all of the footage from tonight."

"Let me guess; yet another one of your many angel powers."

"Indeed. A place such as this will definitely have a generator, which should turn on in about one minute." No sooner had Octavian said it, did the generator fire up. "Now come, poppet, let's get out of here."

As we found our way back to the great hall, some of the guests were leaving, I assume their party vibe killed by Octavian's otherworldly power outage. While it only lasted about sixty seconds, it was enough for some to call it a night. We looked around, finally spotting Elisa, but Dafari was nowhere in sight. There was, however, someone familiar to me standing next to her.

"Elisa, what happened? We got caught by the mayor. Luckily, we were able to…improvise our way out of the situation." I hoped to The One Most High that I wasn't blushing.

Octavian had a sly grin on his face.

"What? Honestly, I didn't see him. He must have used the backstairs because he didn't come this way."

"I can vouch for that. The mayor definitely did not come in our direction," said the tall man with the mocha colored complexion, short wavy hair, and green eyes.

"And you are?" Octavian asked suspiciously.

"Adour-Nuru Citali Daystar. Pleased to meet you," he said, extending his hand to Octavian.

"He's my attorney's, Portia Achebe, law partner," I chimed in, trying to lessen the awkwardness of the moment.

"Octavian Jerrod, brother to Dafari Battle." He shook Adour-Nuru's hand, but I could tell it was reluctantly.

It was if he was staking claim for Dafari since he wasn't here to do it himself. One thing we didn't need right now was a pissing contest.

"Elisa, where *is* Dafari?" I asked.

Looking nervous, she replied, "I don't know. He left a while ago, saying he needed to take care of something urgently, telling Adour-Nuru not to let me out of his sight. He hasn't been back since."

"That is odd, indeed. Something must definitely be amiss," noted Octavian. Suddenly, he had a strange look on his face. "Mr. Daystar, if you will excuse us, I must confer with Tasmin and Elisa…in private," he said, dismissing Adour-Nuru. When he was out of earshot, Octavian said something that had Elisa and me on edge. "Dafari just called out to me. He needs us, now."

CHAPTER 25:
OCTAVIAN

I raced to the hedges where my brother was with Tasmin and Elisa on my heels. Dafari's call was one of distress, and it put my nerves on end. Once there, I found Dafari walking a hole in the earth. He was battle bulked, red-eyes and looked as if he was ready to kill someone. He was pacing as if he were a caged wild animal. His clothes were disheveled, hair unruly and his knuckles were bruised.

"What happened?" I asked him.

"My father," he growled.

"What about him?"

"He was here."

"Here?" Elisa and Tasmin said at the same time.

"Yes, here. He was at the manor, and as usual, full of his head games," he said angrily. "Only this time, he said something that made more sense than I would have liked it to." Dafari took a deep breath as I went on guard. I glanced around the expansive, well-manicured backyard then back at my brother. "Octavian, I think Mother and your father—"

Before the words could leave his mouth, the wind whipped around us, causing the hedges to sway violently back and forth. A small slither of a rip formed in the middle of the air before us, and like someone had parted a curtain, out stepped…my parents. Shock resonated within me as well as confusion. Resignation caused my gut to twist in knots as an overwhelming sense of sadness cloaked me like a soiled blanket.

"What in the world…" I heard Tasmin say behind me as if she was in awe of what had just happened.

Elisa all but gasped loudly.

Whereas Dafari and I had to go through the veil with shadows, my parental units, being full-blooded high-archs, could come directly through the veil, no pretense needed. And just like Demon Daddy, my father was built battle ready. He was well over six feet—two inches taller than both Dafari and me—with butterscotch skin, eyes so startingly black that they gave people pause, and a stern look on his face that showed why he was a general. His tightly coiled hair, like mine, sat in a low tapered cut that put his handsome features front and center.

He was dressed in all black from head-to-toe but dressed down like a normal human male. He stood, feet shoulder width apart, arms at his side. His black shirt could barely be seen under the leather jacket he had on, black denim jeans fit him to the letter, and the black combat boots he had on his feet showed he hadn't come to fraternize as a guest.

My mother, in all her regal beauty, stood like the Dahomey warrior she was. Skin as rich as the darkest chocolate, her long ropey braids hung down her back. She was taller than the average woman, standing at five-ten. She was thick in the hips and backside, slim in the waist with plenty of breasts to match, but she was as toned and fit as my father. She, too, was a general. Dressed similarly to my father, something told me she hadn't come to mingle either.

"What are you doing here?" Dafari asked her before I could.

She turned cool eyes to him and said, "Nice to see you after sixty years, too, Son," she said, a bit of sarcasm in her tone.

He grunted but didn't verbally respond. He and my father exchanged terse nods and nothing more.

"Hello, Mother. I came looking for you," I said dryly. "I assumed Azazel had done something to you. Your flat had been tossed, and you were nowhere in sight. I thought you were in dire straits, but you look just fine and dandy. Go figure."

She looked at me, studied me then turned her nose up as if something had offended her senses. "You speak in a tone that suggests you're accusing me of something, Octavian."

"I haven't accused you of a bloody thing," I said, my voice just as distrusting as hers was cold.

"You're cavorting with the likes of those kind now?" she asked, nodding at Tasmin and Elisa who had been standing silently behind Dafari and me. "You have the stench of witch all over you, both of you," she said jerking her head in my brother's direction. "I expect no less from that one," she continued, pointing at Dafari, then back to me, "but from you? Didn't I raise you better?"

"That's right, Mother," Dafari growled. "Get your jabs and low blows in early. I didn't ask to be born half-caste. *You* made the decision to marry my father." My brother's words had come out more like a snarl.

"I can't tell you how long I've regretted it," she said.

"Me or the marriage to my father?" he asked accusatorily.

"That's enough," my father's booming voice echoed. "We don't have time for petty family squabbles."

"Tasmin and Elisa, meet my parents; arch-angel Michael, my father, and my mother…" Deciding to cut through all the red tape, I cut my eyes at the man whom I looked identical to then asked, "Why?"

"Why what?" Father asked.

"Why did you do this?" I asked, voice louder than I had intended.

"It is something you wouldn't understand," he sneered.

"Try me," I snapped.

He glanced behind me and Dafari to where Elisa and Tasmin were. "They are a ticking time bomb," he said. "Their entire bloodline can cause catastrophes that would end humankind as we know it. Before now, they have been easy to contain, but this town has made their bloodline more powerful than they already were. For the greater good of mankind, I did what needed to be done."

Dafari shook his head then spat on the ground. "Forgive me for my bluntness, High-Arch Michael, but that is utter bullshit. You killed a woman who had done nothing but bring good into this world," he yelled emphatically. "And what about Amabelle Nall-Hunte, her son Duma and his wife, Akasha? For the five years I knew Mama Nall, she was just as kind and as sweet as Ms. Noreen—"

"I've no desire to stand here and listen to you wax poetic about these women," Mother cut in. "We did what had to be done, and we will not stand here and be chastised by our own children who wouldn't know or understand—"

"Stop telling us what we don't or won't understand," I spat. "We understand just fine the dynamics of right and wrong! We can easily conceptualize that we can save humanity and not kill the innocent at the same time! You did not have to do this!"

"That alone proves to us you don't understand as well as you think you do, Son," Father barked. "If you did, then you would know that sometimes, even the innocent have a price to pay."

"That is complete and utter—"

"Bullshit," Dafari cut in, saying what I wouldn't have so bluntly.

"You killed my grandmother?" I heard to the left of me. "My parents?"

Up until that moment, I had forgotten she and Tasmin were still behind us. I had been so focused on confronting my parents that all else got lost.

"Why?" she asked, trying to get around Dafari who had turned to better keep her at bay.

"I was ten," she cried. "Ten...you took them away from me. I was just a child. A child! What could they have done?"

"It is precisely what *could have* been done that we did what we had to do," Father said. "You must understand the magnitude of what could happen with you in the wrong hands."

"They never did one bad thing to anyone," Elisa shouted. "My parents helped whoever, whenever. Mama Nall and Ms. Noreen were saints!"

The pain in her voice matched the pain I fought hard to hide since my suspicions had surfaced about my parents' involvement in the death of Noreen Chadwick. In the same breath, I noticed the winds got more violent as drops of rain hit my face. Elisa, her bracelet glowing, was trying with all she had to get to around Dafari to confront my parents. Who they were be damned, she wanted a confrontation. Anger ruled her emotions, and I couldn't say I blamed her. However, I knew she was no match against two high-archs.

"With the blood of Nephilim," Mother shouted.

"Your markers are too strong! And don't think for one minute that you can't be used for all manner of evils," Father echoed.

Elisa screamed with rage. The tips of her fingers glowed and crackled with lightning like electricity. Dafari was still placed strategically between her and our mother. I heard him speaking to her but couldn't readily pick up on what he was saying. My mind snapped to Tasmin. I turned my eyes to her to see she was standing statue still. I couldn't tell if she was crying or if the rain falling made it appear as if she was. Her arms were at her side, fingers splayed apart as if she couldn't move them if she wanted to. Her eyes were cold and hard. Her bracelet glowed just as bright as Elisa's.

"What gave you the right to do that?" she asked, eyes on my father as she spoke. Her voice was so calm, it was alarming.

I felt a chill run up my spine.

"What gave us the right?" Mother asked through snarled teeth. "What gave us the right?" she repeated again, voice rising an octave with each syllable she spoke. "How dare you speak to us with such insolence, you witch."

Unlike my brother, I hadn't placed myself between Tasmin and Mother. Dark portents were in the air, and I knew what was about to happen before it actually happened. Tasmin's hands shot forward and a burst of energy, the size of basketballs slammed into my mother's chest. The impact knocked my mother's shoulders back, dazing her, which only seemed to rile her anger further. To the right of her, the palms of Elisa's hands glowed with fire that she sent into my mother's abdomen. Mother stumbled backwards, clutched her stomach, but she didn't fall. Her head jerked up and I saw she was in full arch power as her eyes glowed white. Lightning crackled like a whip across the sky as thunder shook the ground.

I jumped in front of Tasmin to try and block my mother's strike, but I was too late. My father's hand jutted forward. His force of motion knocked me into the hedges to the left. I heard Tasmin scream as I hit the ground with a hard thud.

I scrambled to my feet, shocked that my father actually struck me. I jumped up in time to see Tasmin flying one way and Elisa the other. Just like Dafari and I would protect Tasmin and Elisa with our lives, my father made no bones about protecting my mother just the same. Once Tasmin hit the ground, my mother reached over her shoulders and pulled her flaming swords out. She gave the grips a full swirl in her hands, making the flames appear as if they were the swords' wings before advancing on Tasmin.

I didn't have time to think about the fact I was about to attack a millenniums old high-arch angel who also happened to be my mother. She was going after Tasmin, intent to inflict great bodily harm or even death. I called my weapons to me; two handheld bec-de-corbins of pure light energy. They were made of a new magnesium alloy as light as aluminum, but as strong as titanium and had been passed down to me by my uncle; High-Arch Gabriel. To the naked human eye, it looked like the modified head of a hammer with a spike mounted on top of a long pole.

I made a leaping run then went down into a one knee slide to block my mother's blades from coming down into Tasmin's gut. Her swords clashed against mine and she yelled out a battle cry that stilled the night. She made a short retreat while allowing her swords to slide off mine so that she was free to attack. She moved with the grace of the skilled warrior she was.

I had to quickly maneuver out of her swinging range while still protecting Tasmin. While she had been training, and doing quite well, she was no match for my mother. And if I stayed on my knee, I wouldn't be either. I needed to get Tasmin out of her line of fire. As if he had been reading my mind, Dafari came running across the yard. He yanked Tasmin up by her hand then spun her around. He thrust his hand forward and she went sailing in the air, landing softly into a clearing next to a fallen Elisa. I caught a glance of my father bolting through the other side of the mazed hedge as he chased my brother.

The brief distraction gave me a chance to get to my feet. My mother gave a running leap forward then lunged at me with her dominant leg. Her swords aimed at my chest and neck, I brought my weapons up into a cross to block her strike. She then gave a beat attack. She rapped her blades against mine to force me to open up a line of attack. I countered by forcibly blocking her, beating her blades with the forte of my own.

Since I was cherub, I'd been taught to use weapons. It was what all children who were born of high-archs were taught, and I was sure in any other setting, she and my father would have been proud of my show of skill. Tonight, however, there would be no congratulatory words.

Out of my peripheral, I saw Dafari going toe-to-toe with my father. Hand-to-hand combat as if they were mortal enemies as opposed to family. Tasmin and Elisa were right there with him. Elisa tried to attack my father from the right, but he was too fast, too skilled. When she tried to distract him so Dafari could attack him from the rear, father clapped his arms together in the shape of a cross then brought them down. The force of his power knocked her backwards. Her back slammed into hedges. Her leg bent in an awkward manner.

"Elisa," Tasmin screamed then raged after my father like she'd gone mad.

Wrought iron chairs scattered about the yard flew at my father's head. At the same time, Tasmin tried to use her power balls to defend herself to no avail. Just like with Elisa, she was no match. When she tried to swing at him, he grabbed her wrist, pushed her elbow up, causing her to scream in pain then shoved her backwards. She too went airborne again and landed on her face. She wasn't moving. Fury coiled in my guts as I yelled her name. I could feel her pain, her agony. Her wrist had been broken when she landed. Her body's pressure points were pulsing as she groaned out in pain.

Dafari's angry growl lit up the night as he pounced on my Father. Growing up, I'd never seen my father be anything but cordial to my brother. He wasn't overly affectionate in any way, but he wasn't that way with me either. He was stern and fatherly in the way beings of his ilk were. There weren't hugs, there were pats on the back. He told us he loved us freely, but he never treated me better than he did Dafari. To see them fighting as such pained me.

However, not more than being in an all-out battle with the being who birthed me. I couldn't go to Tasmin because I had to keep my mother at bay. Even in the middle of the fight, I still couldn't wrap my mind around the fact I was fighting my mother. Now she had me in a bind. She'd forced one of my blades from a high line to a low one while crossing my center. It left one of her blades free to gut me. I was at her mercy.

An unlikely savior stepped in just as Mother's blade sliced through my shirt. "Now, now… is that any way to treat your son? What a horrible mother you are."

Mother was so shocked, whatever she'd been about to say got stuck in her throat. He'd grabbed the sword she had intended to impale me with. Before I could react, he rammed a meaty palm into my mother's chest and sent her tumbling backwards so violently that she rolled over her head, making her neck bend at an awkward angle.

There was no need for me to think he was on my side. I knew better. Even with that knowledge, when he headbutted me and gave a leg sweep that put me on my back, I was grateful that he had put distance between me and my mother.

"Get away from my son, Azazel," my father growled. "And if you ever lay hands on her again, I will end you."

My father stood over me, guarding my fallen body with his own. I looked for my brother and saw he had been incapacitated, laid out flat on his back with a ring of holy fire imprisoning him.

"No," I groaned, at least I tried to. I didn't know if any words had actually come out.

From my position on the ground, I looked up into my uncle's twisted face. He was in full demon form. His dark-grayish skin was taunt and pulled so tight it looked as if I could see his oversized skeleton underneath. He had a mouth full of jagged fangs. His fingers had elongated with his nails long and sharp like talons. Red orbs glowed where eyes should have been. His leathery black wings had a seven-foot wingspan. He was darn near seven feet in human form. His demon self was much taller, and his bulk was of abnormal proportions.

"Touché ...Brother," Uncle spat. He said the word brother as if it left a bad taste on his tongue. "I saved your son's life. Thank me, you ungrateful bastard. That bitch you married was about to blade him to death." He then let out a maniacal laugh that sent birds flying through the night.

"You're a disgrace."

"Perhaps, but at least I'm not a lapdog."

"You're far worse. You should have been left in the Valleys."

My uncle gnashed his teeth. "I should have been, but why not tell your precious son why I'm here and not there. Why don't you tell him how you and his mother orchestrated this whole thing, and then made me the fall guy. It was quite genius, I have to give it to you. Even I didn't pick up on it at first. But then, I got to thinking…it was far too easy for me to get out of those chains, Brother."

"Of course it was. Do you think a demon of your caliber would have been let out otherwise? I'd have

ordered the guards to strike you down before letting you loose," Father spat. "But what better way to use a Fallen than to have the world believe you're exactly what they think you are; evil incarnate."

"Ah, only this time, I'm not the proverbial bad guy, am I? In fact, all I'm guilty of is scaring those witches shitless…and," he continued with a bitter chuckle, "bringing those powers you and my leftovers didn't want them to know they had to fruition."

My father's eyes went white with rage. "Still jealous you can't have her?"

"I've had her. I've had her so many times, my essence still saturates her womb. That's neither here nor there. Your little plan didn't work. In fact, it is because of your plan Tasmin and Elisa now know the full extent of their powers."

"You have no idea what you've done."

They started to circle one another. "Oh, but I do. I do, dear ole brother. I know exactly what I've done. And to use a woman from Noreen's own coven to betray her? Have you no shame, Brother?" He gave a dark, evil gaping mouthed grin that showed darn near every fang in his mouth.

That sealed it for me. Just as I'd suspected, Martha had been used to betray Noreen. It was why she had blue kyanite on her person. Blue kyanite that only my father could have given her to place her under his protection. I'd bet any amount of my worldly possessions, that she had no idea that she had been used as such. It explained why she had outright refused to speak to me about how she had gotten the crystal to begin with. My father had sworn her to secrecy under the guise that she would be helping the Most High secure the greater good of mankind. I was almost as sure of that as I was that I felt that my parents had betrayed my trust.

"Tell me, Michael, as you and our other brothers sit around Father's table doing his bidding, have you ever stopped to think that doing things for the *greater good* has gotten us nowhere?"

Lightning ripped across the sky, hit trees, splitting them in half and then lit up the grounds. My father pulled his flaming swords from behind him. The blue kyanite swords could do irreparable damage. My uncle, either unfazed or just arrogant, didn't even flinch. "You dare speak such blasphemy in my presence," Father hurled at him.

Uncle roared, "And you dare try to use me as a pawn in this dubious plan of yours! To have my son think even less of me than he already does?"

"Your son has been better off without you in his life. One day he'll thank his mother for keeping you away from him."

Uncle flinched. Father's words had hurt as he'd intended them to. "How does it feel to know my demon essence resides in your son's DNA?" Uncle laughed evilly. "It's almost like he's part my seed."

He didn't have time to gloat. My father attacked him with fervor. As Uncle ducked and blocked Father's strikes, he called his chakrams to him. Forged of titanium that had been washed in The Blood, the blades were round like a discus and sharp enough to cut through bone and diamond. It reminded me that my uncle had been a high-arch before he became a Fallen. It reminded me that he was strategist. He'd taught man the art of warfare. His skills had been legendary behind the veil. And judging by the grunts, moves and countermoves, he hadn't lost the art of fighting.

I gave a low and painful groan as I rolled over then stood on shaky legs. My uncle's touch had done something to me. I didn't know what, but my insides felt as if fire was coursing through my blood. I watched my father shed his leather jacket, roll his shoulders and then transform into his full angel form. He was of pure white light with lions' heads the size of boulders. With wings like those of a sphinx and a span of just over seven feet, his heads of fire were nothing like the pictures humans had of angels on their walls.

My mind screamed for Tasmin. I felt every pain she did. And each time her pressure points pulsed and ached, my anger intensified. All I saw was red. I couldn't get ahold of my senses, couldn't ground my rage. I saw my mother crawl to her knees then gingerly stand. My uncle's attack had weakened her. Still, I saw the rage in her eyes. I saw her intent as soon as her eyes landed on my brother who had awakened.

When Dafari realized he had been surrounded by holy fire, he let out a string of curses that not even Morningstar himself would have been able to stand hearing. My mother got to her feet, grabbed her swords then headed toward him and Tasmin. I knew who she was going after, and before I could react, Elisa dragged herself to her feet. It was safe to assume she thought the same thing I did; Mother was on the attack with Tasmin in her line of vision.

"Tasmin," Elisa yelled, albeit weakly. "Get up."

But I knew Tasmin was seriously hurt. Even as she rolled over and cupped her broken wrist to her chest, I knew trying to stand was futile. My mother was on the move. Elisa yelled for Tasmin to get up again. Another vicious strike of lightning lit the sky. The wind blew so hard that it whistled in the night. Mother advanced on Tasmin. Elisa and I yelled, "No," at the same time as Dafari tried to cross the holy fire. Doing so caused the flames to crawl all over his body. He roared with pain like I'd never heard before. He was, after all, half demon and my father had known the fire would maim, injure or possibly kill him. Mere rain couldn't douse holy fire, just as it couldn't hell fire.

Elisa tried to run for Tasmin, but her injured knee hindered her. She screamed and bent to grab her knee.

"Touch the ground, Elisa," Dafari yelled through the flames.

Elisa looked at him, hurt, pain and confusion in her eyes.

"Grab the earth," he yelled again.

She dropped to one knee, fisted dirt and grass in her hand. As my mother got close to Tasmin, Elisa tossed a fistful of dirt toward my mother. In an instant, tree branches grabbed my mother's wrists, forcing her to drop her swords. Tree roots shot up and surrounded her, caging her inside as she yelled with rage.

I stood, in the middle of chaos. My loved ones were in an all-out war. My parents had caused all of this. Their lies by omission. Their deceit! Their need to control that which should not be manipulated had caused me more pain than I'd experienced since years past. I didn't bloody understand for the life of me why they would do it. To stop some hypothetical end of the world scenario? And now, my uncle and my father were in a deathmatch, fighting like they had no love left for the other.

Mother knew what Tasmin meant to me, but because Tasmin was a witch, her life didn't matter where my parents were concerned. For the greater good, they would cause me hurt, pain, and grief all over again? Before my senses caught up to my rage, I lunged one of my bec-de-corbins at my uncle, the beak of it catching him square in the chest. His eyes widened as blackish bruised blood oozed down his chest. He fell back into the shadows, leaving my stunned bloodied father in his wake.

"Octavian! Octavian," Mother screamed when she saw I'd turned my rage on my father.

I threw my other weapon at him, same as I'd done Uncle, and watched as it pierced his chest just over his heart. His swords lost their flames as they clanged to the dirt and he fell to his knees, blood trickling from the corners of his mouth.

Mother's cries for me to stop did little to quell my rage. The pain in her wails didn't stop me from foraging ahead.

"Octavian, don't do this! Octavian," she wailed from inside her wooden prison.

I spun on her; a stern finger pointed in her direction. "You, you two are the cause of all this madness! You nor he or anyone else will ever take her away from me again."

Somewhere in the back of my mind, I heard my brother call out to me before he hit the ground, the flames doused when I injured my father, but Dafari's burn wounds still smoldered.

"Don't you understand, Son. We had to. We had no choice but to put all this in motion," Mother pleaded as I walked to stand in front of my father. She dropped to her knees, hands gripping the tree roots keeping her in place. "Please, Son…Don't… He's your father…"

My mother had tried to harm the woman I'd loved for centuries. She tried to take something from me…so I was going to take him from her.

"Brother," I heard in my mind. "This isn't you." My brother's voice in my head faltered my steps for a moment. "It's not you. You don't have to do this. It's the demon residue. You have to fight it, Octavian. Fight it."

Who I was at heart was at conflict with the unmitigated rage I felt in my soul at the moment. My jaws felt like they had come unhinged. I felt my teeth elongate and my nails lengthen. I'd show them what it felt like to lose the only love they'd ever known.

"Octavian," Dafari called out to me telepathically. "Come back…"

He said something else, but I couldn't hear him over the den of the memories in my mind. I was back on that plantation…Back to a time when I'd known Tasmin in another life…back when her life, along with another one…one whom we'd loved and tried to protect were snatched from me. I was back in a time when I'd been too late to save her. I'd watched helplessly as her lifeless body swung from the end of a rope, her neck so broken that it looked as if her skin had been stretched to keep her head on the rope…And.I.Lost.It.

I didn't see my father's face before me as I drew my hands back, set to deliver a fatal blow that would surely get me sent to the most bottomless pits of hell. Before my claws could hit their mark, someone's powerful hand gripped mine.

"No. It's not worth your freedom or your soul." I looked up into the red eyes of my uncle.

He was still bleeding from his chest wound, a hole in his chest where my weapon had impaled him. Instinctively I knew falling into the shadows had saved him.

Through his red eyes, I saw my own. I didn't recognize myself and it scared me. I had to get away from here. I couldn't stay here and risk Tasmin seeing me at my lowest. I fled into the night…gone with the wind.

EPILOGUE

DAFARI

Octavian had flown off to who knew where, after almost slaying his father, my father unexpectedly coming between him and Michael, saving him from himself.

"What have you done to my son?" My stepfather yelled between labored breaths, still on the ground.

Father, standing over him, spat on the ground. "What I did was stop him from taking your miserable life, Brother. You should be thanking me."

Michael attempted to stand up, but quickly fell back to his knees, the wound inflicted by Octavian's bec-de-corbins bleeding profusely. "You've turned him in a monster, a monster just like you!"

"No, Brother! You and that treacherous bitch over there did that," my father countered, pointing in Mother's direction. "Your lies, deceit, not to mention murder of innocents, that's *what turned Octavian into what he now is. I may have lit the match, but you two were the ones that started the fire. Congratulations."*

"You've always hated Octavian, Azazel. You've never forgiven me for marrying Michael and having his son."

"No, woman, I've never forgiven you for keeping me from my *son!" Father retorted. "All the while you put your little*

angel on a pedestal and treated my son," he said, looking in my direction, "With scorn. While this was unexpected, I do feel some sort of poetic justice. You took my son from me, now I took yours from you. It's a shame; while I have no respect for either of you, in some ways, I actually respected Octavian."

"I hate you, Azazel," my mother said, head hanging low. She appeared to be sobbing, sobbing for her lost angel no doubt. I had to wonder if I something had happened to me would she have wept so severely, if at all?

My father snickered, walking slowly in my mother's direction, standing in front of her. "I've hated you for centuries. Welcome to my world." He then walked back in Michael's direction. "You know, Brother, with the two of you rendered hors de combat, it would be so easy for me to finish you. First you, then her." As Father said those words, he looked directly at my stepfather, then slowly turned to look at Mother. "But no, I want you to remember this night, the night where your son truly realized who you are and turned away from you."

While my father's words were cruel, I understood his point. Mother's and Stepfather's acts were heinous. On top of it all, while my father was by no means an innocent in any sense of the word, their attempt to scapegoat him was unjustified. They got what they deserved; they lost the one thing that, besides each other, meant the most to them. Unfortunately, that also meant I lost the brother I love.

The hedge maze fell into an eerie silence, save for my mother's sobs. Then, as the rest of us lay there in various states of disablement, bloodied, battered, and bruised, a cone of white light suddenly appeared, enveloping both my mother and Michael. In the blink of an eye, they were both gone. The battle was effectively over, but the effects for all of us were sure to be long-lasting.

I knew in my current condition, I would be unable to carry both Elisa and Tasmin through the veil, especially because of my demon lineage, but I had to get them to safety. Since she was the one most gravely injured, I needed to assess the full extent of Tasmin's wounds. The best way to do that was at my clinic. However, despite the fact that he was hurt, I feared leaving Elisa anywhere near my father. I attempted, with effort, to bring Elisa to her feet. Her knee was red, swollen, and hot; a sure sign that she had at the very least torn some inner structures. She hobbled gingerly as we made our way to Tasmin, who was lying on her back. Though she still appeared to be in a lot of pain, her wounds seemed to be healing, as evidenced by her wrist, which was no longer deformed. Still, the sooner we left this hedge maze the better.

Elisa and I attempted to help Tasmin up, to no avail. Our wounds had severely weakened us both. Suddenly, my father was at my side, the gash in his chest still leaking ichor, but healing rapidly. I was completely perplexed as he opened up a rip into the shadows. Without a word, he looked at me, as if wanting me to follow him. After steadying ourselves, we again tried to lift Tasmin, this time with success. We then followed my father. Before I knew it, we had arrived at my clinic, where we placed Tasmin on an examination table. I excused myself to Elisa, walking into the waiting area, my father directly behind me.

Father and I stood, face-to-face, looking at one other for a moment. "Thank you," I finally said.

"You're welcome, Son."

My father was many things but being altruistic was not among them. I needed to know the motivation for his actions tonight. "Why did you do it?"

"Why did I do what?" he asked. I could tell he was feigning ignorance.

"Why did you help me? Why help Octavian…twice?"

He stood straight, arms folded in from of him. "I helped you because you are my son. As far as your brother goes, I helped him because you are my son. I did it for you, not for him. I also helped to thwart my whore of an ex-wife and my duplicitous brother's plans, thereby saving both Elisa and Tasmin from certain death in the process. Instead of viewing my aid with suspicion, you should be grateful."

I stared at him, skepticism laced in my tone. "If that were really the case, why not just reveal all that Mother and Michael had done, including the fact that they set you up, the moment you figured it out instead of scaring Elisa and Tasmin into discovering their powers, Father? Why all the subterfuge?"

He smiled at me, no pretense in his statement. "Because, Son, it's who I am. No matter how the witches discovered their gifts, this confrontation would have occurred regardless. Only

my way, the evolution of their powers was brought on sooner rather than later. Had I taken on a kinder, gentler approach, your mother and Michael may have been more successful. If I recall correctly, you and your brother resorted to some of the same tactics in order to bring out more of their gifts, with you even fighting your lady love, which brought out her elemental powers. That was a chip off the old block move, if I do say so myself. And in the end, you have to admit, I did help you get your dream girl, did I not?"

I let out a hard sigh, realizing that it was futile debating the topic any further. My father was who he was, and regardless of what he told me, I knew there was an angle in there somewhere; I just hadn't discerned what that was...yet. "I need to get back to Elisa and Tasmin. Thank you for your help, Father."

As a final gesture, I reached out my hand for him to shake. Instead, he grasped my forearm, pulling me into a warrior's handshake. He then backed up, looking at me one last time then he was gone. It was then that I knew, for good or ill, it would not be the last time I would see my father.

That was two weeks ago. Despite the extent of Tasmin's injuries, she was able to heal herself within a day, which in itself was a miracle. I still had no understanding as to why she was able to self-heal, and so quickly at that, but I was determined to find out. She had also healed Elisa. It pleased me to no end to see here walking without difficulty. Both were trying to come to grips with all they had witnessed and learned on that fateful night and were unfortunately going through all the stages of grief at the same time. I truly felt for them and was doing my best to be there for both.

Elisa and I had much to talk about in terms of our relationship, such as it was, but, considering all of our recent turmoil, now was not the right time to discuss our status. Since she was still residing with me, I felt we had plenty of time for that. Her entire family, mother, father, and grandmother, were stolen from her, for no other reason save for the fact that her grandmother and father were witches. And I was sure my mother and stepfather being the culprits made matters that much worse. My only concern was supporting her through her loss.

The day she came to my office just after opening the café, I knew something was wrong. The consummate professional when it came to her business, she never would have left without a valid reason. "Elisa, what's wrong?" I asked, going to her, ushering her into my office.

"Today would have been Mama Nall's birthday," she said, her eyes moist. "With everything going on, I almost forgot. Then I saw the picture from my ribbon cutting ceremony when I opened the shop. It was on her birthday."

Sitting her in a chair, I knelt in front of her, taking her hands in mine. "I am so sorry. I can't image how difficult this must be for you. You've been through so much lately. No one could fault you for a lapse in memory."

"But she was everything to me," she said, tears starting to fall. "After my parents died, she was both mother and father to me. How could I forget something so important?"

I put my hands her cheeks, wiping away her tears. "You are being too hard on yourself. When Mama Nall died, you mourned her. Now, finding out she and your parents were murdered, you're grieving all over again, and if you remember something else, you'll most likely grieve some more. It's understandable."

"I miss her so much. I miss her love, her guidance, and her strength. When I thought she died of natural causes, I figured she was ready to transition because she had done all she could for me while she was on this earth, and that I was ready to handle things on my own. But now…" she said, eyes cast downward.

"Elisa," I began, placing my hand under her chin, raising her head to look at me, "While Mama Nall's physical body was taken from you prematurely, don't think she's still not here, looking out for you.

You, of all people, should know that. Be comforted knowing that she's not just in your heart, but her spirit is here, as well," I said, holding her until she was comforted, at least for the moment.

Tasmin was demanding to know where Octavian was and why he had not returned yet. As she had been virtually incoherent when Octavian had tried to have his father meet his Maker because she was Michael's target, we felt it best to keep that part of the story from her. She had been through enough. Although I did discourage her from going to Octavian, I did tell her where he was. I at least wanted her to have some solace knowing he was safe.

As for me, I was able to heal myself quickly, at least physically. While I was used to being treated like an outcast by her, Mother's words about regretting something, whether it was me being born a half-caste, marrying my father, or both, cut me to the quick. She never answered me as to which she was referring to. Knowing her, that was done purposely. I didn't think I'd ever get past that. I had come to realize that, unfortunately, some wounds never healed.

Then there was my stepfather Michael. Mother purposely alienated me from Father, which, looking back on it, was probably the right thing to do. In lieu of my own father, there was my stepfather, who actually treated me fairly, something mother failed to do. He never looked at me with derision, but instead, treated me like I was his own son. That was why it aggrieved me so to be forced to fight him, but I had no choice. I had to protect Elisa and Tasmin, but it felt as if I was fighting my own father. I didn't know which hurt more, fighting the one adult in our home who treated me like I was worth something, or being trapped by his holy fire. He knew how devastating holy fire could be, knew that it could severely wound me or worse still, kill me. I understood that we were locked in a war of sorts, but it still hurt all the same.

Last, but certainly not least, there was Octavian. I couldn't imagine what it must have been like for him to relive the horror of potentially losing the woman he loved yet again, this time at the hands of both his mother and his father. Then there was my father's touch, triggering the demon residue residing within Octavian's DNA. I was chilled by his ghastly transformation. I could only imagine how he was faring.

After what happened on the plantation over a century ago, I was deathly afraid that this time, Octavian would not be able to come back from this. I feared for his immortal soul. After much difficulty, I was finally able to connect with him. He told me that he was in retreat at the old caves, that he needed to be alone, and had no idea when he would return.

After much inner grappling, I realized that my brother's internal battle was his and his alone. I knew I had to respect that, but if Octavian called for me, no matter what time of the day or night, I would immediately be by his side, helping him in any capacity he allowed me to.

ELISA

People had talked about "the storm" that had come on the night of the jubilee. Townsfolk and partygoers didn't know how the storm had snuck up on them as it hadn't been in the forecast, but apparently, it had torn up the mayor's front and backyard. Some people had even gotten so inebriated that they thought they'd seen big animals fighting in the manor's yard as well. That was the story that was being told, but Tasmin, Dafari and I knew better.

I stood on the wooden steps of a wraparound porch, gazing into the eyes of Cara Lee and Mary Ann. Their eyes held tears that refused to fall. They had on hooded long, flowing black dresses that hung to their feet, and in their hands were wooden staffs with Adinkra symbols that had been intricately carved. I was sure they could be used as weapons if need be. On their faces were grief, concern, a bit of anger, and something else I couldn't name. They held their chins high as if ready to defend themselves if need be. It had taken me two weeks to get up the nerve to come for this visit or confrontation depending on how one looked at it.

I didn't know what I felt. A cacophony of emotions resided within me. On one hand, I knew their eldest sister, Martha, had been fooled into going along with the plans that killed Ms. Noreen, my parents, and Mama Nall. On the other, I wanted to know why she'd been so willing to do Michael's bidding.

"Where is she?" I asked, my voice coming out harsher than I'd intended.

"If you came here to harm our sister, we can't let you do that," Cara Lee said.

I got ready to say something, but Mary Ann cut in. "We know what she did. We wish she hadn't done it. We wish she would have told us beforehand so we could have stopped her. But you have to understand that she genuinely thought she was doing it for the greater good of humanity."

"A celestial being had shown himself to her and convinced her she was chosen," Cara Lee said, this time her tears did fall, and she quickly slapped them away. "She is in more pain now than she has ever been."

I wanted to yell at them to screw her pain! What about my pain? What about Tasmin's pain?

"She made a decision that she has come to regret. We ask that you extend grace to her," Mary Ann said. "We are still of the same coven."

"I guess that meant very little to her in the grand scheme of things?" I said coolly.

The older women stiffened, and their eyes flashed with anger.

"Elisa, you know us," Cara Lee pleaded. "You know our hearts. I know you know in your heart Martha Lee would never—"

"I don't know anything," I yelled. "I thought I did, but I don't know…I just want to know why. Why did she do it? And I need more than she thought she was helping with the greater good of humanity."

Just then the screen door opened. Martha Lee stood in much of the same attire as her sisters, but she was in all white. In the Book of Magic Enchantment, it spoke of the coven wearing all white when they grieved. What in hell did she have to grieve about?

"Leave us," she said to her sisters.

"Martha, I don't think that's a good idea," Mary Ann said, casting a doubtful eye from me back to Cara Lee then back up at Martha.

"Leave us," Martha said again.

After some hesitation, the younger sisters left Martha and I alone. We regarded one another cautiously. She was probably unsure of what I'd come to do, and I wanted answers that made more sense.

"I've been around a long time, Elisa. I've lived through things, experienced things that should have better prepared me for all that has transpired, but I

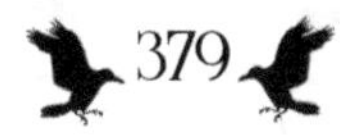

was a fool. An old fool. I'll tell you the whole thing, but I ask that you wait until you're less angry, and I ask the same of Tasmin. I'd rather have both of you here so I can tell both of you at the same time. I know I don't have the right to ask you for anything at all, but please grant me that." I didn't say yes or no, just stared at her. "I also want you to know, I had no hand in your parents' deaths. Not one hand. Like everyone else, I genuinely thought it was a traffic accident due to the storm."

Tears fell down her cheeks and I ached for her. My emotions confused me. Or maybe my anger was misguided. I didn't know why my soft heart felt sorry for her.

"I'm so sorry, Elisa. I am," she said, voice shaky as she tried to hold it together.

I didn't know what else to say so I turned around and left.

A week later, I finally got around to interviewing Rufus. The raw pain I'd felt behind what Martha had done had lessened. As Tasmin and I studied the Book of Magic Enchantment, we started to get more knowledge of who our coven, past and present, were. Octavian still hadn't come out of the caves. I'd gotten concerned as I wasn't sure he was okay, but Dafari assured me that his brother had needed time to process everything his own way.

Dafari and I had been spending more nights together in his bed. Most times with me just needing to be held in order to get to sleep. He'd told me how he still thought his father was up to something but couldn't put his finger on it. He also wondered aloud one night why going through the shadows hadn't negatively affected Tasmin and I, as we were humans.

"Could it be because your father is a Fallen and was our guide that nothing happened?" I asked one night as we lay cuddled in his bed.

"Eh. Could be," he said. "I'll figure it out. Last thing I need is for Octavian to come back and find that something I've done has caused further harm to Tasmin. That's on top of me not wanting anything to happen to you either. I'll figure it out though. My parents, Michael included, will no longer string us along like puppets…"

I still hadn't processed all that had happened the night of the jubilee, but the mayor and his wife had started to regard Tasmin and me with caution. Rumor had it, the mayor had a bone to pick with Octavian as Ilene Suzanne had been telling all who would listen that Octavian had offended her with something he'd said and done.

"Tell ya what, Elsie, just let me make the next batch of confee for these heah customers. If they take a liking to it, then you can hire me. If they don't, you can kick my tuchus right on outta heah. Deal?" Rufus said then held his meaty hand out for me to shake.

I was skeptical to say the least, but I shook on it. Rufus didn't seem like the type to know how to boil water, let alone bake pastries and brew coffee—well confee as he'd called it. I watched as he grabbed an apron then washed his hands. He was humming and doing a little jig as he went along. I prayed I hadn't made a mistake when he almost dropped a mug but caught it quickly. But sure enough, the next five customers who'd come in ordered coffee, took a sip, and then stared wide-eyed at Rufus before ordering an extra cup and promising to tell others to come by and try it.

After the seventh customer had the same reaction, I asked Rufus to make me a cup. He did so with a wide smile that said he was sure of himself. I watched as he poured the brew, measured the sugar, added the cream, a bit of cinnamon and nutmeg then gave it a stir. I cautiously took a sip and got the shock of my life.

"My Loa," I whispered. "Rufus, I think you make coffee better than I do!"

The man blushed and cast his eyes away from mine before saying, "Oh golly, Elsie. You just saying that."

"No, I'm serious. This is freaking delicious! You're hired!"

Later that night, Tasmin and I sat in Ms. Noreen's yard near the willow where Tasmin had poured her ashes. We sat across from one another, holding hands as we chanted a protection spell for us and for Dafari and Octavian.

Together we said, "During this time of uncertainty, we ask that our Ancestors watch over thee. While confusion and anger have clouded our judgement at times, we ask that our Ancestors release the ties that bind. Guide us through this turbulent time so that our hearts remain pure and kind. We call on our Guides to surround us from every direction so that our Ancestors can provide us with much needed protection…"

As the last words left our mouths, the tree produced a golden light that started from the roots and worked its way up to the top of the leaves. It shone bright and wide then washed down over us like a warm embrace.

We looked at our watches and the time read 4:44 in morning.

"All is well," we said as we looked at one another. "All is well."

TASMIN

I couldn't believe how much my life had changed in just a few weeks. I had learned much in such a short amount of time; I was a witch with amazing powers, my practice had burned to the ground under mysterious circumstances; angels and demons existed in real life; and Elisa and I learned that our family members had been murdered by Octavian's parents.

I was still coming to terms with my new reality, one where it appeared I would be staying in Salix Pointe indefinitely. I needed to figure out what I was going to do. I could go back to Brooklyn and rebuild my practice, but that was contingent on an insurance settlement being granted. Considering the suspicious nature of the fire, and subsequent explosion, receiving any monetary remuneration was highly doubtful. I had the bookstore, but that didn't feed me intellectually, medicine did. I was in a quandary for sure.

One thing I did know, I couldn't go on staying at Dafari's. He and Elisa were settling into what could only be described as their own form of domestic bliss, and I felt like the proverbial third wheel. Of course, they never made me feel that way, I just did. There were also too many memories of Octavian there; spending time together every morning over breakfast, our training sessions, even the dreaded teapot incident, all were reminders of him. It was just too much, which was why I had moved back to Aunt Noreen's home.

"You know this is just as much your home now as it is mine, Tasmin," Dafari said, helping me pack the rest of my belongings in my car.

"I really appreciate that, especially since you called us invaders when we first started staying here," I said laughing.

"Ah, yes, the early days," he replied, chuckling. "You have to admit, things were a bit…tense in the beginning, but we eventually learned to peacefully co-exist."

"We did, and I'll miss that, but…it's just not the same," I said, my voice trailing off.

"You mean with Octavian gone," he spoke. I nodded. "Tasmin, he will be back. He just needs time. Finding out your parents murdered four people, including the aunt of the woman you care about, was a lot for him to handle. While we've all been affected by what has transpired, I think it's impacted Octavian the most. Just as you, Elisa, and I had to find ways to cope, he's had to find his."

"I know. I'm just worried about him."

Dafari placed a hand on my shoulder. "As am I, but we have to let him heal in his own way." I closed the trunk, the last of my belongings in the car." Now, are you sure you don't want to reconsider? Elisa and I will miss you being here."

I opened the garage bay then started the car. "I can't. As much as I'll miss you guys, too, I think it's for the best. Besides, I know where to find you both," I said with a laugh.

"That you do," he replied. "But if do decide to come home, just know, the door is always open."

"Thanks, Dafari, I'll remember that."

Even though I wasn't living with them anymore, I still saw Elisa and Dafari frequently, usually at the café. I made a point of stopping by on the days I knew Elisa would be there. She had just hired Rufus, and he seemed to be a big hit with the customers. I stopped in early one morning to chat for a bit.

"Good morning, you two," I cheerfully said to Elisa and Rufus.

Hey, Tasmin," greeted Elisa, filling the pastry counter with the delicacies of the day.

"Mornin' to ya, Tasmania," Rufus said with a wave. I had long ago stopped correcting him. "A hot spiced apple cider and a piece of lemon loaf?"

"You know it, Rufus, and thank you." I took a seat at a booth.

"I got cha. Comin' right up."

Elisa came over, sitting across from me. "We miss you at the house. Things are so quiet without you and…" Her voice tapered off.

"It's okay, Elisa. You can say his name. I won't fall apart."

Elisa put her hand over mine. "I know you won't, although I couldn't blame you if you did. I know this has been hard on you wondering when he'll come back. You two had just started getting close."

Rufus walked over to us, my spiced apple cider and warm lemon loaf in hand. "Here you go, Tasmania. Just the way you like it. Enjoy," he said, shuffling in a dance-like manner back to the counter.

I took a sip of the apple cider; it was sheer perfection with just the right amount of cinnamon, nutmeg, ginger, caramel, and whipped cream. The lemon loaf with its lemon-flavored icing melted in my mouth. Rufus was by and large worth his weight in gold.

"I just want him to be okay, Elisa."

"I know you do. It's hard worrying about someone, especially when you have feelings for them."

The morning rush was just beginning, and customers were starting file into the café. "I don't know what I'm feeling for Octavian," I said, finishing my cider and lemon loaf.

"I think you know," Elisa said with a smirk. "You're just afraid to admit it, even to yourself. Like you said to me about Dafari a while back, me thinks the lady doth protest too much. Anyway, I have to go help Rufus, but we'll talk later." She took my trash, threw it away then walked behind the register.

As I walked to the bookstore, I thought about what she said. I really was unsure about my feelings for Octavian. We never had a chance to explore anything further after our…encounter in the mayor's office the night of the jubilee. While I was unsure of any romantic feelings I had toward Octavian, I did know one feeling that was coming through loud and clear; guilt.

I felt extremely guilty for Octavian's current plight. I never told Elisa or Dafari, but I heard what happened when I was injured in the hedge maze the night of the battle, heard both Elisa and Octavian yell as someone was coming for me; heard his mother begging him to spare his father's life. It was only when Dafari's father, Azazel, intervened did he stop attempting to strike down his father. Octavian was willing to take on, and, if need be, kill his own father, an arch angel, in order to protect me. And for that, I was guilt-ridden. I didn't ask him to protect me; nonetheless he did, against his own parents at that. And now he was grappling with the aftermath.

Because of my guilt, and perhaps because of some unresolved feelings I had for him, I had been visiting Octavian at the cave daily for the past few weeks, leaving a basket with food and drink for him, talking to him for a few minutes before leaving. He never responded, but I knew he was there because when I would return the following day, the basket would be sitting at the cave's entrance, empty food containers and thermos inside. I kept my visits a secret because I knew Dafari and Elisa would probably try to stop me.

Today I stopped at the bookstore first, preparing a thermos of hot tea just the way he liked it. I had cooked spaghetti with a vegetarian tomato sauce the night before. I packed that, along with the tea and some macadamia nut cookies, into the basket.

I drove part way to the caves, making the rest of the trek on foot, which was my usual route. The weather appeared to be transitioning from fall to winter, the early morning air being cold and crisp. Standing in front of the cave entrance, I placed the basket down then sat on the large rock just outside the left of the cave.

"Good morning, Octavian," I said, knowing he wouldn't answer me back. "I hope you're doing well today. I stopped by the café this morning. Rufus has been doing a great job working for Elisa. I know you think he's an odd little man, but he's really very sweet and can make a mean cup of apple cider," I said with a laugh. "Elisa and Dafari are doing well. I check in with them all the time. I should tell you that when you get back, you might want to avoid the mayor. Rumor has it he has a few choice words for you. Apparently, Ilene Suzanne is running around town telling people you said and did something offensive to her at the jubilee. Just giving you a heads up."

I talked for a few more minutes before preparing to leave. "Octavian," I said, standing at the entrance to the cave, "Before we left the mayor's office the night of the jubilee, you said we needed to talk. I'm still going to hold you to that. I'll be back tomorrow."

When I was injured during the battle, I heard Octavian say something that confused me. He told his mother that neither she nor his father nor anyone else would even take me away from him again. I didn't understand why he would say that considering we had never met until I came back to Salix Pointe. I needed answers, and this was on the top of my list if and when Octavian emerged from his self-imposed exile.

After I walked back to my car, I climbed inside, turned it on, cranking up the heat. With winter on the way, I wasn't sure how much longer I would be able to come out to the cave, but I would for as long as possible.

I had no plans to open the bookstore today, so I went back home. I decided I was going to do some light housecleaning then take a deep dive into the

Book of Magic Enchantment. That was the plan anyway. As I was dusting in the living room, I heard someone fiddling with the front door. I had changed the locks, so no one had a key save for me, Elisa, and my parents, who I had mailed a set to. It was still early in the day, so I knew it wasn't Elisa, and my parents were back in Brooklyn. I dropped my duster, putting up my hands, ready to blast whoever was trying to come into my home. That was until I saw who it was.

"Mommy? Daddy? What are you doing here?" I asked, surprised by their sudden arrival in Salix Pointe.

Not even making time for pleasantries, my mom said, "Tasmin, we need to talk."

OCTAVIAN

It took me days to come back to my normal self. I could smartly surmise that the demon residue left behind from the time Mother carried Dafari had finally reared its ugly head. I couldn't bear to look at myself, let alone show myself to anyone else. It took seven full days for my anger to release me, and in that time my demon transformation finally retreated. I used the water in the cave as a mirror to see my reflection.

I looked like my old self minus scrapes and bruises from the fight with my mother. However, I knew I'd never be the same again. I wanted to get away, but not too far away that I wouldn't be able to protect Tasmin and Elisa, and even my brother, if I needed to. My parents had shaken my faith. Before smelling the burned cinnamon and seeing the blue kyanite at Elisa's place, I would have never guessed my parents to be the bad guys. It was hard for me to even think about it after the fact.

As I looked at all the degrading food Tasmin had been bringing me, I wondered what life would be like for me after all was said and done. I'd have to pay for my actions toward my parents, specifically my father. If Azazel hadn't stopped me, I would have indeed struck my father down. Now that anger wasn't clouding my judgement, that bothered me. But it would be something else I would have to deal with when the time came.

I stayed in that cave for weeks. I grieved my own way. I waited patiently each day as Tasmin brought me food and talked to me. It showed how big her heart was that she knew I wouldn't respond, but she kept coming back to leave me food and libations. I didn't want her to think I'd completely abandoned her or that I was ignoring her, so after she left each day, I took the food and left the empty basket. She'd said she still wanted to talk, but it wasn't the time. It would have to wait.

For weeks, I prayed. I cried out. I yelled to the heavens for answers that I knew I wouldn't get any time soon. Two weeks before Thanksgiving, I got a visit from an unlikely source.

"Finding out your parents aren't the perfect beings they pretend to be isn't easy, is it?"

His voice had startled me awake. I shot to my feet, calling my weapons to me. After all, I had tried to kill him. I didn't know if he was out for revenge just yet. I didn't see him fully, but his golden eyes were as clear as the night was black.

He chuckled as he stepped out of the shadows. "Stand down, dear nephew. I come in peace," he said.

He was dressed in a bespoke gray suit. Underneath the suit jacket was a blood red collarless shirt. His wavy black hair was pulled back into a ponytail. A golden pinky ring was on his finger. It matched the one my brother never wore but kept in a lockbox in his closet.

"What do you want?" I asked nastily.

"Only to talk. Offer a listening ear maybe? Answer any questions you may have…"

"I don't need anything from you."

"The pain in your aura says differently. However, I won't pick at an already open wound. I came to deliver a message; I never intended to hurt the witches. In fact, I still have no reason to harm them. So I have no beef with you or my wayward son. Can you believe he questioned why I saved you?"

"Yes," I said. "Yes, I can believe it. It's not like you've given many reasons as to why he should trust you."

"Perhaps if your mother had actually allowed me to see him—"

"Spare me the theatrics, Uncle. I have no quarrel with you…as long as you stay away from Tasmin and Elisa, especially Tasmin where I am concerned."

He held his hands up. "Hey, say less, Nephew. But just so you know…word's out in the underworld about you and your brother's pretty little witches.

That power surge on All Hallows Eve put a pulse into the air that lead right back to them. I'd advise you to come out of this cave. Stop wallowing in pity and get back to your brother's. Once otherworldly beings start trickling into Salix Pointe, those witches and this town will need all the help they can get."

I studied the Fallen whom I shared a bloodline with. I didn't know how to take what he was saying. He was a lot of things, but a liar I'd never known him to be. Still, the way he always spoke in riddles chapped my backside.

"Have you told Dafari this?" I asked.

Uncle laughed while shaking his head. "Now, why would I do that?"

"Why wouldn't you do that?" I asked, befuddled by the method to his madness.

Uncle laughed haughtily as he turned and headed back into the shadows. His last words were just as chilling as they were confusing. "Why indeed, Nephew. Why indeed…" Then he disappeared just as he'd come.

It took another week and a few days later, but I left the caves in search of my brother. Apparently, Tasmin had gone back to Noreen's house weeks before and soon after, once Elisa's home had been remodeled, she, too, had gone back home. I was grateful for that as I didn't want to come face-to-face with Tasmin as of yet and didn't need Elisa running to tell her I was out of the cave and back at Dafari's.

I heard my brother moving around his house as I stepped through the veil and entered his front room. I didn't have to make any grand announcements as I knew he would feel me in his place soon enough.

"You look…a gotdamn mess," he greeted me once he walked into his front room and flipped on the lights.

I hadn't really thought to give a damn about my appearance. So when I glanced at myself in one of the mirrors on his wall, I did a doubletake. I'd grown a full beard and my clothes made me look like a pauper. I was dirty and looked worn. My eyes were a bit sunken, and I was sure I would need more than a bath to rectify the situation.

"I can't say I've cared very much about my appearance since that fateful night, Brother," I said, not caring enough to be embarrassed.

"I can smell that," he said as he turned his nose up, but still walked over to me and embraced me. "I missed you, Brother."

I returned his embrace. "And I, you," I said. "How's Tasmin?" I asked once we pulled away.

"Worried about you for the most part," he said, patting my shoulder. "She asks me about you every day. Starting to think you've abandoned her."

"I haven't."

"I know. She doesn't know what to think. It's your responsibility to fix that. Nothing I can tell her will assure her at this point."

I nodded, knowing I had to make up for my absence with her. "And Elisa?"

"Besides worrying about you, too, she's fine as one can be after all that happened. We had a big fight about her leaving my home where I can better protect her. Bull headed woman… She's also busy with Tasmin studying their book and their family histories." He walked over to his liquor cabinet and poured two fingers of rum into two tumblers. "Tasmin's parents are here…and I can't quite put my finger on it, but there is something about her father that gives me pause."

"What do you mean?" I asked as he handed me the libation.

"He's put up some sort of…shield, dare I say, to hide something about him."

I grunted then told Dafari about my visit from his father.

After he and I clinked tumblers and took the drink to the head, my brother shook his head angrily. "I knew he was up to something."

"We have to stay on our toes around him," I said.

"That's for sure," he said then eyed me. "Even with all we have to still discuss, I refuse to stay in this room with you a minute longer. You smell as if you've been wallowing in a pit of horse manure and hog slop. Please go free yourself of your filth before we talk any further."

Normally, I would have had a snappy comeback. Tonight, I had none. I excused myself to the facilities and proceeded to wash away as much grime, grief, and sadness as I could. As the water washed over me, I heard my brother stop in the hallway, say a prayer for me, and move on. I felt a calm that I hadn't felt in weeks. I knew that soon enough, I'd have to deal with the aftermath of what my parents had done and what I'd been about to do to them. Until then, I had to get back to a semblance of my sanest self so that I could get back to protecting Tasmin and Elisa…and from what Uncle had hinted to, Salix Pointe.

I didn't know what was coming, but I knew one thing was for certain: whatever and whoever thought they would come and cause harm to Tasmin and Elisa had surely better think again.

Printed in the USA
CPSIA information can be obtained
at www.ICGtesting.com
LVHW040941070524
779566LV00002B/282

9 781955 916042